"Perhaps you'll like Daphne,"

she heard herself say.

"Very unlikely. I suppose I'm not being very kind, but I've thought of her as a double bagger. To be blunt, a dog. Probably a very sweet dog, but a dog nonetheless."

She was trembling. It's all your own fault, she repeated silently to herself. It's like eavesdropping. You never hear anything good about yourself. But a *dog!* "Maybe," she said viciously, "she'll think *you're* a double bottle."

"No, double *bagger.* You could be right. I shouldn't be saying things like that to you, Lucilla, since you're her cousin. It's just that I'm furious about the whole situation. Are you here to stay? Since you'll inherit the hall, I should stop with my plans. They should be your plans."

"It's not up to me, I can assure you of that. None of it will be mine, since I'm not—"

Brant was seized by a very funny feeling. "You're not Lucilla?" he said in a controlled voice.

"No, I'm not, my lord." She swept him an insulting bow. "I'm Daphne—the double-bagging dog."

AFTERSHOCKS:

Right place, right woman—wrong time. Georgina was just too young for him, or so Dr. Elliot Mallory tried to tell himself. Not to mention the issue of what she did for a living! So why was he unable to forget this woman who ought to seem wrong but only seemed right?

AFTERGLOW:

Head-in-the-clouds Chelsea and here-and-now David were a complete mismatch. They had nothing in common and no reason to listen to the friends who'd matched them up and now insisted they made the perfect couple. No reason at all—except love.

THE ARISTOCRAT:

Viscount Quarterback? It sounded crazy to football star Brant Asher, but it was true. Unfortunately, along with a title and an English estate, he'd also inherited the obligation to marry ugly duckling Daphne Asherwood. Daphne, however, was not quite what she'd been rumored to be, and she was ready with a few trick plays of her own!

The Aristocrat

Catherine Coulter

Silhouette® Books

Published by Silhouette Books New York

America's Publisher of Contemporary Romance

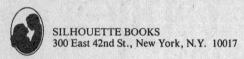

SILHOUETTE BOOKS
300 East 42nd St., New York, N.Y. 10017

THE ARISTOCRAT

ISBN: 0-373-48261-2

Published Silhouette Books 1986, 1992

Prologue

The New York Astros' offense stood helplessly on the sidelines, gripping their helmets, their eyes glued on the players on the field as the Steelers' field goal kicker, Karpatian, sent a high, slicing kick from the forty-third yard line toward the uprights. Brant Asher watched the ball sail inside the right goalpost by no more than inches and watched tensely for the signals.

The kick was good.

Guy Richardson, the Astros' kicker, threw his helmet to the ground and stomped his feet in disbelieving frustration. "*Damnation!* I don't believe it, for God's sake! He couldn't get the other two up in the air! Fifty-three yards!"

Karpatian jumped a good three feet in the air and disappeared into a mob of teammates.

"The fans here in Three Rivers Stadium are going bananas!" screamed the excited field announcer. It felt, Brant thought blankly, as if the stands were trembling.

Brant heard some vivid cursing from his teammates, but most of them stood quietly, their heads lowered. He looked over at the final score flashing on the electronic scoreboard: 24 to 21. This play-off game was over; it was history. Their chance at the Superbowl was down the tubes. He shut out the noise from the crowd, clutched his helmet tightly in his hands and made his way to Sam Carverelli, the Astros' coach. He looked as rotten as Brant felt. His bushy gray eyebrows nearly met over his forehead, his shoulders were slumped, and his lips were a thin white line.

"Jesus," Brant heard him whisper. "Now I've got to go congratulate that polecat Howard! A damned fluke! Karpatian is the biggest mistake he ever made!"

Brant wrapped a muscled arm around his coach's shoulders. "Luck's the next best thing," he said, for want of anything better.

Sam Carverelli pulled himself together by a thread and blinked up at his prized quarterback's face. "Hell, Brant, it isn't fair. Our second winning season—oh, what's the use? Let's get over there before this crowd goes ape."

Most of the Astros were already on the field, congratulating the Steelers. The tension was over. The Steeler fans would soon forget this football game, for they had another game to think about in only a week. The Astros would be home watching the rest of the play-offs and the Superbowl on TV.

They'd played well today, for the most part, Brant thought as he jogged toward the center of the field to congratulate Joe Marks, the Steelers' quarterback. If

Eddie Riggs hadn't fumbled in the second quarter on the Steelers' thirty-eight yard line, if he hadn't thrown that one interception in the first quarter. Too many damned ifs. He'd had twenty-four completions today, including two for touchdowns to Lloyd Nolan, and Washington Taylor had rushed for over a hundred yards. But it hadn't been enough. He was deaf to the incredible noise as he trod over the football field, unwary now of the uprooted clumps of turf that could easily trip up a quarterback. There would be no more football until next summer.

Joe Marks was so euphoric that he didn't at first recognize Brant. "Lordie, Lordie," he shouted over and over again, clapping Brant on the back until he realized who he was. He doused his elation and clamped down on his competitiveness. He was the winner. "We lucked out, Brant, didn't we?"

"Sure did. Good game, Joe." *How sweet it is.* He almost grinned at Jackie Gleason's famous quote. Sweet for Joe and the Steelers.

The two longtime competitors shook hands, and Brant stepped back, letting Joe return to his moment of glory. The locker room scene with champagne soaking sweaty uniforms, plastering everyone's hair to their heads with booze, would be his today.

Brant fell in with a group of his silent teammates on their trek to the Astros' locker room. He was thirty-one, at the height of his career. He thought for one depressed moment that maybe it was time to retire from football, retire with dignity. Then he thought of Kenny Stabler, the Snake, still out there, taking on all comers. He wondered how the Snake felt, seeing those huge young men on the field, eager to stomp all over him. Age, he'd begun to realize once he reached thirty, wasn't a relative thing in football. Even at thirty-one, he faced men eight years his junior. He grinned for a brief moment. He imagined that Joe Marks, over thirty himself, wasn't thinking about being at all old right now.

The locker room was subdued. Suddenly Brant wanted to yell at all his glum teammates that losing in the play-offs wasn't the end of the world, for God's sake. They'd had their second winning season in a row. The owner might be crying now, but he'd made a lot of money with the Astros the past two years.

Brant Asher, all-pro quarterback, jumped on one of the benches and shouted, "All right, you turkeys! Before the press breaks down the doors, I want you to stop acting like I've just screwed your wife!" At least I'm getting their attention, he thought, willing the bummed-out athletes to respond to him.

"There wasn't a damned thing we could do about Karpatian's kick. At least the man still has a job—next year, anyway."

A laugh came from Nolan Lloyd.

"He can't even speak English," growled Guy Richardson, "and he's got a beer gut."

"And a lucky foot," Brant said. "Listen up, you guys, we're going out winners. George, give a towel to Lance. I saw a *person* of the press out there, and we don't want Lance to scare her. Give the lady something to wonder about."

Good, Brant thought as he stepped off the bench, seeing a few grins. He briefly turned an eye toward the horde of reporters filing into the locker room. He watched Lance Carver, a huge lineman, quickly wrap his towel around his waist.

Because he'd won and lost countless games since high school, and been on the receiving end of endless pushy questions during his first three years in pro ball with a consistently losing team, Brant fielded the press's questions with aplomb. He saw from the corner of his eye that one of the media people had managed to get Tiny Phipps, only twenty-two and a rookie, in a lather of emotion. He quickly answered several more questions, then made his way to the young linebacker, clapped the two-hundred-seventy pound player on the back and said to the reporter, whose microphone was inches from his nose, "You'll be seeing Tiny next year, folks. This guy's got a helluva future." In Tiny's ear he whispered, "Don't give them what they want, Tiny. Just give 'em a victory sign and send it to your mother."

It was a good forty-five minutes before the press left the team in peace. Brant stood under the shower, letting the hot needles of water soak into his sore muscles. His right arm was in agony. Maybe he'd need an operation next season, maybe he'd lose his famous snap... *Stop it, you fool! Why don't you listen to your own speech!*

It was close to another hour before he was free of his teammates and out of the Astros' locker room. They were flying back to New York tonight, and he wanted the quiet of his hotel room for a couple of hours.

But he wasn't going to get it. The press *person* he had spotted earlier was waiting for him. She was a forceful, no-nonsense woman, and her eyes fastened on him like a vulture's who'd just trapped her prey. She was elegant-looking, of course. All the female press corps who covered sports were.

"Mr. Asher," JoAnn Marrow said, her pencil poised over an open notebook. "I wanted to speak to you just a moment." She gave him a wide smile, and he noticed that her front teeth were so perfect they defied nature. She gave a high, grating laugh. "I guess you'll want to be called Viscount Asherwood now!"

He blinked at her. It was a moment before he saw her TV crew stealthily ease up behind her. Before the microphone was hooked up, he said, "What did you say? Viscount?"

Her artificial laughter floated upward, picked up by the microphones. "You didn't know? It just came over the wire service. Your great uncle has just died in England and left you an estate and a title."

"Hey, Brant," one of the crew called out, "you're an English aristocrat!"

There was good-natured laughter.

"Make that the top of the line: 'Brant the Dancer—Aristocrat!'"

"Brant the Dancer runs for ten yards in the House of Lords."

"What do the English call that book of theirs? Oh yeah, DeBretts. You're a star, Dancer, and not in the Football Hall of Fame!"

"I can just hear them on the tube next season: 'Now, folks, our star quarterback, my lord Asherwood'!"

Brant stared vacantly at the lot of them, faded memories flooding his mind. Asherwood. Lord Asherwood, an ancient old relic who'd more or less commanded his appearance in England last year. He hadn't gone, put off by the obnoxiousness of the old man's letter to his heir. Now he was dead. He'd never had a whit of interest in England, or his father's unobtrusive relatives, unobtrusive at least until a year ago. Brant's grandfather, Arthur, had come to the United States in the early twenties and shortened his name to Asher, and Brant had never thought of himself as anything but an Asher and an American. Good God, he thought blankly, who the hell cares if I'm Lord Asherwood or Count Dracula?

There was a microphone in front of his face. JoAnn Marrow was waiting for his comment. He pulled himself together and said pleasantly, "I haven't heard a word about this. But," he managed a thin smile, "I am not surprised that you are way ahead of me. The press always has the jump on everyone else. I'll have a statement when I find out exactly what has happened."

"But you knew, didn't you, Brant, that you were heir to an English title?"

He gave JoAnn as big a white-toothed smile as she was bestowing on him. "Yeah, I knew. I'll be certain to invite all of you to a big bash when I get everything straightened out."

He wasn't allowed to get away that easily, but finally, by dint of simply shutting himself in his rented Corvette and revving the powerful engine, he blocked them out. He knew he couldn't go back to the hotel. They'd be waiting for him. He drove around Pittsburgh, not really seeing the sights, until he had to return to his hotel and pack for the return flight.

He managed to sneak in the back way. On the way out of the hotel, buried in a group of his teammates, he saw the six o'clock news blaring loudly on a color TV in the lobby. He shook his head in disbelief as he watched himself and JoAnn Marrow. Lord Asherwood had upstaged the game! He felt the nudge of an elbow in his ribs and gave Nolan Lloyd a bemused shake of his head.

Brant was feeling closer to sixty than thirty-one when he finally drove into the underground parking garage of his west-side New York condominium. His muscles were stiff, and a bruise on his ribs from a crunching tackle throbbed. He focused his thoughts on his Jacuzzi as he retrieved his suitcase from the trunk of his Porsche. And then bed, to sleep for a good twelve hours. He would turn on his answering machine and bolt the front door. No press, no questions until he could call his mother and sort out what had happened. Who, he wondered, had spilled the news to the press?

His two-bedroom condo was on the thirty-fifth floor, and the elevator had never seemed slower. Two residents were in the elevator with him, and they were solicitous about the loss to the Steelers. They said nothing, bless them, about his newly acquired dignities.

He unlocked the front door, stepped inside and firmly closed it behind him. Home, he thought as he fastened the extra chain-lock in place. He strode through the living room, not bothering to turn on the lights as he flipped on the answering machine and went straight to the immense bathroom. He'd stripped off his clothes and lowered his grateful body into the hot swirling water of his Jacuzzi when he heard a noise. He cocked one eye open and turned toward the open door of the bathroom.

Marcie Ellis stood there, her tall, charmingly formed body silhouetted in the bathroom light. He started to smile, but didn't have the chance, because she said abruptly, "I can't believe you didn't tell me, Brant! I look like an utter fool with that bitch JoAnn Marrow getting the jump on me!"

"Marcie, I was kind of busy with the game, just like everyone else. Who cares who interviews the loser, anyway?"

"I'm not talking about the ridiculous game. You an English lord and I knew nothing about it!" Her dark brown eyes flashed magnificently, and she tossed back her thick auburn hair with an impatient hand.

"Ridiculous, Marcie? I promise my body doesn't agree with you, at least at the moment. It is how I make my living, you know."

Marcie flushed and lowered her eyes. She knew Brant well enough to realize that when he spoke very quietly, his voice nearly emotionless, he was angry. "I—I'm sorry, darling. I was dreadfully disappointed that the Astros lost. I know how much it meant to you and the team." She shrugged slightly, one thin strap of her nightgown falling down her arm. "You'll make it next year; I know you will."

"Yeah, it's possible," he agreed. "What are you doing here, Marcie? You know that I'm half-dead after a game."

She rarely considered deception, particularly with Brant, because he had an uncanny ability to see through it. "I hadn't intended to come," she said truthfully, "but after I saw the news, I wanted to know why the hell you hadn't told me yourself."

That was one thing he liked about Marcie, other than her exquisite sensitivity in bed. If suitably encouraged, she could be frighteningly blunt. It was a quality that made her an excellent reporter. "I really never thought about it," he said with equal honesty. "I knew the old bird was getting older, but I don't care about English titles. Good God, I'm as American as the stadium hot dogs. In fact, I can't believe the media are making such a fuss about it."

"Don't be stupid," Marcie said sharply. "It's not like you're Joe Schmuck from Kansas!"

"I'm not Joe Montana from California, either."

"You're still famous, and people eat up a story like this. I can just see JoAnn's headline now: *Athletic Aristocrat.* It isn't fair. If only I'd known!"

A lot of things weren't fair today. "I think I'd prefer something less cutesy, like nothing at all."

"You can take your preferences and flush them, Brant. It'll take a good week for all this to cool down."

The other strap fell, and the gown slithered down a good three inches. He felt his muscles ease miraculously. Lord, he loved her breasts. "Tell you what," he said, rising from the tub and reaching for a towel, "I'll give you an exclusive interview when I find out what the hell is going on. Okay?"

Marcie forgot her snit for a moment as her eyes traveled down his body. "There's an ugly bruise on your ribs," she said.

"Yeah," he said, giving her a wide grin. "Do you think you can limit yourself to the north and south?"

"Primarily south," she said on a slow smile.

Chapter One

Daphne Claire Asherwood sat cross-legged on her blue flowered beach towel, watching the tourists, mainly German, board the small motorboat tied to the dock of the Elounda Beach Hotel. They were off for a day of fishing and swimming on one of the many deserted islands off the northeastern coast of Crete.

As usual, the Greek sun was so hot she could feel her knee caps beginning to burn after only thirty minutes. Blast her fair complexion, she thought, reaching for her bottle of sunscreen. As she rubbed the thick cream into her warm flesh, she smiled ruefully at the two brief strips of bright orange nylon that covered her. Uncle Clarence would have had a seizure if he'd seen her in something so very revealing.

Uncle Clarence, dead now, and with no more control over her life. She felt little grief at his passing at ninety years of age, only an occasional expectation of hearing his voice, commanding in his querulous way for her to fetch something for him. He's a lonely old man, she'd told herself when she'd felt the familiar spurt of resentment. He really can't help that he's hateful and treats me like a housekeeper, nurse and servant, a possession to be at his beck and call at any time, day or night. I owe him because he took me in when my parents died. It was a litany that had become more difficult over the years. Now she was free of him. She sighed and carefully fastened the cap on the sunscreen. Aunt Cloe would tell her roundly to stop dwelling on those long, empty years at Asherwood. "Life," Aunt Cloe would say grandly, "life, my dear little egg, awaits you!"

Well, Daphne thought, thrusting her chin upward, I'm ready for it . . . I think. But how did one go about grasping life if one had no notion of what to grasp at? What was she going to do when she returned to England? I am an adult, twenty-three years old, she told herself yet again, a new litany in response to the thorny question. An adult always thinks of something. She looked down her body at the bikini and shook her head, bemused. She would never forget the look on Aunt Cloe's face when she'd emerged from the posh dressing room in an Athens department store, slinking forward, her hands furtively trying to cover herself.

"Merciful heavens!" Aunt Cloe had exclaimed. "And here I thought you a skinny little twit! Goodness, love, what a bosom! Now that I think of it, your dear mama was marvelously endowed. I shan't despair, no indeed, I shan't despair."

Despair about what? Daphne had wondered. It was true about the bosom, hidden for so many years beneath her loose jumpers and oversized windcheaters. She personally thought she looked lopsided, particularly since the rest of her was so skinny.

"No, love, not skinny," Aunt Cloe had said sharply, demolishing Daphne's tentative observation. "Fashionably svelte! Like a model, at least from the seventh or eighth rib down."

And now here she was in Greece, on the island of Crete, a place she'd dreamed for years of visiting, sitting on a beach and looking like a model, from the ribs down. Eighth rib.

Why, she groaned silently, running one hand distractedly through her long hair, did I let Aunt Cloe talk me into this? Not that Crete wasn't one of the most beautiful places Daphne had ever seen, for it was. Aunt Cloe had known for years that Daphne had spun dreams of visiting the Acropolis and the Greek isles, and particularly King Minos' palace, now partially restored, on the outskirts of the capitol of Crete, Herakleion. And, of course, Aunt Cloe knew she would simply adore the exquisite small village of St. Nicholas with all its colorful fishing boats and quaint canals. "Well, little egg," Aunt Cloe had said to her in mild exasperation when she'd dithered, "do you intend to rot here by yourself at Asherwood until you're booted out by the new viscount? It's time, my girl, to do something for yourself!" Daphne had let Aunt Cloe sweep her away from England after Uncle Clarence's funeral. I'm like a limp noodle, she told herself in silent disgust. Always bending to the stronger will. But at least Aunt Cloe wanted her to have fun.

Suddenly aware that a man was looking her way, his dark eyes resting with a good deal of interest on her bosom, she eased herself quickly into a robe and skittered from the beach. Men, she thought, another problem. What did one *do* with them?

Where the dickens was Aunt Cloe?

Cloe Sparks was busy making an appointment with the French hairdresser in St. Nicholas, Monsieur Etienne.

"She has looked the *jeune fille* for all her life, *monsieur*," she was explaining. "Now she is twenty-three and still looks fourteen. You know, too gamine. We must have something dramatic, scintillating, oh, something *je ne sais quoi*!"

"I understand, *madame*," Monsieur Etienne said, the veil of boredom glazing his dark eyes. These pushy Englishwomen and their deplorable, heavy-handed French! Undoubtedly this gamine was a squat, depressingly plain girl who was probably better off just as she was. "When would you like to bring the young lady to me?" He picked up his appointment book and gave her one of his special intimate smiles.

"Tomorrow at nine o'clock," Cloe said firmly. On the taxi ride back to the Elounda Beach Hotel, Cloe chewed her lower lip, painfully chapped from the relentless Greek sun. She'd forced Daphne into this trip, whirling her willy-nilly away after the old curmudgeon's funeral to Athens, then on to Crete. She'd taken advantage of the girl's sweet biddable nature, just as the old curmudgeon had always done. But, dammit, it was for her own good. Yes, she thought, resolutely, Daphne had to have her chance. She wasn't plain, not by any means. She still had to get Daphne out of those ridiculous glasses of hers and into contacts. She drew a deep breath. One thing at a time, Cloe, she told herself. Everything was right on schedule. She had to remember, she reminded herself, to send a cable to Reggie Hucksley in London. She needed another week, at least.

*   *   *

Brant hugged his mother tightly. "Peace and quiet at

last, lots of tender loving care, and no hassles. It's so good to be home. You look beautiful as ever, Mom." She usually teased him when he told her that, because he was her masculine counterpart in looks.

Alice Asher said nothing for a few moments, feeling an equal surge of affection for her splendid son. Thank heaven he wasn't like his father, embarrassed to show his feelings, as if that would make him less than a man. "Welcome home, Brant. It's so good to see you again. In addition to tender loving care, I've made you your favorite dinner—stuffed pork chops and homemade noodles."

"My body will think it's died and gone to heaven with a home-cooked meal, Mom." He gave her another hug and released her.

"There's lots to talk about."

Her eyes searched his face for a moment. He looked tired and, oddly enough, wary and uncertain. "Yes, I imagine there is. But first, honey, why don't you just relax for a while?"

Brant sat down and leaned back against the soft cushions of his mother's infinitely old and comfortable velvet sofa. He grabbed one of the cushions, shoved it behind his head and closed his eyes.

"It's been a hard several days I would imagine," Alice Asher said, her eyes, as brilliant a blue as her only son's, resting sympathetically on on his tired face. "I'm glad you managed to get here in secret. The press has been hounding me, too. Luckily, they haven't managed to track Lily down."

"She's cruising the Aegean, right?" Brant asked, cocking an eye open.

"Yes, this time with her husband," came the tart response.

"It is her honeymoon, Mom," Brant said, grinning at her.

"Her third! And of all things, Danny, Patricia and Keith are staying with *his* mother."

"Don't fret," Brant said. "I like Crusty Dusty, and so do the kids. Lord knows he's rich enough to give her whatever she wants."

"He's closer to my age than Lily's!"

"You know as well as I do that Lily needed someone like Dusty, someone older to keep her in line."

"You should hear his Texas accent!"

"I have. You're not turning into a snob, are you, Mom, just because you're now a dowager viscountess, or something? The way the nobility address each other is craziness."

Alice Asher smiled ruefully. "You're right. I'm a regular old fool, and I sound like an obnoxious mother-in-law." She sighed deeply, clasping her hands in her lap. "I wonder what your father would say to all this."

"He'd laugh, a big belly laugh, and tell them to go shove it. The ridiculous title and the moldering estate."

"Moldering?" Her fair left eyebrow shot up. "What do you know that I don't, Brant?"

He felt a surge of restlessness and bolted up from the sofa. He said over his shoulder as he strode to the bow window that looked into the beautifully landscaped front lawn of his mother's Connecticut home, "I spent several hours yesterday with my lawyer, Tom Bradan, and a *solicitor*—as they say—who'd come all the way from London to 'inform me of my good fortune,' which is exactly what he said in that affected accent. Fellow's name is Harlow Hucksley, of all things! About my age, I'd guess, acts like a pompous nerd, and covers himself with tweed. And skinny as your azalea stems, not a muscle on him."

Alice Asher laughed, picturing Harlow Hucksley with no difficulty. Her splendid athletic son didn't think much of men who were "soft as mulch." She imagined that with his teammates he would be far more specific and excessively graphic.

"He was the jerk who spilled the beans to the press, dam—*darn* him."

"You gave him a tongue-lashing, I suppose."

Brant turned and gave her a crooked grin. "Well, Tom did run a bit of interference for the guy. I tried to out-flank him, but it didn't work. He expected me—no, he really *demanded*—that I fly to London and get everything squared away."

"You will go, of course," Alice said calmly.

"Why the . . . heck should I?" Brant said sharply. "It makes no difference to me what happens to any of it."

Alice Asher gave her son a long, thoughtful look. "I know your father never spoke much about his English relations, and neither did your grandfather, for that matter, but England is a part of your heritage, honey. You are more than half-English, you know, because I've got a drop or two in there somewhere. Remember that letter he wrote you last year? The old man knew a lot about you."

"Obnoxious," Brant said.

"Perhaps. I reread the letter, you know, after you phoned me. It was really rather pathetic."

"Mom, listen. Harlow told me very little, but I gather there are no estates, and no money. Just this moldering old house in a place called Surrey, and maybe some worthless acres surrounding it."

"The house is called Asherwood Hall, and its located in a quaint village, East Grinstead."

"And don't forget that the title had to come to me, so Harlow Hucksley says. The old coot had no choice about that. The rest of it he probably willed to me because it's worthless, and he realized that the American branch had some money and would pour it back into his tomb of a house."

"Well, son," Alice said logically, "you do have money. It really wouldn't hurt for you to at least go see the place. The season's over, after all. You are at loose ends for a while, aren't you?"

Brant shrugged. "I'm supposed to do a commercial for a sporting goods company, but not right away."

"At least it's not shaving cream!"

Brant laughed. "True. Lily told me she'd never speak to me again if I bared my face to the world covered with white sh—stuff." He shot his mother a guilty look from the corner of his eye.

"Don't feel guilty about your...lapses, dear," Alice said, rising. "I expect it'll take you a while to get yourself under control. Last year, if I remember correctly, it took about two months. As for your sister's language—" She shrugged, slanting her right shoulder just as her son did.

"Look, Mom," Brant said, fighting what he knew was now a losing battle, "maybe you should go. You could take charge of things and tell me what you think."

"Brant," she said, her blue eyes sparkling with mischief. "I already have culture. It's time you acquired some. Roots, Brant. They are important. As a personal favor to me, honey."

"Damn," he muttered. "It's not as if I didn't have any culture, for God's sake! I have been to Europe, and I did go to college."

"Yes, dear, I know."

"I didn't have to be tutored like a lot of the athletes!"

"Yes, dear, of course."

"My degree isn't totally worthless. Communications. Maybe I'll go into announcing when I retire from football."

"Yes, dear, an admirable choice."

"Duke isn't a second-rate college."

"Of course not. You exhibited tremendous foresight. I am quite proud of you, as was your father, of course. Now, why don't you think about it for a while? I'm going to go stuff the pork chops."

He gave up the battle and said, mimicking her, "Yes, dear, an excellent idea."

Brant was feeling full and mellow when he answered the phone after dinner. Lily, exuberant from a distance of five thousand miles, yelled over the phone, "Lord Asherwood! As I live and breathe! Lordie, does that make me a countess or something, brother dear?"

"Hello, Lily," Brant said. "How are Athens and Dusty?"

"Both unbelievably warm, darling," Lily said, laughing deeply.

"Yeah, I bet. When are you coming home?"

"To Connecticut or to London, darling?"

"Texas. That is where your husband lives?"

"Houston, Brant. It's hot there, even this time of year. I don't know if I could take it." She giggled. "All right, stop screwing up your mouth. I can just see you now! How can you be so disapproving, and you a jock? Of course, it's only because I'm your sister, I know. Maybe an English lord should be straitlaced, but—''

"Lily," Brant broke in, "as a personal favor to Mom, I'm going to London, all right? The end of next week. Do you want me to buy you anything?"

Brant had to hold the phone away from his ear at her crow of delight. He could hear her yelling to Crusty Dusty in the background. "I've talked him around, lovey! All he needed was some good reasons for—'' Thankfully, he couldn't hear the rest of what she said, because Dusty Montgomery grabbed the phone away from his bride.

"Good, Brant," he said in his slow, measured drawl. "Hey, boy, sorry about the play-off game. It'd be a lot easier for you if you played for the Dallas Cowboys. But I'll tell you, that pass to Nolan in the second quarter was mighty impressive. And that draw play, what a call!"

"Thanks, Dusty. It was a good game, despite the outcome."

"Damned foreigner and his toe," Dusty said, and Brant could picture him shaking his head in mournful disgust.

"Yeah. Well, you guys having a good time?"

"There ain't no other kind around your sister, Brant. Place is old, though. Not an oil well around. Maybe we'll see something on the cruise. These ruins are getting to me."

Speaking of ruins... No, I can't say that, even as a joke, Brant thought, and quickly asked about the islands they were going to visit.

"Thank you, honey," Alice Asher said to Brant after she'd spent some ten minutes more talking to her daughter.

"No reason to thank me," Brant said.

"Yes, of course there is. I know you're going for me, and I appreciate it." She paused a moment, wiping her hands on her apron. "Will you take Marcie with you?"

Marcie, beautiful Marcie, who'd decided only a week ago that it would suit her just fine to marry a somewhat famous jock who was also an English viscount. "No," he said, surprised, "of course not."

"She's called twice today."

Brant ran his hand through his thick dark hair, the color of his mother's mahogany piano, she'd always told him. "I was hoping she'd cool down a bit."

"You're thirty-one, Brant. Marcie is serious, isn't she?"

"You hoping for another grandchild, Mom? I promise you, Marcie isn't into children. After all, she does have a dynamite career, to be fair about it."

"Yes, that's true enough," Alice said with the utmost composure. "But that really isn't the point. I've never been particularly blind, Brant. So many years now you've gadded about like the gay bachelor. So many women."

"Yeah, most of them out to have their names and faces in the paper with a famous jock."

"And a very handsome and kind man. It's too bad, you know, both for those women and for you. I think you've gotten the least bit cynical. It's understandable, I suppose. I'm glad you're going to England. Come here a moment. I want to show you a family album that you haven't seen in years. I dug it out of the attic just before you arrived."

"You didn't need to drag out the album, Mom. You knew you'd convince me without it."

"It never hurts to have reinforcements, just in case."

Brant sat beside his mother on the sofa, balancing a cup of coffee on his knee.

"So many people that we never even met."

There were faded photographs of great uncle Asherwood, looking irascible and formidable, even in those old pictures from the twenties. He looked as unremittingly stern as any hellfire minister, but no more stern-faced than the flock of females surrounding him, whoever they all were.

"This is your poor Uncle Henry, who died in World War II when he was only twenty-one years old. And your Aunt Loretta, who passed away in 1976, I believe it was. She never married. So, you see, your great uncle had no one left in his direct line. And this is Asherwood."

Brant was surprised that it was so impressive looking. But it looked dark and uninviting with all the tangled ivy covering it. There was an unpaved circular drive, and an old 1940's car parked in front of the house. He felt absolutely no sense of his touted roots as he stared at the house.

"Here's your grandfather, Edward Charles, as a little boy."

Brant laughed. "He certainly improved with age!"

"Indeed he did. Incidentally, you were the picture of him at the same age."

"You know that's not true!" Brant laughed. "You've always told me I'm the spitting image of you. You can't have it both ways, Mom."

There were more pictures of children, dressed in styles suited to the twenties. There were no pictures of Brant's grandfather as a young man.

"Why?" he asked his mother.

"Well, he came to the United States in 1919, just after the war, with his English bride, Melanie. I think there was some sort of falling out between the two brothers shortly after your great grandfather died. He never talked about it."

"Asherwood must have been furious that his title would pass to an unwashed American, particularly if he and my grandfather weren't speaking to each other."

"Yes, I imagine he was somewhat disappointed."

"I suppose all that damned ivy has roots, anyway," Brant said slowly, his forefinger tracing over the photo of Asherwood Hall. "Are you sure you don't want to come with me, Mom?"

"No, Brant. They're not my roots, just yours. I'm almost pure Bostonian, remember? A provincial colonist of no worth at all."

Chapter Two

"I can't believe it's really me!" Daphne Asherwood stared at herself, openmouthed, in the mirror. Her contacts had been tinted according to Aunt Cloe's instructions, and her eyes shone back at her a vivid green. A fake green, she thought rebelliously, but only for a moment. She'd never known a moment's vanity in her entire twenty-three years, until now. She rather liked it.

"It's you, my pet," Cloe said, quite pleased with the results. Cloe, in fact, couldn't believe it was the same young woman. "Your green eyes are lovely with your tan and your blond hair."

"Streaked blond hair, Aunt," Daphne said. "Monsieur Etienne, well, he was most thorough, wasn't he?"

"Oh, indeed, my pet, most thorough, but look at the result! I'm glad he left your hair long; it's so lovely. Are the contacts comfortable?"

"I don't even feel them," Daphne said, rolling her eyes about and blinking rapidly. "And the doctor says I can wear them for a full week or so without even taking them out."

"I won't remind you of all the witless arguments you gave me, my pet. Now that you see I'm right, we're off to pick up your clothes from Mademoiselle Fournier."

"I haven't been to Paris since I was fifteen," Daphne said. "Then it was only for three days. Uncle Clarence let me come over one summer with the rector and his family. It's so very lovely, isn't it, Aunt?"

Actually, Cloe thought, gazing for a moment at the heavy dark clouds, Paris in February was a rather dreadful, dank place, and bloody cold to boot. "Yes, indeed, love," she said. She efficiently flagged down a taxi outside the eye doctor's ornate office on the Champs Elysee and directed the driver to the Place Opera. "*Numéro quatorze,*" she said in ringing tones.

"*Bien,*" said the French taxi driver, not looking up.

As he zipped them through the snarled traffic in a most intoxicating fashion, Cloe listened to Daphne's expressions of delight at everything in sight. Poor child! Three days with the rector! Good lord, how utterly like Clarence, her impossible father. How dare that old man keep Daphne in that damned tomb of a house, denying her everything! Friends, school, fun. She'd pleaded with him to let her take Daphne to Scotland to live with her, but he'd refused.

"Impossible!" her father had roared more than once. "She'd come back to me one of those insufferable modern chits! I won't have it!" She thought of the terms of his will and stilled her niggling guilt. Only she and Reggie knew what was afoot. She pictured the photos she'd studied of the new viscount as she'd sorted through everything Reggie had found out about him. Utterly handsome fellow. Lord, think of the things he could teach Daphne! She flushed at her thoughts, but only slightly. After all, she wasn't that old. She'd decided irrevocably on her present course after Reggie had told her the terms of the will and asked her advice on how to proceed with Daphne. "The girl's not up to snuff, Cloe. I haven't the foggiest notion of how to carry on."

But Cloe did. In a flash of inspiration she had realized exactly what she must do. Then Reggie had given her the report old Clarence had prepared on young Brant Asher. "Here you are, Cloe, all the information old Lord Asherwood gathered on Brant, including newspaper articles and photos of him. He's no brainless fellow, as one might expect from an athlete, particularly one from America. Quite the virile bachelor, I'd say. Look at the women he's with in this picture. He's got money, though, and that might prove to be a problem."

"There's no such thing as having too much money," Cloe had said firmly. "He'll come through. And don't you dare get cold feet, Reggie! I'm going to have enough problems with Daphne!"

But what about Lucilla? Damn Clarence anyway! Why Lucilla? Obviously he wanted the same thing I want. Why couldn't he just let me handle everything? No, she thought, I won't worry about Lucilla; there's no need. Maybe. And she turned to smile complacently at Daphne.

To Cloe's utter delight, when she handed the surly taxi driver the requisite francs for the fare he didn't even count them, his eyes fastened like a dazed famine victim's on a succulent Daphne.

Hoorah! She'd always thought of French cab drivers as the most blasé men in the world.

* * *

There can be no more dismal a place than London in February, Brant thought, trying to make out details of the landscape below as the 747 circled Heathrow. It looked cold, foggy and depressing. He didn't think about the blackened snow that had made Boston look equally depressing when he'd left. It had been a smart move, leaving from Logan. The press had expected him to take off from Kennedy.

The man seated next to him was still dozing peacefully when the plane swooped down at Heathrow. One of the flight attendants, ever-smiling Laurie, was more observant, and Brant caught her eye on him, studying him closely. He quickly put his sunglasses back on.

At least in London, he thought, he could lose himself in the crowd. He grinned, thinking he'd have to buy himself a tweed sports coat to ensure that he'd blend right in.

He was met as he left customs by none other than Harlow Hucksley himself. He wondered briefly if all Englishmen were so tweedy and twirpy. The designer glasses he wore were the final touch.

"Ah, Lord Asherwood, such a pleasure to see you again!"

"Mr. Asher is just fine, or Brant."

"Then call me Harlow. I fancy we're going to become quite chummy before all of this is settled." He laughed, and his protuberant adam's apple bobbed.

"Fine, Harlow."

An underling appeared at an unobtrusive nod from Harlow, and Brant's luggage was taken away. Brant arched a thick brow.

"Old Frank will see to it, nothing to get uprooted about," Harlow said.

Brant was greeted outside the airport by a blast of Arctic air and swirling snowflakes.

"Bloody awful weather we're having," Harlow said, unconcerned.

"Yes, bloody dreadful," Brant said.

"London's knee deep in muck, but it won't bother you. The limousine is at your service, of course."

"First class treatment," Brant said, eyeing the gas-guzzling black car that pulled up alongside the curb.

"Certainly," Harlow said over his shoulder as he climbed into the back seat and unfolded his long, skinny legs.

"Compliments of the firm, Harlow? Didn't you tell me there was no money involved in my inheritance?"

"Scarce a sou, old chum," Harlow said. "Even so, my father insisted that you be treated appropriately."

"Very nice of him," Brant said.

"Not really, just good business. At least, that's what he told me. The Old Man's always alert. By the by, Brant, I had thought this car monstrous, but with you in it, it looks like one of those little German boxes. Most impressive, your size."

"I'd have been in trouble if I weren't this size."

"Are all American rugby chaps as big as you?"

"Football, Harlow, football it's called. Actually, I'm something of a shrimp compared to the men on the line. A mere one hundred ninety-five pounds."

Harlow fell into intense thought. "That's a goodly number of stone."

"Probably a whole bagful. What's a stone?"

"A stone is around fourteen of your American pounds," Harlow said. "Equates to the size of Jonah's whale, in your case. Odd business, this." Before Brant could seek clarification, Harlow continued blandly,

"Yes, indeed. Who would have imagined an American athlete claiming an English title? You'll be in for some raised brows, old boy. Talk's already around, you know. But don't worry, no one knew exactly when you were to arrive. The Old Man insisted that mum's the word!"

"Good for the Old Man," Brant said. "I assume he's your father?"

"Indeed. Reginald Darwin Hucksley. Very proper sort, and no relation to *the* Darwin," he added.

Brant stared out the limousine window at the cramped, boxlike rows of houses they were passing. The light, swirling snow made them look quite quaint, but he imagined that when the snow melted the black smoke that belched from the pot-shaped chimneys, their charm dwindled fast.

"The Old Man's been trying to round up your relatives."

"Relatives," Brant said sharply, turning to face Harlow. "You said nothing about relatives in New York."

"Well, no, actually. We weren't quite certain how many there were, or where they were. The Old Man doesn't like to spring things without being certain of his facts. I told him they'd be dribbling out of the lamp shades if there was any money involved, which of course there isn't, at least not enough to fill a hat, so my father told me."

"My mother didn't mention any relatives," Brant said. "Who are they?"

"You Yanks do spread yourselves out so, don't you? Lose track of people, and all that. Well, let me see. There's an aunt legging about somewhere in Scotland. Glasgow, we think."

"An aunt," Brant repeated blankly, beginning to feel like a damned parrot.

"Righto. An adopted daughter of old Lord Asherwood, married a chap named Sparks, Carl Sparks, a Scot. Dashed ridiculous name I told the Old Man, but there you have it. Sparks, Cloe Sparks, widow. She was an Asherwood, of course, until she married this bloke, Sparks."

"Any more relatives hanging about in the wings?" Brant asked.

"Quite. There's a young female in there, your father's younger brother's wife's first cousin's offspring."

Brant was silent, weaving his way through this morass of genealogy. Uncle Damon, whom he'd never met. He'd died when Brant was a young boy. His wife's first cousin's kid. "And what, may I ask, is her name now?"

"Ah, she was a Bradberry, but after her parents were killed in an auto accident in 1974, old Lord Asherwood took her in and had her name legally changed to Asherwood. Can't remember what her first name is. The Old Man will know. She grew up at Asherwood. Then, when your great uncle cocked up his toes, she popped out—to Greece, we believe."

"I can't believe the old coot forced her to change her name to Asherwood!"

"Well," Harlow said reasonably, "it certainly gave the girl a leg up, you know. Asherwood's a much more cushy name than Bradberry."

"Still, it seems to me that people are entitled to keep their true names."

"I don't know, old chum, look at your name. Asher, not Asherwood. Incidentally, there's one other female, a *femme fatale*, if you get my meaning."

"Yes, I get it," Brant said. He was startled that Harlow could manage a leer. Did Englishmen poke you in the ribs when they made a dirty joke?

"She comes off one of the old bird aunts. Loretta, I think, or maybe not. I'm really not certain. Named Lucilla. Dashed goer from what I hear."

"Does she have a confounding last name?"

"Oh no, changes her names like her jumpers. She's married to a rich German industrialist by the name of Meitter and lives in Bonn. That's the lot of them. Doubt you'll have to worry about them barging in and queering your lay. No money and all that, just the bloody house."

"Hall," Brant corrected blandly. "Asherwood Hall, I believe."

"Quite, old boy, quite!"

"Where are we now?" Brant asked.

"Coming up to Westminster Bridge. The Old Man said I should show you some of the sights. He wants you to feel at home. That gray matter swishing down below is the Thames."

Brant perked up to take in Big Ben and all the government buildings. The driver gave them a quick spin along Downing Street, then turned back onto Horse Guards Road.

"St. James Park, old chum. Thought you'd like to see it. Soon we'll be coming up to Buckingham. The queen's in residence now."

Traffic was incredible. Much like New York, Brant thought, except all the cabs were black and on the wrong side of the road.

"Here, Brant, is Hyde Park. See over there..."

Brant closed him out. He was tired, beginning to feel wrung out from jet lag, and wanted nothing more than to sack out for a while, without any "quites" or "indeeds" sounding in his head.

"Your hotel, old chum. The Stanhope. Quiet, and quite private. No nosey blokes hanging about here. You can walk in Hyde Park and sort out your mind and all that.''

Curzon Street, Brant read silently. It was a beautiful tree-lined street, calm and restful. The snow fell like a lacy white curtain, obscuring anything that might dilute the serenity. The Stanhope was small, old and reeked of Victorian atmosphere. The lobby was empty, which was just as well, because Brant couldn't imagine very many guests managing to weave their way through the dark, heavy stuffed sofas and chairs. A thin, tweedy clerk was at the desk. He eyed Brant with a good deal of interest.

''They don't get many foreigners here,'' Harlow said kindly. ''Particularly blokes your size. Here now,'' Harlow continued to the clerk, taking charge, ''this is Lord Asherwood. Reservations for your best room.''

Brant handed over his passport and signed his name to an ornate old-fashioned register. From the corner of his eye he saw a hunched old man struggling with his luggage.

''Let me help you with the elevator,'' Brant said, striding over to the old trouper.

''Eh?'' the grizzled old man asked.

''The lift, old chum,'' Harlow said. ''I had the same trouble in America. I kept asking for the loo! Wouldn't believe the tooty looks I got.''

Brant closed his eyes for a moment, wishing he'd never come to England. He turned and stuck out his hand to Harlow. ''I think I'll tuck up for a bit, Harlow.'' He grinned, liking his choice of words. If it wasn't English slang, it should be.

''Righto, Brant. Follow the fellow upstairs. I'll send the limousine for you tomorrow, say about ten o'clock?''

''To see the Old Man?''

''Quite,'' said Harlow.

* * *

"Welcome to London, my boy! Sit down, sit down! Betty, fetch a cup of tea for Lord Asherwood."

Brant felt as though he'd stepped into the last century. The law offices of Hucksley, Hucksley and Maplethorpe on Salisbury Court, were somber, dark and, Brant guessed, admitted only male solicitors through their staunch portals. As for the Old Man, he was heavily jowled, nearly bald, and wore stiff wire-rimmed glasses. They were anything but designer frames. He wore a very conservative dark suit, the jacket buttoned and stretched over his ample stomach. Brant had no difficulty picturing him with one of those curled white wigs on.

"Mr. Hucksley," Brant said, shaking the older man's hand. "A pleasure to meet you, sir."

Brant was aware that he was being scrutinized closely and bore up without shifting a muscle.

Mr. Hucksley said to his son, "You didn't tell me Lord Asherwood was such a demmed good-looking sort. The girls will be swarming all over him, starting with pop-eyed Betty."

Pop-eyed Betty did gape at him a bit, but nothing more obtrusive than that as she handed him his tea. Thank God, Brant thought, staring at the repulsive brown liquid, he'd drunk two cups of black coffee for breakfast.

There were amenities to be sorted through and Brant stilled his impatience. Oddly enough, by the time Mr. Hucksley sat back in his huge leather chair, Brant felt relaxed.

"Now, my boy," the Old Man said, his voice shifting gears to a businesslike tone, "it's time to discuss what's to be done with you."

Brant cocked a thick dark brow. "Done with me, sir? I'm afraid I don't quite understand. Harlow has told me that there's only the house and nothing to go along with it, except, of course, the title."

Reginald Hucksley picked up a gold pen and began to tap the side of his impressive nose with it. "That's correct, to a point." He sent a bland look toward his son.

"Point, sir?" Harlow asked, popping forward in his chair like an eager schoolboy.

Brant had the sudden feeling that this scene had been played through many times between them in the past. Obviously the Old Man kept some things, probably some very important things, to himself. Poor Harlow looked for all the world like an eager puppy waiting for a meaty bone from his master.

"Well, you see, there are some stipulations in the late Lord Asherwood's will."

"Stipulations?" Harlow asked, as if on cue.

Brant said nothing. What the hell is going on, he wondered. He felt himself tensing.

The Old Man's gold pen moved more slowly over his nose. "I assume, my lord, that Harlow here told you about the three women?"

"Yes," Brant said. If Hucksley senior wanted to make a drama out of this, he didn't feel like helping him.

"Humph," said Reginald Hucksley, the only sign that he was at all disappointed by Brant's cool reaction. "Actually, only the two young ones are of any concern. Daphne Claire Asherwood and Lucilla Meitter. Both distant cousins of yours, my lord. More disparate females I've yet to see. Rather than read you your great uncle's will, which I must admit is a bit difficult to grasp, I'll explain it to you."

"I understood from Harlow," Brant said slowly, "that there was really nothing to be concerned about. And I will be frank with you, sir, the only reason I came to England was as a favor to my mother."

"Perhaps I should begin with an apology, my lord. I must admit that I have held some things back, as per the late Lord Asherwood's instructions. You see, your great Uncle Clarence most seriously desired that you come to England, and I was to use any means at my disposal to get you here."

"Then I suggest, sir," Brant said very quietly, "that you get on with your explanations. I expect I'll be leaving London soon, quite soon."

"Well, yes, indeed, my lord," the senior Hucksley said. "First, dear, sweet Daphne Claire, a very properly brought up young lady. Lucilla Meitter, on the other hand, well, she's a bird of very different plumage! Just received word yesterday that she's indeed free and clear of her German husband—indeed, she was back in business before the old lord passed on—and is wending her way back to London after getting over her, ah, disappointment in the South of France."

"You didn't tell me!" Harlow said, looking much aggrieved. "I told Brant she was still married!"

"Ah, didn't I? Well, now you know, my boy."

"What," Brant asked, his voice ominously quiet, "do they have to do with me? And with these stipulations?"

The gold pen slowly descended from the Old Man's nose, and he sat forward in his chair. His shrewd eyes glittered from behind his glasses.

"The long and short of it is, my lord, that old Lord Asherwood did leave a bit of money. After all the taxes, it comes to about 400,000 pounds. That would be about half a million dollars."

"Sir!" Harlow nearly shouted, jumping up from his chair. "You didn't tell me!"

"Well, my boy, now you know. Do sit down. Now, my lord, you will inherit all the money and Asherwood Hall, if—"

"If?" Brant wanted to leap over the Old Man's desk and throttle him. Of all the ridiculous charades!

"If you marry Daphne Claire Asherwood, the dear, sweet young lady."

Brant stared at him, one incredulous brow raised a good inch.

"Isn't that clear, my lord?"

That's ludicrous! He nodded, tight-lipped.

"Very good. Now, listen carefully, sir. This is, ah, rather detailed and quite specific. If, my lord, you refuse to marry Daphne, you will get nothing, Daphne will inherit a mere five hundred pounds, Lucilla gets half the money and the Hall, and the other half of the inheritance goes to the old lord's favorite charity, the Foundation for Abandoned Foreign Children."

Brant wished at that moment that old Lord Asherwood was there. That old fool!

"Is that clear, my lord?"

That's even more ludicrous! "Oh, yes," Brant said, "quite clear." He sat back and crossed his arms over his chest. "I can't wait to hear the rest of it."

Hucksley Senior ignored his sarcasm. "Now then, if, on the other hand, the impossible happens, and Daphne refuses to marry *you*, then you get nothing, Daphne receives only one hundred pounds, and Lucilla inherits everything."

Brant's stare became more pronounced. Suddenly he threw back his head and burst into laughter.

"I say," the Old Man said, looking shocked, "surely you understand! Really, my lord, you must realize that the estate isn't entailed. Old Lord Asherwood could do anything he wished with it."

So, Brant thought, sorting through this maze of insane information, if he married Daphne the Dog—Daphne, the dear sweet young lady—he got the money, the Hall and a wife. If he refused to marry her, he got nothing and Daphne got practically nothing. Ah, Lucilla! If Daphne refused him, he still got nothing and she was out on her ear with one hundred pounds in her pocket. "Jesus," he muttered, "my great uncle must have been insane!" He raised his eyes to the Old Man and asked, "What does entailed mean?"

"Ah, you Americans!"

"It means, Brant," Harlow said, eager to be able to contribute to the unfolding drama at long last, "that old Lord Asherwood didn't have to bequeath anything except the title to the next male in line. By law, he could do whatever he pleased with his money and the Hall."

"Perhaps you know why my great uncle made such a ridic—ah, unusual stipulation?"

"He didn't want the future viscountess of Asherwood to be an American. He wanted his bloodline to continue."

"But a viscount who's an American is all right?"

"In that, he had no choice," Hucksley Senior said primly. "But after all, your blood isn't entirely diluted."

"Quite good," Harlow said. "All the pitter-pattering little feet should have British blood."

Pitter-pattering little *what*? Jesus, I've got to wake up soon! But nothing occurred to end the scene, and Brant asked, "And what happens to the money if both I and my far-removed cousin refuse to marry each other simultaneously?"

"Everything goes to Lucilla. Understand, my lord, that old Lord Asherwood wanted Daphne cared for."

Is she incompetent? A half-wit? "That, sir, is quite obvious. It's also blackmail of the lowest sort." He felt another surge of anger at his great uncle well up in him. Not for himself, but for his whatever-degree cousin, Daphne. He didn't give a damn about the wretched house or the money. But to leave the poor girl stranded if either of them didn't cooperate with the insane will…! He said with furious irony, "It is obvious that my great uncle was truly fond of this Daphne. So fond of her, in fact, that he's trying to condemn both of us, with me the villain if I don't marry her! This is unbelievable!"

"Now, now, my boy," Hucksley Senior said, adopting his most placating tone, "I must admit that old Clarence did go a bit far. As for Daphne, my lord, I can't frankly consider her refusing to marry you. And, as you say, if you do the refusing, well, as you know, both of you lose everything. And Daphne, I'm afraid, would be left penniless and homeless."

"But what if we find each other equally repellent?"

"Not possible," Harlow said firmly. "It isn't as though you parade about looking like a gnome."

Brant bit back a wild surge of sarcastic laughter. "Another question, sir. What if I had already been married? What would have happened to all these stipulations then?"

"Old Lord Asherwood knew you weren't married. It never came up."

"What if I were to tell you that I'm already engaged to be married—to an American?"

There was a moment of stunned silence. "Surely you are jesting, my lord," the Old Man said, his eyes narrowing in disapproval. "Of course the old lord had you thoroughly, er, investigated, as I believe you Americans put it. We know that you're seen with a lot of women, but no one woman in particular."

Brant rose from his chair. "I think, sir, Harlow, that I'm going to pay a visit to the Tower of London. Check out all the torture devices and see if the block is still there. Good day, Harlow, Mr. Hucksley."

"But—"

"I say, old chum—"

"I'll talk to you later," Brant said over his shoulder.

"Don't miss the royal jewels!" Harlow called after him.

Brant turned suddenly in the doorway. "It sounds to me like my great uncle wasn't playing with a full deck. That means queer in the attic," he added at the blank expressions. "Loony, off his rocker, ready for Bedlam."

"Ridiculous!"

"Not to be thought of. Really, my boy, four hundred thousand pounds isn't to be sniffed at!"

Brant sniffed, wheeled about and strode from the room.

"The boy's a bit upset," said the Old Man.

Chapter Three

"Harlow, you're pushing me, you know."

"Now, old chum, it's but another hour and we'll be there!"

"That's not what I mean, and you and the Old Man know it! I've given this entire...mess a good deal of thought. I am quite willing to settle some money on Daphne. She won't be destitute then, and she can go on with her life without—"

"Good God, Brant! You can't do that! I mean, it's not what the Old Man, that is—"

I'm getting tired of arching my eyebrows, Brant thought.

"Ah, Brant, you can't think of legging it now! You'll love the old place, you'll see. You've got to see it before you decide anything, and Daphne—"

"Have you ever seen it, Harlow?"

"Well, actually, old boy, that is..."

"I thought not. I, on the other hand, have seen a photo of the place, and it didn't turn me on."

"Turn you on?"

"I was indifferent to it, Harlow. I could probably shine it on without a second thought."

"Shine it on?"

"Dismiss it, ignore it, send it to hell."

"Ah, well, just another forty-eight minutes."

Brant sat back in the comfortable limousine and closed his eyes. The scenery was beautiful, but he didn't want to gaze at another perfect quiltlike field or another perfectly trimmed hedgerow. Hucksley Senior, the old devil, had held him in London for a full week before insisting that he come to Surrey to see his *ancestral home*. Every damned play he'd sat through in Drury Lane he'd already seen in New York. You're being a jerk and an ugly American, he told himself, and not honest. Westminster Abbey had moved him deeply, as had, oddly enough, the British Museum. Who wouldn't be moved at seeing an original of the Magna Carta? Whenever he could shake the ubiquitous Harlow, he'd roved all over London, enjoying Great Russell Street just as much as Piccadilly. Even Madame Tussaud's on Marylebone Road had fascinated him.

Asherwood Hall. Old, bringing back the dim past. Hucksley Senior had duly filled him in on the history of the place over a formal black-tie dinner at the Savoy. Unlike Harlow, the Old Man had visited Asherwood Hall on many occasions.

"Old red brick, my boy, mellowed in tone, contrasting so well with the green things that clothe or neighbor it. What charm! The River Wey winds all about the place in the most romantic fashion. As to particulars, Brant, Sir Richard Worton was granted the land by that old demon, Henry VIII. There was an immense brangle with the king and Anne Boleyn, but the family survived, even prospered under Elizabeth. The Wortons died out in the direct line in 1782, and a gentleman of Herefordshire, John Gebbe, took over the name. Ah, the transoms and the mullions. Some of the best examples of Tudor architecture in all of England. There are even some painted glass windows with the rose *en soleil*, don't you know, from Edward IV.''

"*En soleil?* Why, how unusual! You're certain it's not a fake?''

"Really, old chum,'' Harlow had said, frowning at Brant's sarcasm, "there's nothing like it, believe me!''

"How many rooms are there?'' Brant had asked when the Old Man paused in his monologue to eat his mushroom soup.

"It's not large at all, actually. Not more than twenty rooms.''

"Hardly enough room for pets,'' Brant had agreed.

After that night at the Savoy, Brant simply couldn't contemplate leaving, for there was to be a formal reception for him, given by the Earl and Countess of Rutherford.

"I say, old chum,'' Harlow said, tugging at his suede jacket. "That's the Wey. Dashed lovely, eh?''

"Utterly dashed,'' Brant said, eyeing the sluggishly winding river, its water brown from the winter mud.

"We're now driving through Guildford. Be there in just a sec!''

Guildford was another sleepy little village with lots of sturdy, leafy trees and quaint pubs set around a common green. There were even ducks strolling about the brackish pond in the center of the green.

Brant felt restless. He wanted to go home. He didn't even want to meet the dog, Daphne.

He asked suddenly, "You said that Daphne is in Greece?"

"That's what the Old Man told me."

In that case, Brant thought, the girl could be anywhere!

"And she doesn't know the terms of the will?"

"That's what the Old—"

"Yes, what the Old Man told you."

"Ah, we're here! I think."

The limousine turned into a drive between two high stone pillars. Overhead on a rusting circular iron grill were the scrolled words, Asherwood Hall. The wide graveled drive was surrounded on either side with more sturdy, leafy trees. Oaks, he thought, or maybe beeches. Suddenly, out of nowhere, he felt a very odd sensation, as if he'd been smashed by a lineman in the stomach. It was something of a déjà vu, an inescapable feeling that he'd been tied to this place, somehow, in the distant past.

He stared at the huge house. Slowly he climbed out of the limousine, his eyes never leaving the graceful old structure before him. It was three stories high, not quite square, with ivy climbing up to the chimney pots on the sloped roof and twining about the many steep gables. A surge of pride, of possession, washed through him. He wanted suddenly to scrub the dirty panes of glass in the mullioned windows until they sparkled. He wanted to cut away the ivy and bring light into the rooms. He wanted to lovingly replace each of the torn slates on the roof.

I'm turning into a senile fool.

He wanted to run his hands over the huge oak double doors and peel away the rot, then stain them to their former splendor. He wanted to polish the huge brass griffen-head door-knockers.

I'm losing my damned mind.

He drew a deep breath. Suddenly the doors were pulled open, and he heard them creak on their hinges. They have become warped through the years, he thought. How will I fix that?

A scrappy-looking old woman emerged, wiping her hands on her apron. She looked for all the world like an over-the-hill wood sprite. "Eyuh?" she said, staring at Brant and Harlow warily, as if they were there to collect on an overdue grocery bill.

"Mrs. Mulroy, I believe," Harlow said. "This is Lord Asherwood."

"Eyuh," Mrs. Mulroy said. To Brant's surprise, she dropped him a curtsey. "Welcome, my lord." Her voice sounded as creaky as her old bones likely were. Brant heard himself mutter something.

"You were expecting us, weren't you, Mrs. Mulroy?" Harlow asked.

"Oh, uh," said Mrs. Mulroy. "'Tain't much of a homecoming for his lordship, but me and two girls from the village been cleaning out the muck, just as Mr. Reggie instructed. As for Mr. Winterspoon, he's still on holiday. Old Maddy agreed to cook for a bit until his lordship could find someone permanent. It'll taste like fly paper, but ain't nothing for me to say about it. My, but you're a grand fellow, my lord! I ain't never seen a lord as big as you, if you don't mind my saying so."

"No, I don't mind." The front stone steps were chipped. He supposed there were masons in England. He hoped they'd know what to do about that, and where to find the right kind of stone.

"Well, righto! Do you want to see the inside, Brant?"

"Yes."

He was aware that Harlow was looking at him somewhat oddly, but he didn't care. Indeed, Harlow barely impinged on his conscious thoughts.

The old wood sprite scratched her thin gray bun and led the way into the huge, black-and-white marbled entryway. Were there special cleaners to shine up the marble squares? Brant wondered. The ceiling was simply the underside of the roof, some forty feet above. Directly ahead was a beautiful old oak staircase, winding to the second-floor landing. He drew closer and ran his fingers over the smooth old wood. He swore for a moment that he could feel the warmth from hundreds of years of hands that had touched the bannister.

"This here's the Armor Hall," Mrs. Mulroy said, not a hint of awe in her voice as she creaked toward the open doors to the left.

Brant turned reluctantly and followed her, Harlow behind him. He stepped through the twenty-foot-high double doors and sucked in his breath. He'd never before imagined that a room like this could exist. It appeared to be at least forty feet long and some twenty-five feet wide. It had thick beamed ceilings, a huge fireplace against the far wall, tall narrow windows that gave onto the front drive, and a very odd mix of furnishings. Suits of armor, many of them missing parts, were both standing and sitting along the walls like an array of drunken soldiers. Maces, lances, long bows, battle-axes and other pieces of assorted medieval fighting equipment whose names he didn't know were affixed to the paint-peeling walls above the drunken soldiers. One battle-ax had obviously fallen at some time, conking a suit of armor on the head, and had been fixed back on the wall with a crooked knot. Brant moved forward to examine a medieval-type chair, caught the toe of his shoe in the thread-bare carpet, and went flying.

"Yoicks!" Harlow shouted. "Careful there, Brant. The place isn't quite all up to snuff!"

Brant picked himself up and grinned at the wizened guffaw that erupted from the old sprite. He shook off Harlow's hand and began a closer examination. Lord, the work he'd need to do in here! How did one replace armor parts? He couldn't imagine wandering into London's equivalent of Macy's and asking for a steel arm, circa 1500. The fireplace was huge enough to roast a whole cow, and so blackened that it looked like an immense dark cavern. The heavy, hewn-oak furniture looked as if it hadn't been polished for at least two centuries.

"Eyuh, my lord," Mrs. Mulroy said in a commanding voice, "'tis time to see the rest of the place. Can't be spending an afternoon in each room. Those lazy girls are in the kitchen, likely drinking tea without me to tell them what to do."

He was tempted to give the old sprite a salute.

There were ten odd more rooms on the ground floor: a long, narrow dining room that would be a perfect setting for candles and ghost stories; a large ballroom that boasted haphazard groupings of heavy Victorian sofas and chairs; and the Golden Salon. Again Brant felt that odd, unsettling feeling when he walked into the room. He knew next to nothing about architecture, but in this room he felt generations of loving care. There was no decay here, no musty smell or peeling paint. It was light, spacious and, he noted, would be wonderfully airy if the damned ivy were cleared away from the wide windows. There were cherubs and other such things along the molding in the ceiling, and an exquisite light marble fireplace that some fool had painted gold! The furniture was grouped in small conversational arrangements, each grouping from a different bygone era. Delicate white and gold pieces by the windows; heavy dark mahogany pieces he suspected were Victorian; and even some light-wood sofas and chairs from this century. There was bric-a-brac everywhere, and a line of photographs on the mantle. His feet drew him forward, and he studied the faded black-and-white pictures. So many people he'd never known! There were several more recent photos: one of an older woman who had fascinating eyes that seemed to mock the world, and another of a young woman who was squinting at the camera through ugly thick glasses, had her hair scraped back from her face in a fat bun, and wore a shapeless, dowdy jumper. Suddenly he smiled. The signature at the bottom of the photo was "Daphne Asherwood." The dog! Then he stiffened. He was supposed to marry *that*? His hands felt clammy and he thrust them into the pockets of his corduroy trousers. As he followed Harlow and the old sprite from the room, he noticed that the floors were in awful shape. How, he wondered, would he be able to bring them to their former beauty?

"Eyuh, my lord," Commander Wood Sprite said, "time for the upstairs."

The next thirty minutes passed in rather a daze. The half-dozen rooms on the second floor were in depressing shape, but each one of them fascinated Brant. There were endless little nooks and cupboards, even a priest's hole that the old wood sprite pointed out proudly. There was a long, narrow portrait gallery, filled with centuries of paintings, many of them so dark that the faces were difficult to make out. Brant gulped. It would cost a fortune, he guessed, to bring in an expert to clean them up. *It would eat well into the 400,000 pounds.*

There was only one bathroom on the entire floor and it was a shrine to the inefficient opulence of the last century. He was still fretting about how to modernize the bathroom when Mrs. Mulroy led the way into old Lord Asherwood's suite.

My God, Brant thought, still somewhat dazed, this is my room! It was as rich and splendid as the Golden Salon downstairs, a strange combination of styles that fascinated rather than repelled. He immediately strode to the heavy burgundy draperies along the west wall and jerked them open.

I've got to paint the walls a light color, and get rid of that ridiculous dark wall paper.

"Aubusson, they call it," Mrs. Mulroy said, pointing at the beautiful red carpet that stretched a good twenty feet in each direction. The bed was canopied, a monstrosity that was raised, of all things. Brant suddenly pictured himself climbing into the thing, and smiled. The crimson spread would have to go. Moths had taken their yearly meals here for two generations at least.

"I hope you're not too disappointed, Brant," Harlow said as they wended their way back downstairs. "The place is in dreadful shape, something the Old Man didn't mention to me. But it's filled with tradition—"

"Yes, roots."

"I hope you're not too disappointed."

Disappointed! Brant stared at him as if he were crazy. "It is perfect," he said simply, and turned away, his mind buzzing with plans.

Chapter Four

"I don't see a photo of my cousin, Lucilla Meitter."

Mrs. Mulroy sniffed loudly. "She ain't here often," she offered by way of an answer. "Two years ago it was Outrake, and before that, Vargas."

Brant grinned. "A woman of international tastes. No photo of her?"

"If it 'tain't there, 'tain't one, I don't imagine. His old lordship was vastly amused by Miss Lucilla, used to tell her without a husband, she was like a cup of tea without the lemon. Why, look ye here! It's Mr. Winterspoon, my lord."

Winterspoon?

"My lord!"

Brant stared at the short, very chubby little man whose bald head came even with his chin.

"I'm Winterspoon, my lord, Oscar Winterspoon. I was the old lord's valet." His bright blue eyes took in every

inch of Brant. "I'm here, my lord, to take care of you."
Goodness, his look said clearly, do you ever need it! "I
do apologize for not being here when you arrived yesterday, but I was on holiday. Bath, you know."

"Stuffy sod," Mrs. Mulroy sniffed under her breath.

Winterspoon drew himself up to his full height, looking so dignified that Brant had the momentary urge to
salute. "Are all your things upstairs, sir? If so, I'll see to
your unpacking."

A valet, Brant thought blankly. Then he smiled, re-
membering one of his favorite authors, Wodehouse, and
the inimitable valet, Jeeves. *I hope this vintage dapper
doesn't think I'm mentally incompetent.* He stuffed the
hand that wanted to salute into his jeans pocket and said,
"I'm not certain actually, er, Winterspoon, that I'll be
here at Asherwood Hall all that long." His eyes fell on
the peeling paint around the floorboard, a detail he
hadn't noticed on the first tour he'd taken the previous
afternoon. *I've got to scrape that and stain it.*

"Certainly, sir, but doubtless you'll remain until Miss
Daphne arrives?"

"And Mrs. Cloe, don't forget," Mrs. Mulroy snapped.

"Indeed, Mrs. Sparks. And Mrs. Meitter also, I understand."

"I say, what's all this?" said Harlow, stifling a yawn
as he strolled into the Golden Salon. "Just who, my good
man," he asked, staring hard at Winterspoon, "are
you?"

"Winterspoon, sir."

"My valet," Brant added smoothly.

"My father didn't tell me about the valet," Harlow
said.

"Well, Winterspoon," Brant said, turning to the dignified little gentleman, "let us say that you stay on as long as I'm in England. All right with you?"

"Yes, sir. Most proper. In my last position, with Lord Culpepper, I also acted in the position of butler, sir, when his lordship's finances took something of a downturn." He cast a deprecating eye toward Mrs. Mulroy. "Since Mr. Hume, his late lordship's butler, won't be returning, perhaps you would like me to assume his responsibilities now?"

"Eyuh!" Mrs. Mulroy said. "As if I can't answer the door!"

"Perhaps," Brant said to both his retainers, "it would be best, Mrs. Mulroy, if you spent your time getting the house to rights. I imagine it will be up to Mrs. Meitter to decide about the future disposition of Asherwood Hall."

"Mrs. Meitter!" Mrs. Mulroy exclaimed. "What about poor Miss Daphne?"

Brant didn't wish for the moment to strangle himself in explanations, and said only, "We'll speak of it later. If you would both see to your responsibilities for the moment..."

The vintage dapper and the wood sprite left the room, Mrs. Mulroy calling over her shoulder that breakfast was ready in the breakfast room.

"We'll be right there," Brant said.

"Where," Winterspoon asked with awful calm, "is Mr. O'Reilly?"

"Who is Mr. O'Reilly?" Brant asked as he entered the breakfast room.

"His old lordship's cook, my lord."

Brant bent an eye toward Mrs. Mulroy. "He bagged it," she said. "Took a case of his old lordship's best brandy with him. Bloody blighter!"

"He is Irish, my lord," Winterspoon said by way of explanation. "I trust, Mrs. Mulroy, that the kitchen is in competent hands?"

Mrs. Mulroy drew herself up, looking like a bantam-weight fighter.

"I'm certain that all hands are competent enough," Brant said quickly.

"Did you sleep well, Brant?" Harlow asked once they were alone.

"Yes, I slept very well."

"No ghosts or strange noises?"

"No..." *It was like coming home and sleeping in my own bed. Only better.* "It was a noble experience sleeping in a huge bed three feet off the floor."

Over a rather uninspired breakfast of one egg, too well-done, soggy toast and weak coffee, Harlow said, "The Old Man wanted me to tell you that expenses for the staff would be picked up by the estate, until...everything was finally settled."

"Too bad O'Reilly bagged it," Brant said, wincing as he gingerly took another sip of coffee.

"If you like, Brant, I can call up an agency and see about getting you a proper cook."

Brant's attention was on the stained and faded wallpaper in the breakfast room, and the hideously dark wainscotting. Lord, he was thinking, this room could be flooded with light. *I must do something with it soon, since I'll be eating three meals a day in here.*

"I say, old boy, is that all right with you?"

"What? Oh, certainly, Harlow. Tell you what, drive me back to London this morning and I'll rent a car for myself."

"You don't mean you're leaving Asherwood today!"

"I'm coming back. There's so much to be done, you see. Oh, one thing you can do for me, Harlow. I want you to contact an agency or whatever, and find me a cook."

Harlow chewed thoughtfully on his toast, wondering if it were an American trait to be witless in the morning. He said only, "For what period of time, Brant?"

"Make it two weeks, why don't you?" He glanced at the wallpaper, smiled to himself, and said, "No, a month."

My God, what has happened! Daphne stared open-mouthed as the cab drove through the gates of Asherwood. The drive was cleared; there were two men trimming bushes; and another was mowing the dead winter grass. The thick ivy was gone, all of it, and the windows sparkled in the bright February afternoon sun. She saw another man, wearing old, faded jeans, a wool shirt and sneakers, high on a ladder, doing something to the roof.

"This is the place, Miss?" the cab driver asked, turning to see the young lady staring fixedly at the house.

"What? Oh yes, thank you! Please, just put my suitcases on the drive."

None of the men turned, and she realized they couldn't hear the taxi over the low roar of a buzz saw. She stood in the drive a moment, staring about her, wondering yet again why Aunt Cloe had insisted that she had things to do in London and had sent her on ahead.

Brant didn't know what made him turn on the ladder, but when he did he saw a taxi leaving through the front gate, and a gorgeous young woman standing in front of the house, looking blankly about her.

Lucilla Meitter, he thought. Lucilla the Vamp, he added to himself. Lord, what a face and figure! He climbed slowly down the ladder, jumping the remaining few feet to the soggy ground. He stared at her a moment, taking in the waving streaked blond hair that fell softly to her shoulders, the incredible wide green eyes, and her endless stretch of legs. She was wearing a soft blue wool coat that was belted at her narrow waist.

"What," Daphne asked, eyeing the staring man, "are you doing?"

Brant gave her a crooked grin, knowing he was gaping at her like a horny goat. "The gutter was filled with leaves and other things. I was cleaning it out."

"It appears that the new viscount has taken control. The house looks so different, quite lovely, really, without all that tangled, depressing ivy."

"Thank you, ma'am. I—we are all doing our best."

Daphne studied the man more closely, suddenly aware of his strange accent. He was a lovely looking man, too, and it pleased her that he was smiling at her. "Are you a friend of Lord Asherwood's? You sound American, I think."

"Oh yes, we're quite close." Brant thrust out his hand. "Actually, we're one and the same person."

Daphne blinked at him, and gave him her hand without thinking. His grip was warm and firm. "Oh, I'm sorry! I suppose I hadn't expected you to be clambering about on the roof. You're the football player."

"That's right." He paused a moment, clasping her hand a bit tighter, and said, "I don't think I have to ask your name. You're my cousin, Lucilla Meitter, right?"

Lucilla!

She gave him a thin smile and removed her hand. "Why do you think that?"

Brant thrust his hands in his jeans pockets, and Daphne's eyes followed his movements. She gulped. He was a beautiful man, and so well put together! *But he thinks you're Lucilla.* He gave her another lovely smile, and she just looked at him, waiting.

"Well, actually, it didn't require a great deal of intelligence on my part. I was informed that my cousin Lucilla was the beauty, and, of course, I've seen a photo of my other cousin, Daphne."

Daphne thought of the single picture of her in the Golden Salon and winced. Ugly, ugly, ugly! Still, he didn't have to be so...

"I understand that Daphne has changed a good deal," she said, clutching her purse tightly, and wishing her newfound self-confidence weren't plummeting to her toes.

"Has she? Well, like this house, I imagine that any change would improve matters. Do you know her well?"

"Oh yes, quite well, as a matter of fact."

"Then you also know the terms of the infamous will?"

Daphne shook her head. "No, I didn't stop in London to see Mr. Hucksley. Aunt Cl—that is, I imagine I'll find out soon enough."

"Good grief!" Brant said. He began to laugh. "Well, since Asherwood Hall will doubtless be yours quite soon, may I recommend that we adjourn to the Golden Salon? Unfortunately, the old spr—er, Mrs. Mulroy is in the village right now, so I can't offer you any refreshment."

Brant picked up her suitcases and strode to the open front doors saying over his shoulder, "I'm expecting a cook shortly. I was informed by Mrs. Mulroy that O'Reilly bagged it with a case of his old lordship's brandy."

For a moment Daphne simply stared after him, not attending to his words. What did he mean that Asherwood would shortly be Lucilla's? Impossible! It was his; it had to be.

She followed him numbly into the house, at first not noticing the shining marble floor. Then she did, and blinked.

"Come on in here, Lucilla," Brant said. "I just finished the Golden Salon two days ago. I started there first, since there wasn't too much to be done. I've also been working on the breakfast room. Hopefully, you'll approve my changes. If you don't..." He shrugged.

She couldn't think of a word to say. If the house was Lucilla's, why was he doing all this work? She paused in the doorway and looked around. The large room was filled with clear winter sunlight. The walls had been repainted a cream color, and the furniture had been reduced to the Regency settings. All the heavy mahogany pieces that she'd hated were gone, as were the piles of ugly bric-a-brac.

"It's beautiful," she said. "And the carpets are so clean! I never realized they were so lovely."

"Thank you. I'm glad you approve. I was surprised myself that they came out so well. I was certain they'd have to be replaced. Here, let me help you off with your coat."

He slipped it off her shoulders and placed it on a chair back. "Won't you sit down?"

Daphne sat in her favorite chair, a small, high-backed blue satin-covered affair that had been relegated, before Uncle Clarence's death, to the far corner.

She crossed her legs, unaware that Brant was studying each exposed inch.

"So," he said, forcing his eyes to her lovely face, "you don't know about your good fortune?"

"No," she said, "I don't. Perhaps you'd be good enough to tell me about the will."

She didn't have the look of a swinger, he thought. Nor did she look old enough to have gone through three husbands. She looked fresh as sunshine, and . . .

"The will?"

"Forgive me," Brant said. "It's just that you're something of a surprise. I knew, of course, that you were . . . lovely, but I thought you'd be older."

"I take good care of myself," she said, trying to keep her voice light. *Tell him who you are, you fool!* But she said nothing more.

"Ah, the will. Shouldn't we wait for Hucksley Senior?"

"I don't see why we should."

"It's quite complicated, actually, and in my opinion, odd in the extreme. Basically, it all boils down to this: I inherit all the money and Asherwood Hall if I marry my cousin, Daphne Asherwood."

"Marry Daphne! Why, that's ridiculous!"

"My feelings exactly," Brant agreed in a dry voice. "Evidently old Lord Asherwood wanted her taken care of. Why he didn't leave her the money to take care of herself is quite beyond me! From what I've heard, though, it's likely the girl doesn't have a notion of what to do."

"But what if you don't wish to marry Daphne?"

"Ah, then the fun begins! If I refuse, then you, Cousin Lucilla, and a charity, split everything, and poor little Daphne is out with only five hundred pounds in her purse. If she refuses to marry me, then we're both out, and this time it's all yours."

Everything fell into place. The scales have fallen from my eyes, she thought, utterly distracted. Uncle Clarence muttered something about taking care of me, but this! Oh no, it can't be true! Aunt Cloe must have known; she must have! Why else would she have insisted that I needed to be redone, top to toe? "How much money is there?" she asked.

"If you're not a rich woman now, Lucilla, you soon will be. The estate amounts to four hundred thousand pounds."

"Four hundred thousand pounds! But why didn't Uncle Clarence spend some of that precious money on the Hall? I begged him and begged him not to let it fall into ruin! Oh, that impossible old man! I'd like to strangle him!"

"You're a bit late," Brant said.

"Daphne is supposed to marry you," she repeated blankly. "But I ... she doesn't even know you! And you don't know her!"

"I can't say I'm particularly looking forward to our meeting," Brant said.

"Why is that?"

Brant shrugged. "I think that is rather obvious. The will, my great uncle's ridiculous stipulations, Daphne herself ..."

"What," she heard herself asking in a shrill voice, "about Daphne herself?"

"I've seen a photo of her, as I told you," Brant said with disarming frankness. "She is not what I ever envisioned my wife to look like, nor do I expect her personality to be particularly invigorating. I've heard her referred as 'that poor, sweet young lady.'"

Conceited, arrogant beast! Jerk! Cad! Her mental list of insults came to a grinding halt. Ah ha, bastard!

And true, all of it!

"Why, if you have no intention of marrying Daphne, are you spending your time here, doing all this work?"

Brant clasped his hands together between his thighs. "I don't know," he said, honest puzzlement in his voice. He raised his eyes to hers. "I didn't even want to come to England. I didn't want to see this house, but when I did..." He shrugged. "It's like I've been here before, long ago, perhaps. I have these pictures in my mind of how it should look. Sounds dumb, doesn't it?"

"No," she said. "No, it doesn't, not at all. I'm delighted that you kept the Regency furniture in here. It is my favorite. Many times I've pictured myself reclining gracefully on that sofa, pretending to be a rich, beautiful lady of 1810, dressed perhaps in a soft muslin gown— oh! You must think I'm bonkers!"

He was smiling at her, open approval and liking lighting his blue eyes. "I don't think either of us is dumb or bonkers." He rose and paced across the room, Daphne's eyes following his progress. "Then you feel the draw of the house, too?" he asked.

"Draw? Oh, do you mean that I feel an affinity toward it? Why, yes, I suppose that I have always felt that way. That's why it always made me so angry that Uncle Clarence was letting it fall down around his ears." She added, without pause, "You don't look like a viscount."

He thrust his hands into his jeans pockets, drawing the pants down further, which made her mouth feel strangely dry. "Wait until you meet my valet, Winterspoon. Likely he's hiding in a closet right now, bemoaning the fact that I'm such an ugly, informal American, but just wait until evening. He turns me out in fine fashion, whether I want it or not."

"Winterspoon is here? How marvelous. I've missed him."

Brant sent her a quizzical look. "I wasn't under the impression that you'd visited Asherwood Hall all that often."

Daphne forced herself to shrug. She couldn't believe that she was actually carrying on a conversation with a man. It's what Lucilla would do, she told herself. Daphne would sit huddled up, looking and acting like a tongue-tied fool.

"Perhaps you'll like Daphne," she heard herself say.

"Fat chance!"

"What?"

"Very unlikely. I suppose I'm not being very kind, but I've thought of her as a double bagger."

"A double what?"

"American slang. Forgive me. To be blunt, then, a dog. Probably a very sweet dog, but a dog nonetheless."

She was trembling. It's all your own fault, she was repeating silently to herself. It's like eavesdropping. You never hear anything good about yourself. But a *dog*! "Just maybe," she said viciously, "she'll think *you're* a double bottle."

"No, double *bagger*. You could be right. I shouldn't be saying things like that to you, her cousin. It's just that I'm damned mad about the whole situation." He raked his fingers through his thick hair. "Are you here to stay? Since you will be the owner, I should stop with all my plans. They should be your plans."

The bitterness in his voice made her blink. He had indeed fallen in love with the Hall. Well, to hell with him! Lucilla would get the "dump," as she'd always stigmatized Asherwood Hall. She rose jerkily to her feet.

"No," she said, "it's not up to me, I can assure you of that!"

"I tell you, I won't be marrying Daphne! I'll be returning to the United States shortly, and it'll be all yours."

"None of it will be mine, since I'm not—"

There came a gasp from the open doorway. "Miss! Lawks, you're home! And just look at you—what a stunner!"

"Mrs. Mulroy," Daphne said, smiling at the beaming old woman. "How good it is to see you again. His lordship has been telling me that Winterspoon is here, also."

Brant was seized by a very funny feeling. Something was wrong here, quite wrong. He looked from Lucilla to Mrs. Mulroy and back again.

"You're not Lucilla Meitter?" he said in a very low and controlled voice.

"No, I'm not, my lord!" She swept him an insulting bow.

"Mrs. Meitter!" Mrs. Mulroy gasped. "Certainly not, my lord. This is Miss Daphne!"

"Yes," Daphne said with furious calm, "the double bagging dog."

Brant flushed deeply, and cursed very softly and very fluently under his breath.

Chapter Five

They faced each other across the dining table in the formal dining room. Brant was dressed according to Winterspoon's notions, in a dark suit and white dress shirt. Daphne wore a dark gray wool dress that Aunt Cloe had insisted upon in Paris. It hugged her body like a York glove, and gave additional oomph to her magnificent bosom with its small pleats splaying downward like an opened fan from a circular neckline. She wore no jewelry; she had none. For once Daphne didn't feel like hunching her shoulders forward. She sent Brant a studied, insolent look, one that she'd been practicing, and sipped from her wineglass.

She'd walked out on him that afternoon, and this was the first time he'd seen her since their debacle. He'd managed to whip himself into a fine state, and her nasty silence egged him on.

He said, his voice as cold as her stare, "You should have told me immediately who you really were. Your behavior was infantile, like a schoolgirl wanting to write her own Shakespearian scenes, with all the silly mix-ups and people at cross-purposes."

Daphne's fingers tightened on her glass. Oddly enough, for the first time in her twenty-three years she didn't feel at all embarrassed or intimidated by being in a man's company, alone. She was too furious. She pulled back her shoulders, with the result that her breasts could not help but draw his attention. "I," she said finally, in an equally cold voice, "have never thought much of Lucilla's looks." *Lord, what a lie! I've been jealous of her since I was ten!* "On the other hand, my lord, you were just as I knew you'd be: brash, rude, insulting, arrogant, conceited—"

"Well, that certainly must cover it!"

"—and you were wearing disgusting American clothes!"

"So you liked my jeans, huh?"

"I don't know how you could bend over! What's more—"

"Don't strain your brain for more charming adjectives!"

"I never *strain my brain*."

"Perhaps you should consider straining it a bit more in this particular instance. I repeat, Miss Asherwood, your behavior was every bit as ridiculous as mine, no, more so. And yes, I admit that I was out of line."

"Is that to be construed as an apology?" she asked sweetly.

"Construe it as you like," he said, and forked down a bit of leathery roast beef. "Surely you can't take exception to my clothes this evening. Winterspoon assures me that this is what the well-dressed English lord wears to dinner.''

"Clothes," she said, "do not make the lord."

"But clothes," he said, eyeing her bosom with lecherous interest, "do tell me a lot about what a woman has to offer."

She choked on her roast beef, too angry to think of a retort, and frowned at the taste. "Oh, how I wish O'Reilly were here!" she exclaimed. "This is terrible. How have you managed to survive?"

"I keep asking for hamburgers. They're hard to screw up."

"Who would want to screw a hamburger?"

"I've never wanted to screw a hamburger. What I mean is that hamburgers are hard to ruin, to mess up."

"Oh."

"Now I suppose you'll tell me that I can't speak proper English."

"Oh no. It appears that you already recognize your...lacks, at least in that area."

Brant dropped his fork and leaned against the high-backed chair, folding his arms over his chest. "Why don't you tell me why the hell you don't even remotely resemble that *double bagger* in the photo? Was it all some elaborate joke? Who is that girl?"

Daphne toyed a moment with a slice of bread. "I'm not certain to which photograph you are referring."

"The one of the girl who looks frumpy, dowdy, unappetizing, completely without style, with a face that could sink a thousand ships—"

"Now, I believe *you* can cease with *your* sterling adjectives! Actually, that photo is of Lucilla, taken when she was much younger. Her first husband saw to it that she was done over. I haven't seen her for quite a while, but I've heard that she looks much different now."

"Just why is the photo signed Daphne Asherwood?"

She looked at him with wide, innocent eyes, and stared limpidly into his suspicious, narrowed ones. "Is it? Well, perhaps it was added as a joke, you understand."

"And why are you referred to by everyone as 'poor, sweet, little Daphne'?"

She surprised herself by giving him a saucy grin. "Well, it does appear as if I now am poor. What is it, five hundred pounds?"

"Only if I refuse to marry you!"

"And I'm certainly sweet."

He stared at her breasts. "But not little!"

I will not let him embarrass me! "I'm not all that tall," she said blandly, surprising herself even more.

"Perhaps," he said, with a wolfish gleam in his eyes, "we'll see just how you size up."

"Size up?"

"How you fit against me."

Her eyes widened; she couldn't help it. She felt a flush rising from her neck to her cheeks. "Are all Americans so abominably conceited and rude?"

"Do all English women turn into little red roses when they can't stand the heat?"

"Little red roses! What heat?"

"You're blushing, and you haven't retorted with much aplomb," he said. "Thus, I applied the heat, and you couldn't handle it."

"Have I mentioned how very muscular your chest looks with the shirt buttons straining so...so provocatively?"

He threw back his head and laughed deeply. "Bravo! My little English rose is getting into the swing of things!"

Where is Daphne? she wondered for a brief moment, marveling at herself. She should be under the table by now. "I very much enjoyed watching you thrusting your hands in your jeans pockets." She rolled her eyes. "What a treat!"

"I'm glad you thought so. I think I'd prefer *your* hands thrusting in my pockets, though."

Her eyes fell from his face as fairly specific images flitted through her mind.

"Gotcha!" he said. "Now, if you're through fencing about with me, a poor mortal man, perhaps we can get serious."

"Serious about what?" she asked, relieved that he'd changed the subject. But then again, she felt so alive, so sparkling...

"Serious about why my Great Uncle Clarence produced such an outrageous will."

She set to crumbling her bread into small bits. "I believe he thought me incapable of doing anything on my own."

Brant shook his head. "Was he blind? You're beautiful, you're witty, and I can see you being capable at anything you tried."

The string of compliments, said quite seriously, stunned her for a moment. Am I really beautiful and witty, she wanted to ask him. "You don't understand," she said, sighing a bit. "I came to live at Asherwood when I was very young. I grew up here, alone, except for Uncle Clarence and the servants, of course."

"Surely you went to school."

She looked stricken for a brief moment, a look not lost on Brant. "Uncle brought in a tutor, an obnoxious little man who treated me like a half-wit. He left when I turned seventeen. Uncle had other uses for me then."

"Like what?"

She swallowed and forced her voice to indifferent calm. "Oh, I sort of ran things here at the Hall. You know, housekeeper, fetcher, bill-payer, gardener, and anything else he wanted of me."

"General all-purpose slave, in fact."

"Nothing quite so...degrading. And, of course, he let Aunt Cloe come to see me on occasion. I even went once to Scotland to visit her."

"You must have died of excitement," Brant said. Miserable old codger!

"Aunt Cloe loves me. In fact, she took me to Greece just after the funeral."

"Where is Aunt Cloe?"

"In London, I think. She sent me on ahead. She said something about business with Mr. Hucksley."

"Ah."

"Ah, what?"

He didn't reply for a long moment. Instead he gazed at her, a thoughtful expression on his face. "That is your photo, isn't it?"

"Yes," she said, "it is. I lied about Lucilla; she's been beautiful since she was born. I was the one who needed doing over, and Aunt Cloe saw to it, I guess you'd say."

"She couldn't have achieved this result if all the ingredients hadn't been lurking about, ready to come together."

"My eyes aren't really such a vivid green. They're kind of a washed out hazel. These are colored contacts. Aunt Cloe insisted."

"Confession time? Your lovely hair... is that a wig?"

"No, it's mine. Monsieur Etienne streaked it."

"And your clothes?"

"Aunt Cloe took me to Paris."

"This transformation began just after the funeral?" At her nod, he continued. "Look, Daphne, I'm delighted someone cared enough about you to do something. Obviously, all you needed was a bit of a boost."

"You are kind to say so."

"No, on the contrary, I'm being honest." Suddenly he grinned. "Obviously your Aunt Cloe knew what she was about, as did Reginald Hucksley, I'll bet."

Daphne's eyes drew together. "I don't understand."

"Don't you, yet? I would imagine that she and the Old Man—Hucksley Senior—plotted this together. You see, Aunt Cloe wanted you to have your chance, to present you in all your glorious new plumage to the new Lord Asherwood."

"That's...ridiculous! I don't know you! You're an American!"

"I wondered why Hucksley kept insisting that I remain in England," Brant continued, ignoring her spate of words. "He ran me all over the place, then insisted that I come here, to Asherwood Hall."

Daphne didn't reply. She was thinking about what he'd said, and she knew he was right. They'd planned to truss her up like a Christmas goose and present her on the new viscount's platter! Her hands flew up to her face, and she pressed her palms against her cheeks.

"This is awful! Why, you don't even like me!"

"I don't?" he asked blandly.

"No! And I think you're...well, I won't insult you! But what about me and my feelings?"

It was a wail of fury and chagrin.

"Eyuh! You all finished, my lord?"

Brant cast a distracted, impatient eye towards Mrs. Mulroy. "Yes," he said shortly, "we're finished. Coffee in the Golden Salon, if you please."

Daphne pulled herself together with an effort. "It was quite fine, Mrs. Mulroy. Thank you."

"Well, little Miss, you didn't eat much," said Mrs. Mulroy, judiciously eyeing Daphne's plate.

"It must be all the...excitement," Brant said. "Will you come along now, Daphne?"

"But I made some singin' hinnies for you, Miss Daphne!"

"Singin' what?" Brant asked, bending a fascinated eye on the old wood sprite.

Daphne said smoothly, "They're scones. Very fattening, indigestible, and really quite delicious. Just wrap them up, Mrs. Mulroy, and we'll enjoy them tomorrow."

"Eyuh," said Mrs. Mulroy, and left them, shaking her head.

Daphne rose and took Brant's proffered arm. "Perhaps you can tell me what 'eyuh' means," Brant said, smiling down at her.

"It's an all-purpose word that can convey anything from dire chagrin to immense joy. I meant to tell you," she continued after a brief pause, all too aware of the strength of his arm beneath her hand, "the entranceway looks marvelous."

"Yes, it does, doesn't it?" he said smoothly. "Stop a moment, Daphne."

She did, looking up at him, a question in her eyes.

He drew her toward him, very slowly, very gently. "You aren't too tall, even with your heels on. A nice fit, though, a very nice fit. Probably perfect in your bare feet."

He saw the surprise in her widened eyes, then the uncertainty. "Come along," he said. "Let's continue our discussion over coffee, such as it will be."

Once Brant managed to remove the old wood sprite from the room, he sat back on the sofa and said, "Won't you sit down? You're prowling about like a caged tiger. Tigress, rather. Not that I'm not enjoying the view, of course."

"No, I don't want to sit," she snapped at him. "I'm too mad."

"Oh? You didn't seem at all mad in the entrance hall."

"Stop drawing me! You have realized their...plot! But what about me? Am I supposed to fall into your arms and beg you to marry me? I don't even like you!"

"As I recall," Brant said, eyeing her closely, "I believe you were even referred to as being dreadfully shy. Odd, I haven't noticed any shyness in you at all." *Except when I brought you against me.*

Daphne drew up short, her hands on her hips, her head cocked to one side. "You're right," she said, her voice puzzled. "I am shy, dreadfully so, as you said. At least, I always thought I was. Uncle Clarence always called me his bashful little peahen. I don't understand..."

"I imagine that starting out our relationship as Lucilla the Vamp helped you get over it. And then you were so angry with me, you forgot to act like the old Daphne. Incidentally, Uncle Clarence was a complete and utter idiot and fool."

She frowned and waved a dismissing hand toward him. "But why did he write his will in such a way? I guess he knew you weren't married, but you must have friends, women friends."

"Yes," he said, "I do, but no one terminally serious. Undoubtedly Uncle Clarence did something of a work-up on me. As Harlow told me, he must have believed this the ideal way to have pitter-pattering little British feet running about Asherwood Hall. You, I take it, are all British?''

''Yes,'' she said absently. She flopped down into a chair and crossed her legs. ''What,'' she said, raising her eyes to his face, ''are we going to do?''

I think I should get the hell out of Asherwood Hall and out of England as soon as I can, he thought, pulling his eyes away from those glorious long legs. Instead he said coolly, ''Let's not worry about it now. You've just arrived. Perhaps I can draft you into helping me with the house. There's a great deal to be done.''

''Lucilla's house? Why bother? As soon as she takes ownership she'll turn it over to the National Trust. That or sell it.''

''Perhaps you're right,'' Brant said. ''Still, I don't have to be back in the U.S. for another month. It amuses me to work on the house. Besides, I'll bet you've got some great ideas.''

''Why would you bet that?''

''You love it,'' he said simply. ''It must have made you furious to see it go to rack and ruin.''

''I planted the rose garden in the back. It's not impressive now, but wait until spring.''

''Roots,'' Brant said.

''Yes, of course rose bushes have roots.''

''No,'' he said smiling as he rose, ''I meant roots as in where a person hails from, belongs.''

''You're rooted in the United States, aren't you?''

''I'm not quite certain. Actually, I'm really not certain about a whole bunch of things right now. Are you ready to sack out?''

''Sack what?''

''Go to bed, sleep.''

"Yes," she said without guile or wiles, "I would like to go to bed. It's been a terribly enlightening day, hasn't it?"

"Frighteningly so," he agreed. "Incidentally, do you have any idea where I can find replacement parts for the armor?"

She burst into merry laughter. "I worried about that for the longest time! I told Uncle Clarence that I wanted to reassemble them, taking parts from one knight to make another one whole." She paused a moment, a sad glint in her eyes. "He didn't let me."

"Screw Uncle Clarence," Brant said.

"As in screwing hamburger?"

"As in damn and blast Uncle Clarence, and let's forget him."

"You Yanks have the oddest way of talking," she said, grinning up at him. "Screwing this and screwing that, all with different meanings! How do you keep it all straight?"

"That particular expression," he said, appearing much struck, "does have many different meanings. There's one special one, though, that tops them all."

"And what is that?"

"Perhaps," he said slowly, "I'll tell you, someday."

Chapter Six

"You had the *nerve* to criticize my jeans?"

Daphne skittered to an abrupt halt in the doorway of the Armor Room at the sound of Brant's teasing voice. "Oh dear," she said, feeling suddenly as if she were on display, "I shouldn't have used that as an insult." She wanted to cover herself somehow, but she didn't know where to put her hands.

"No," he agreed, gracefully coming to his feet. "You shouldn't have." His eyes traveled from her bulky cream wool sweater to the very new designer jeans she was wearing. Not wearing, he thought, dazzled by the sight. Poured into was more like it. Endless long legs, lovely shape, no bulges, no... He shook his head and said abruptly, "You ready for some breakfast?"

She nodded, saying impishly, "Maybe Mrs. Mulroy has put out the singin' hinnies!"

"Lord save us!"

She fell into step beside him. "Or maybe some kedgeree, or some bangers, or—"

"How 'bout some plain eggs and bacon?"

"Impossible! Too provincial. I think I'd prefer some angels on horseback."

"You got me on that one," he said, grinning into her twinkling eyes. "All right, what are angels on horseback?"

"Oysters wrapped in bacon. But, if you substitute prunes and chutney for the oysters, you have devils instead of angels."

"How about a combination of the two? Too much of one or the other would be boring."

"I have this odd feeling that you're no longer talking about oysters."

"No, and you're not boring. Not at all."

She gave him a sudden, dazzling smile, revealing small white teeth. "Nor am I shy," she said proudly, and blinked.

He wanted to kiss her, run his hands over her bottom and up under her sweater. He wanted... "Oh no," he said, "more soggy toast."

"Shush," Daphne giggled. "Mrs. Mulroy will hear you. Old Maddy does try, Brant, truly she does."

"The new cook is arriving today, hopefully. Winterspoon agreed to pick her up at the train station. Then we can pig out."

"Pig what?"

"Make gluttons of ourselves, eat until we're stuffed."

"We can't. We wouldn't be able to get into our respective jeans. Aunt Cloe told me I shouldn't do anything but drink tea when I wear these."

I'd just as soon see you out of them anyway. "Good point."

"It's raining," Daphne said, looking toward the fogged up windows.

"We've got plenty to do in the Armor Room. You up for fitting armor puzzles together?"

"I'd adore it." She fell silent, dipping pieces of her toast into a cup of tea, tea laced with milk, for God's sake, he observed, wincing at the sight.

"What's the matter?" he asked after a moment. "Your jeans hugging a bit too close?"

She smiled, but only briefly. "Lucilla. Perhaps we shouldn't be changing things, since Asherwood Hall will be hers."

"There is that," he agreed. "I like your hair," he added abruptly.

She smiled tentatively, as if surprised by the compliment.

"And your scrubbed face."

Her scrubbed face fell. "You mean I look like a prim schoolgirl."

"No, that isn't at all what I meant. I don't like much makeup on women. And you're lucky. You don't need it."

"I am wearing eyebrow pencil," she said, thrusting up her chin. "My eyebrows are too light without it. Aunt Cloe told me so."

"I'll have to take a closer look to see if I approve."

She remembered in very specific detail how he'd been quite close for those few moments the night before. Her breathing quickened. She said, her voice full of reproach, "You're making sport of me."

"I? Surely not. I'm merely trying to keep your self-confidence up." Just as I'd like to pull your jeans down. How, he wondered silently, surprised at himself, could he be so horny? Daphne—ridiculous name—was lovely, no doubt about it, but take Marcie, for instance. Now, she was beautiful, perfect body... and full of herself.

"Brant, what is football?"

He grinned, waving his fork at her. "Football and baseball are the two most popular American sports. It's similar to rugby, I guess, though I don't know too much about rugby."

"I don't either, so we're even. But what do you do in football?"

"I'm a quarterback," Lord, where to begin? "Tell you what, Daph, I'll call up my mom and have her send over a couple of films of my games. We can rent a projector somewhere around here, can't we?"

"Certainly. You're not in the wilds, Brant. Are you famous? Like a cinema star?"

"I'm not exactly a household word, but I'm fairly good at what I do."

"And you love it."

"Yes, I do. Immensely. But I'm getting old."

"Old! What a silly thing to say. What are you? Thirty?"

"Thirty-one. In football, that's getting up there. It's a very rough contact sport. And every year I get older and my competitors get younger. I've probably got four or five more years, barring any serious injuries."

"Oh no! You get hurt?"

He grinned wryly. "The opposing team loves nothing more than to cream the quarterback. That is," he added, quickly translating, "their objective is keep me from gaining yardage. If they can bury me under a pile, they succeed. Pile of bodies, that is."

"Have you ever been hurt?"

He unconsciously flexed his throwing arm. "On occasion. My teammates are good about protecting me."

"It sounds like the Romans and the Christians."

"It does a bit, doesn't it? In my early professional days I was quarterback for a consistently losing team. I was usually sore all season. No big deal, really," he added, seeing her eyes darken with concern. "I realize it's difficult for you to understand until you see the game. I'll explain everything to you then. Okay?"

She sighed, sitting back in her chair. "While you were playing this game and making money, I was rotting here, wondering what was going to happen to me when Uncle Clarence died."

"And you still wonder?"

"Of course, wouldn't you? Five hundred pounds won't last long, after all. I don't have any skills."

Her voice was matter-of-fact, not an ounce of bitterness or self-pity, which he would have expected. He said lightly, "You'll probably marry a nice young Englishman."

"I'll miss my rose garden," she said, ignoring his words.

"I'd like to see it."

"Not today. I don't have a brolly big enough to keep us from drowning."

"Brolly?"

She looked startled. "You know, Brant, one of those things you raise over your head when it's raining."

"Ah, an umbrella."

"Exactly," she said, giving him an approving look. Like I'm a bright schoolboy, he thought.

"You finished?" he asked, rising. "Ready to attack the knights?"

"Onward!"

They worked throughout the morning, assembling matching arms and legs to form a half-dozen proper suits of armor. Their laughter floated out of the room, reaching Mrs. Mulroy's ears as she dusted in the entrance hall. She smiled benignly.

"Oh, you've a spot of smut on your face." Daphne raised her hand and rubbed his cheek with her fingertips.

Brant felt an alarming jolt of desire at her touch. She was so close he could see her contact lenses. Slowly he raised his own hand and stroked it through her hair. Silky smooth, he thought, and so thick.

Daphne's hand dropped. She looked at him, confusion written all over her face.

"I was just checking to see if you had any spots of smut," he said smoothly, leaning away from her. He had no intention of seducing the castle maiden.

"In my hair?"

"One never knows." He jumped gracefully to his feet and stretched. "I'm ready for some exercise. How 'bout you, Daph?"

"Daph? Is that a common nickname in America?"

Her voice sounded a bit breathless, for she was watching the play of muscles as he stretched his arms over his head.

"No, it's my own. I've never known a woman named Daphne before. It's nearly stopped raining. Why don't you get the um...brolly and let's take a look at your rose garden."

"Righto," she said. "I'll be back in a moment."

He watched her walk gracefully from the room; he couldn't seem to take his eyes off her swaying hips.

Daphne found him a few minutes later in the Golden Salon, standing in front of the fireplace.

"I'm ready," she said.

He turned, and she saw that he was holding the god-awful photo of her in his hand. "I think we can burn this," he said quietly.

"But she still exists, I'm afraid."

"Does she?" He handed Daphne the photo. To his delight, after staring at it for a moment, she giggled. "Goodness," she said, raising eyes brimful of laughter to his face, "what a double bagger!"

They spent the evening seated on a carpet in front of the fireplace. It was cosy, intimate and utterly enjoyable.

"I talked to my mother. She's sending a couple of films express. You want a bit more brandy?"

"I'm already tipsy. I'd better not."

"I like your dress. I know, Aunt Cloe insisted that the English Rose should wear peach silk."

"It is silk, my very first silk anything. And yes, conceited man, she did insist. At the time I thought it a bit..."

"Sexy? Too revealing?"

"I'm not in the habit of exhibiting myself to such an extent," she said tartly. Her hand moved to cover the deep V of the neckline.

"No, don't," he said, and grasped her hand, drawing it down to her lap. "I'm a simple man, and the sight gives me pleasure."

She flushed, embarrassed, pleased and confused by his manner and his words.

As for Brant, he thought, I'm acting like an idiot. I won't seduce her. Nothing could be more stupid than that. She's not the seducible type. She's revoltingly innocent. I'm leaving England shortly. I'll never see her again. Not those beautiful breasts, not those gorgeous legs . . .

"Do you have any brothers or sisters?" she asked, turning slightly, so her breasts weren't directly in his line of vision.

"One sister," he said easily, leaning back against the chair. "Her name's Lily, and she's a character. I also have two nephews and a niece. They all live in Texas with Lily's new husband. He's an oilman."

"Just like on the telly? Is he another J.R. Ewing?"

"I'd heard *Dallas* was popular over here." At her excited nod, he continued. "I call him Crusty Dusty. I imagine he's ruthless enough if the situation calls for it. But he loves my sister, and that's good enough for me. I told him before they married that Lily needed a keeper more than a husband, and Dusty drawled that as long as she was housebroken, it was fine with him."

"Housebroken? You mean like a burglar?"

Brant groaned. He clasped her hand and drew it to his mouth, kissing it lightly. "No, not like a burglar. Have you ever had a puppy?"

"Yes, when I was a little girl."

"Well, housebroken means that you train the puppy not to relieve himself on the floor or on the carpet or anywhere in the house. Like breaking a horse, I guess. Get him tamed and under control."

"I'm beginning to get quite fond of American. How long do you think it would take me to speak it fluently?"

"It would all depend on your teacher, I expect."

"You said that you're going home in a month. Will you play football?"

"No, it's the off-season. Practice starts in the summer. No, when I go back, I'm making a commercial for TV."

"For the telly! Oh, I am impressed. Whatever will you be selling?"

"I'll be pushing sports equipment."

Daphne came up on her knees, resting her hands on her thighs. "Do you want to know a secret, Brant?"

He arched a thick brow at her, forcing himself to keep his eyes on her face.

"It's about my Aunt Cloe. Well, you mustn't tell her I told you, but she adores young men. I remember her nearly choking when she saw a poster of one of your American athletes wearing nothing but sexy undershorts."

"Ah, and did you nearly choke, Daph?"

"I was too busy watching her reaction. When she noticed that I'd noticed, she hauled me away." She grinned at him, shaking her head. "I can't wait to see what she does when she lays eyes on you!"

"Shall I greet her in my underwear?"

"She'd love it, but perhaps you'd better not."

Would you love it? "I can see it now," he said lightly. "English Viscount Arrested for Indecent Exposure. Aunt Cloe in Hospital for Severe Palpitations."

Daphne was still laughing when she rose to her feet. "Well, we'll soon know what she thinks about you. She should be coming here soon. Now, my lord, I'm off for bed. My weak head is spinning from that wicked brandy."

"I'll walk up with you," Brant said. He laid his hand lightly on her shoulder when they reached the bedroom. "Do you ride?"

"Of course. Every Englishwoman who lives in the country rides, I'll have you know."

"Fine. If this blasted rain stops and it's not too cold, shall we go out tomorrow morning?"

"I'd love to. I'll even wear my new riding togs."

"I know, Aunt Cloe insisted."

"No, I did. I can't imagine getting on my mare, Julia, in my new jeans."

"I can," Brant said, patted her on her cheek, and walked down the corridor to his room.

The morning was cold, but not overly so, and the sky was overcast, but there was no rain. Brant's mount, borrowed from a neighbor, was strong and fast, and Daphne, astride her Julia, looked good enough to eat in her tailored tan riding pants and jacket. An Englishwoman to the tips of her riding boots.

They galloped and cantered, and he saw her life through her eyes. A circumspect life, he thought. A limited world. She took him into East Grinstead, and he saw the fondness of the locals for her, and their surprise at her appearance. They dismounted and walked along the River Wey, talking about nothing in particular.

"Daphne," he said abruptly as they readied to return to Asherwood, "have you ever dated?"

"Me?" He saw a fleeting glint of anger in her eyes, but it was so quickly gone that he might have imagined it. And there was light amusement in her voice as she replied, "Well, there was the rector, Mr. Theodore Haverleigh. Uncle Clarence let him into the house a couple of times and allowed him to take me to a church picnic."

"Did you like him?"

"Theo? Goodness no! He had no shoulders and no chin, and he was terribly puffed up with himself. I'm sure at the time he honestly believed he was doing me a favor, and perhaps he was...."

"At the time. Now, he'd probably start slobbering at the sight of you."

She gave him a pert salute. "Very true," she said, and lightly dug her heels into Julia's fat sides.

She felt marvelous. Full of humor, full of life. Until they reined in in front of the Hall.

"Oh dear," Daphne said. "That's Lucilla."

Brant gazed toward the woman standing on the front steps looking toward them. She was tall, with raven-black hair, immense blue eyes, and a figure that would stop a train.

"Indeed," he said. "Shall we take the horses to the stable?"

Daphne nodded numbly. She'd seen the admiration in Brant's eyes. Life as she'd known it for the past two days was over. She wanted to howl her disappointment. Instead, she followed Brant to the stables.

Chapter Seven

"Darling! How good to see you again! My, don't you look the smart bird! Whatever happened?"

Daphne suffered herself to be hugged and pecked on her cheek. "Hello, Lucilla. You're looking well. This is Brant Asher, the new Viscount Asherwood."

She's responding to him just as I would if I only knew how, Daphne thought with a stab of resentment.

Lord he's handsome, Lucilla thought as she calmly shook his hand, but her eyes were wide with admiration as she took in every inch of him. "Welcome, my lord, to England and to Asherwood."

She's already acting like the queen of the castle!

"Thank you, Lucilla. May I call you that?"

"Certainly, Brant. Has our little Daphne been showing you around?"

"We've been out riding, if that's what you mean, Lucilla," Daphne said. *Condescending bitch! Why do I feel* as if I've just gained weight in my thighs, got greasy hair, and my contact lenses have turned red?

"Why yes, dear, that's exactly what I meant. I hope," she continued, her eyes on Brant, "that you don't mind my dropping in unannounced?"

"Since Asherwood Hall will belong to you, Lucilla, how can we mind?"

"Oh yes," Lucilla said slowly. "The will."

"As you say," Brant said. "Shall we go in, ladies?"

It would all be extremely amusing, Brant thought, as the three of them sat over tea in the Golden Salon, if Daphne weren't losing her self-confidence by the second. It wasn't that Lucilla was obviously unkind to her. On the contrary, she was all that was gracious, as if she were addressing a sweet, but simple child.

Lucilla said over her tea cup, "The changes you've made, the improvements, Brant, are remarkable. The old tomb looks marvelous. Daphne, would you please hand me a biscuit? Thank you, dear. The entranceway is so very tip-top sparkling. And what you did to the suits of armor—why I would have tossed the lot out!"

"His lordship is quite creative," Daphne said dryly.

"What a lovely thought," Lucilla said, giving him a long, intimate look.

"I expect you saw Mr. Hucksley in London?" Brant asked.

"Oh yes. It's all too remarkable, isn't it? You mustn't worry, dear," she continued to Daphne, gently patting her hand. "I'll see that things are put right. I thought about it all the way up here. Perhaps a trade school, or a try at interior decorating, now that you've got yourself together. You'd enjoy that, wouldn't you, Daphne? Why, there's even business. You'd make an adorable secretary."

"Actually," Daphne said, getting a firm grip on her insecurities, "I think I might try my hand at modeling."

"Why, my dear girl, what a remarkable idea!"

If she says remarkable one more time, I'll yank off her panty hose and strangle her with them! Instead Daphne said, drawing herself up a bit straighter, "Not so remarkable. I certainly have the figure for it."

"Do you, dear? Well, I suppose I must wait to see you in a dress. Riding clothes are so...minimizing, aren't they?"

"I believe, ladies, that it's time for lunch," Brant said, rising. He looked toward Daphne, but her eyes were on Lucilla, who was gazing raptly at the zipper on his jeans.

At the sight of an unappetizing lunch of slipshod-looking sandwiches and thin potato soup, Brant said, "A new cook is arriving this afternoon."

"It's just as well," Lucilla said gently. "It will help us girls keep our weight down, won't it, dear?"

"Quite," Daphne said.

There were several minutes of blessed silence. Lucilla asked, "How long will you remain in England, Brant?"

"Another month, perhaps less."

"I understand from Mr. Hucksley that you're an athlete?"

"Yes, I play professional football for the New York Astros."

"How remarkable! You've certainly the...build for it. I thought you'd probably look grand in your title."

Daphne choked on her soup.

"I also understand that you've a *chère amie* waiting for you in New York, a lovely, independent career woman?"

Brant started to tell her that he had several gorgeous women waiting for him in New York, but he was aware of Daphne's eyes searching his face. "I'm fortunate to have many friends, both men and women."

"And all American, too. You must find our ways very strange."

"Not at all," Brant said pleasantly. Lord, is she playing both sides of the fence, he thought. "Though I will admit that Daphne is giving me quite an education."

"Daphne?" Lucilla's beautiful arched brows arched a bit more over incredulous light blue eyes.

"Yes," Daphne said, goaded. "I think Brant looks charming in his title too."

Lucilla laughed merrily. "My little peahen—as Uncle Clarence so sweetly called her—is changing before my very eyes! How utterly remarkable. Haven't you done something with your eyes, dear?"

"Yes," Daphne said, "I've finally learned to see with them."

"Well, I'm very proud of you, dear." She turned to Brant. "I talked of Daphne to my husband, you know, and he wanted to meet her, take her in hand and all that."

"You're too late, Lucilla," Daphne said. "Aunt Cloe already did."

"Dear Mrs. Sparks. I imagine that she'll be arriving here soon. To keep an eye on her investment, so to speak?"

Why do I feel like the sacrificial goat? "The more the merrier," said Brant. "Now, if you ladies will excuse me, I want to do some planing on the front doors. They're a bit warped."

Daphne's eyes followed his progress from the room. She stiffened when Lucilla said in a pitying voice, "Such a temptation, Daphne, but surely you have some pride?"

"What do you mean, Lucilla?"

"Surely, dear, you wouldn't consider marrying a man who only wanted you for money and Asherwood Hall? A good deal of money, I might add."

"Why not?" Daphne said, angry color staining her cheeks. "After all, it's either that or... trade school! I'll call Mrs. Mulroy to show you to your room, Lucilla."

"A marriage of convenience, dear. Really, what an appalling thought."

"Haven't you done it three times?"

"Why no, dear, not entirely. All three husbands were remarkably virile, you know. Just like Brant. I imagine that he knows every trick to make a woman swoon for him. Don't you agree?"

"Excuse me, Lucilla."

"Remember, Daphne," Lucilla called after her, "Brant is quite experienced with women. I do hope you won't make a fool of yourself over him. Seriously, dear, have a care. Hasn't he already turned your little head, just a bit?"

No, he's just made me feel very good about myself.

Daphne left the breakfast room and went immediately upstairs to change into her jeans and a sweater. Afterward she found Brant working on the front doors.

"Hi," he said, glancing up at her briefly. "Did you survive the first salvo?"

"What's a salvo?"

"A burst of rapidly firing artillery."

Daphne worried her lower lip for a moment, then burst out, "Do you need money, Brant?"

"Ah, that's very stiff cannon fire. No, as a matter of fact, I've got quite enough money."

"But I've heard that Americans view money as a sort of god, that they can never get enough of it."

"I wasn't aware that view was confined to the United States," he said. "As you well know, Daph, this estate runs about four hundred thousand pounds. Nearly a half million dollars. That's not chicken feed. Hand me that piece of sandpaper, will you?"

"This thing? Lucilla's so beautiful."

"Yes, she is. How old is she, anyway?"

"About thirty, I'd say."

"Listen to me, Daph. She's got a tremendous potential investment, all of it riding on what you and I decide to do. Don't let her rile you. If you were in her shoes, you'd likely do the same thing." He grinned at her. "Only not as well."

Daphne sighed. "Why do I feel as if I'm thirteen again, and fat and plain and dowdy?"

"She's quite good. Why don't you just sit back and enjoy her machinations? You might learn something useful."

"You're cynical, aren't you?"

"A bit, I guess. I just want you to use your wits and not get all sullen and defensive. You have got wits, you know, plenty of them."

"So, in other words," Daphne said slowly, "you want to keep her in . . . suspense?"

"I hadn't thought of that in particular. But it just might be fun. And, Daph, don't worry about your future. I won't let you starve. I'll see that you're set up in whatever you want to do."

"Marvelous," she muttered under her breath. "No, thank you, Brant. It's time, I think, that I looked after myself."

She walked away. She heard the grating sound of the sandpaper against wood cease, and knew he was looking after her.

* * *

If Brant felt like the main meal with Lucilla, he definitely felt like a very fattening dessert with Aunt Cloe. She'd examined every inch of him in great, interested detail, a dreamy look in her eyes. He noticed, gazing at her across the dining table over a delicious meal prepared by Mrs. Woolsey, that she was a tall, big-boned woman, with a strong nose and chin, and penetrating light blue eyes. When they looked at him, they both sparkled and looked speculating. She wore her thick salt-and-pepper hair the way his mother did, in a classic chignon. Her humor was dry, her smile charming. She has a lovely voice, he thought, listening to her speak of her trip.

"Ah, what a delight Paris was. All that gray sky and muzzling rain, but no matter. Such a relief to be home again. In the bosom of my family so to speak. I must say, Brant, you're everything I expected."

"I hope your expectations weren't set too high, Aunt Cloe," he said dryly, grinning at her. She'd arrived but three hours after Lucilla. He wondered if she'd hot-footed it here, knowing that Lucilla would be doing her best to making things unpleasant for her little chick, Daphne.

"Dear boy," Cloe said, wishing she were thirty years younger, "when you've lived as long as I have, you learn to be wary in what you expect. Photos help, of course. I must say, I like to see a man togged up for dinner. Very elegant."

"How long will you be staying, Aunt Cloe?" Lucilla asked, her voice as flat as her enthusiasm. "You must have so much waiting for your attention in Glasgow."

"What an excellent gunner you would have been in the war, Lucilla. Such marksmanship, such precise . . . yes, well, you know, I've been thinking that I will visit America. I will wait, of course, until Daphne gets settled in."

Brant blinked at her double-edged words. Lucilla gritted her teeth.

Daphne said, "That shouldn't take long, Auntie."

"Yes," Lucilla said. "We will all move her into a nice flat in London. Not long at all."

"Perhaps I'll study to be a carpenter," Daphne said. "I learned today how to plane a door."

"Or," Brant added, "you could work for the British Museum, keeping their armor exhibit in good shape."

"I thought that was probably your idea, Daphne," Lucilla said. "As I said, I should have tossed the lot."

"Oh, I don't know," Brant said. "I suspect the new owner of Asherwood might be delighted at such antiquity."

Cloe gave him a bland smile. "Indeed, my dear boy."

"But then again," he added, shooting her down, "one never knows, does one?"

He wished he'd kept his mouth shut, for Lucilla gave him another one of her patented intimate smiles. He wondered if he should lock his bedroom door tonight. He forked down another bite of the delicious Yorkshire pudding, listening to the well-bred backbiting going on between Aunt Cloe and Lucilla.

"How did you leave your dear third husband, Lucilla?"

"I left him, period, Aunt Cloe. I would have sworn you knew that."

"German men are so fierce and dominating, don't you agree?"

"Basically, Carl was a dear. But," Lucilla added, shooting Brant a honey-coated smile, "he was too old for me. Why, his daughter was Daphne's age, and his son, Dieter, well, such a possessive young man.'' She gave a little shudder.

''And Brant's age?''

''A bit older, actually. I just hope he doesn't follow me here.''

Brant studied Daphne from beneath half-closed lids. She was toying with the fresh peas on her plate, eating little, saying even less. She'd reverted to the old Daphne, he suspected. Withdrawn, shy, all self-confidence obliterated. He wanted to shake her, to draw her into his arms and comfort her. No! If he had half a brain, he knew he'd leave in the morning, early.

''I say, a jolly good dinner,'' Aunt Cloe said. ''Shall we have coffee in the sitting room?''

I've got to get Daphne alone, Cloe thought, as she watched her rise from her chair and walk from the dining room, like a prisoner going to the gallows. I've got to knock some sense into the girl!

To her utter delight Brant said, ''Unfortunately, Daphne and I haven't time for coffee. We're going into the village to see a movie. Are you ready, Daphne?''

Daphne stopped dead in her tracks, wondering if she'd heard right. He was rescuing her! She turned and gave him a dazzling smile. ''I just have to get my coat.'' She was off like a shot, nearly running up the stairs.

''I hope you'll forgive us, ladies, for leaving you on your first night here.''

''Not at all,'' Cloe said. ''Not at all.''

Lucilla was frowning, but just for a moment. She said with just an exquisite touch of wistful disappointment, ''I suppose one must keep one's promises. It's very nice of you, Brant, to see to Daphne.''

Daphne was looking at herself in the mirror. I don't look like a frump, she said under her breath. I won't let Lucilla make me feel like a refugee from a turnip patch. I won't! However, when she returned to the entrance hall, there was Lucilla, her hand on Brant's arm, laughing up at him. And he, damn him, was smiling down at her.

"Ah, here you are, dear," Lucilla said, turning to give her an approving look. "How lovely your coat is. I've always thought brown such an enduring color, and wool so very wearing. Now, Brant, don't keep her out too late, will you?"

As if I'm some sort of backward adolescent!

Aunt Cloe gave her a quick hug, whispering in her ear, "Don't you dare regard anything she says, love! You look charming, make no mistake about it."

"You ready, Daph?"

"Yes. Good night, Lucilla, Auntie."

The evening was clear and cold, a quarter moon lighting the drive. "I've always liked enduring things," Brant said, grinning down at her. "Would you drive, Daphne? I still don't trust myself on the wrong side of the road."

She nodded and slipped behind the wheel. "It's a lovely evening," she said inanely.

In response Brant sighed deeply and leaned his head back against the leather seat.

"What's the matter, Brant? Too many salvos?"

"For sure," he said, his eyes closed. "I've never before felt like a duck in hunting season."

And I'm one of the hunters, she thought, suddenly depressed. He must despise the lot of us. "What movie do you want to see?" she asked, forgetting there was just one cinema house.

"Turn on the heater and let's go parking."

"Parking? You mean, stop the car?"

He gave her a long, lazy look. "Yes, find a nice spot with something of a view to liven things up and pull over."

She drove on in silence.

"I told you that you shouldn't let Lucilla get to you."

Her hands gripped the steering wheel. "You invited me out because you didn't want me to continue making a fool of myself. You were feeling sorry for me," she said flatly.

"No, I was feeling sorry for myself. And you're a cute fool."

"Ha! I thought men just loved so much female attention!"

"At least you've got your sharp tongue back."

She shot him a look of pure dislike.

"Also, I invited you out because I'd like to beat some sense into you. Good, I've got your attention. Watch out for that ditch! This looks like a good spot. Pull over here."

She obeyed him and turned off the engine. Daphne had stopped on a slight rise overlooking the Wey. Naked-branched beech trees surrounded them.

"Now, turn around and look at me. I've got lots of things to say to you."

"You sound just like Uncle Clarence," she said, her voice as nasty as she could manage it.

"Do I? Unlike Uncle Clarence, I won't ask you to do anything you don't want to do. Well, maybe that's not totally the case. Why the hell did you regress again? I thought we'd straightened all that out after our memorable lunch."

She stared at him, unable to find the words to explain her feelings.

"How do you expect to get along if you can't handle all different kinds of people, and that includes women who patronize you?"

"I'll get along," she said. "Why do you care, anyway?"

"Sometimes I think you need a keeper."

He sounded mildly angry, and that surprised her. "Things are different with Lucilla here," she said slowly, trying to explain it both to him and to herself. "Before, with just the two of us—"

"Daphne," he interrupted, his voice impatient, "Lucilla's really a great deal of fun if you'd just forget all your old stored up envy of her. There's a whole world of people out there that you have to deal with."

"Just stop it!" she hissed at him. "Just leave me alone, okay? I don't need you to tell me what's wrong with me. And I'm not envious of Lucilla!"

She twisted the ignition key, and the engine turned over. Suddenly his hand was over hers, and the engine died. "Damn you," he said, and pulled her into his arms.

Daphne was too surprised to resist. She opened her mouth to say something—what, she didn't know—and felt his lips cover hers. She stiffened at the attack, and immediately he gentled the pressure. His tongue glided lightly over her lips; his hands stroked up and down her back.

"You taste like Yorkshire pudding," he said against her cheek. He returned to her mouth, gently nibbling, tasting, and slowly she began to relax, and respond.

"That's it," he said softly. "You're a beautiful, intelligent woman, Daphne, and I don't want you to forget it again." *And you're such an innocent I feel like I'm being unfair even kissing you.*

He released her and smiled at the dazed, uncertain look in her eyes. He gently rubbed his thumb over her jaw. "This," he said, "is what we Americans call parking."

"It's . . . different."

"You sound a little out of breath. Let's try again. Trust me and relax."

She did, without a second thought. He was careful, very careful, well knowing she didn't have a bit of experience. He didn't want to frighten her or put her off. He kept his hands on her back and his kisses light, undemanding. He broke off and gently pressed her face against his shoulder. He thought her breathing was a bit faster.

He stroked his fingers through her soft hair. I've wanted to do that since I've met her, he thought. He leaned his cheek against her temple and breathed in her sweet womanly scent. He heard himself say, "I want to make love to you, Daphne."

She raised her face and gave him a puzzled but glowing look. "You mean, you want to go to bed with me . . . and . . ."

He grasped her upper arms, cursing himself silently. "No, that isn't what I meant to say." He dashed his fingers through his hair. "I want you to realize that you're a marvelous person who can do anything she wants."

"Then why did you kiss me?"

Because I'm horny and any port in a storm!

But that wasn't true. He wanted her, only her. He had no idea why. His idea of a good time had never been the company of a repressed female with the experience of a Victorian maiden.

"Did you kiss me because you thought that would give me self-confidence?"

"Yes," he said without thinking.

Slowly she pulled away from him. "Lucilla's right," she said. "And I'm a fool."

"We're both fools," he said in a distracted attempt at humor. "And Lucilla's been right about only one thing I can think of."

"What is that?"

"She's afraid of you," he said slowly, studying her face in the dim shadows. "And she has a right to be."

Daphne shook her head, an abrupt, angry movement. "I just don't believe this. Everything revolves around you; at least, that's the way you see it. All of us are like hens bowing and scraping in front of the cock! Well, I don't care! I intend to see to myself, do you hear? I don't want your help, or Lucilla's help, or Aunt Cloe's! What I would like from you, my lord, is your refusal to marry me. That way I'll get five hundred pounds rather than just one hundred."

Brant clenched his jaws together. How dare she fly off the handle at him like that! Damn her! Accusing him of being some kind of a conceited sheik with a harem! He wanted to help her; he wanted to make her realize how much she had to offer, to... He said quietly, very quietly, "I doubt you'd even know what to do with fifty pounds. I doubt you would even know a checkbook if it bit you. You'd probably last no longer than one week on your own. You want five hundred pounds, lady? Fine, you've got it!"

Chapter Eight

Brant opened his bedroom door quietly, not bothering to turn on the ancient overhead light. He was still angry with Daphne—ridiculous Victorian name—and her dumb accusations. Why should he care, anyway? What she did with her life had nothing whatsoever to do with him. Hell, he'd be home soon, and good riddance to all of them!

Cock, indeed!

He turned on a Victorian lamp with a red velvet shade that sported thick red fringe, and methodically began to strip off his clothes. At least Winterspoon wasn't waiting for him. The thought of his valet helping him out of his pants was unnerving.

"I knew you'd look marvelous in your title."

His fingers stilled over the zipper. He turned slowly to see Lucilla wearing a tight silky thing, lounging pajamas, he supposed, a saucy smile on her lips.

"How 'bout title and trousers?"

"Sounds like the name of a painting," she said. "Perhaps we could frame you and put you up for the Royal Academy."

He grinned at her. "What are you doing in here, Lucilla?"

She shrugged, and one of the straps slipped off her lovely shoulder. He suddenly had the image of Marcie in his mind, standing in his bathroom doorway, wearing finally, after both straps had fallen, nothing but her enticing smile.

"It occurred to me, after seeing you in person, of course, that there were more options, shall we say, than the simple ones presented."

"I think," he said, "that you'd better explain that."

She shrugged again, but fortunately for his peace of mind and body, the other strap stayed put.

"You love this house," she said simply.

"Yes," he agreed, "I do. I'm not certain why, but I do. It's as if," he continued thoughtfully, trying yet again to put his feelings into words, "the house has been waiting for me, as if the house needs me, just as I need it." Roots, his mother would have said.

"The house also needs quite a bit of money to reinstate it to whatever its former glory was," she said dryly, giving him an odd look, one he was certain he deserved. It did, he admitted to himself, sound a bit crazy that he'd feel so strongly about what, after all, was only a pile of brick, windows and stone. He mustn't forget the chimney pots that were in dire need of scrubbing down.

"That's true, too."

"I will inherit the house and more than enough money."

Only if I don't marry Daphne.

"I see," he said only.

She chewed on her lower lip a moment, as if uncertain how to proceed. "I think perhaps," she said finally, "that you and I could join forces."

"In what way, Lucilla?"

"I think a nice start might be a vacation to, say, the South of France. St. Tropez, perhaps, or Nice."

"To get to know each other better?"

"Much better. We might just discover that we could do quite well together, Brant. Yes, quite well indeed. You are, I think, a man who appreciates a woman who knows her way about, a woman who would please you and appreciate you also. You are a very nice-looking man, Brant."

And I'd look just dandy on your arm, huh?

"Thank you," he said aloud.

Lucilla walked nearer—glided was more like it, he thought, watching her warily as she came to a halt a half inch from him. She placed her hands on his bare chest. "Very nice," she murmured, stroking him lightly. One hand dipped down, her fingers slipping beneath his shorts.

"Lucilla," he said, grabbing her hand and pulling it away, "I don't think this would be such a good idea."

"Why not?"

He watched her tongue glide over her lower lip. *Because Daphne's in the house and she would find out and she would be hurt.*

"I have a headache," he said.

She burst into merry laughter, but didn't move away from him. "Well, why don't you think about it, Brant? We could, I think, make very nice music together."

He said nothing, and her forehead furrowed into a slight frown. "Daphne, you know," she continued in a sincere voice, "is a very English sort of girl. I do think it a pity that Uncle Clarence kept her so tied up, but what can one do? In fact, I can't imagine taking Daphne to the South of France. And in America she would be lost as a lamb, and desperately unhappy. You know how shy she is."

"Daphne seemed to do okay in Greece," he said in a neutral tone.

"With Aunt Cloe telling her what to do and when and how to do it, she should have done all right. But in your society, Brant? In your particular group of friends? No, it wouldn't do at all, you know. Not at all."

But Daphne wasn't at all shy, he thought, not until you came. He wanted to tell her that Daphne wasn't retarded but she was sliding her hands up his arms to lightly clasp his shoulders. "I fully intend to take care of little Daphne. You mustn't feel guilty about it."

She stood on her tiptoes and kissed him. He felt her darting tongue probe at his closed lips, felt the length of her pressed against his body, and he responded. But just for a moment. His breathing was a bit heavy when he grasped her arms and set her away from him.

"I don't have to leave you tonight, Brant," she said softly, her eyes luminous in the dim light.

He got a hold on himself. This was ridiculous, damn it! He didn't want to make love to Lucilla; he wanted to make love to... Oh no, you don't, he nearly shouted at himself. Oh no.

"I don't think so," he said finally. "I think you should leave now, Lucilla."

"Ah, I was forgetting about your headache. Will you think about things, Brant?"

"You can be certain of it," he said. He didn't move until she had quietly closed the bedroom door behind her.

* * *

"Here is your coffee, my lord."

Brant cocked open an eye to see Winterspoon standing patiently by his bed, a tray on his outstretched arms.

"You don't sound too approving," he said, yawning mightily.

"You are an American, my lord."

"I agree. In that case, it should be black and thick and grow hair on my chest."

"The hair is there, my lord—on your chest, that is—so I assume it is all of those things."

"You don't have to wait on me, Winterspoon," Brant said as he sat up and leaned against the thick pillows. "I could have gone down to the breakfast room."

"I don't think that would be such a good idea, my lord."

"Do you know something I don't?"

"Doubtless there are many things, my lord, but it is my job to... protect you from unpleasantness."

"Unpleasantness, huh? Is there a cat fight going on over the scrambled eggs? Delicious coffee. I needed it."

"Cat fight?" Winterspoon shuddered delicately. He looks just like Jeeves must have looked, Brant thought, when Bertie said something gross. But so tolerant.

"I shouldn't have phrased it exactly like that, my lord. But if you're referring to the ladies, I suggest you keep to your room for a bit longer."

"That bad? Well, what can they be doing?"

"I believe, my lord," Winterspoon said very carefully, his eyes trained on the spot above Brant's left shoulder, "that Mrs. Sparks was accusing Mrs. Meitter of trying to—" He cleared his throat and looked heavenward.

"Trying to what, Winterspoon?"

The amusement in his voice earned him a reproachful look. "Mrs. Sparks saw Mrs. Meitter go into your room last night, my lord."

"Ah." His amusement suddenly died, and he stiffened. "Was Miss Daphne there?"

"Yes, my lord."

"Oh no. Damn it!" He pulled back the covers, spilling the remains of his coffee. Winterspoon quickly handed him a robe, his eyes on Brant's adam's apple. "I set out pajamas for you, my lord," he said.

"I can't stand them," Brant said shortly, shrugging into the robe and belting it.

"I noticed, my lord. His old lordship was very fond of that pair. He never wore them, in fact. Saving them for a special occasion, I suppose. I've drawn your bath, my lord."

"I'd give a bundle for a shower," Brant grumbled. "Who wants to sit in their own dirt?"

"I couldn't say, my lord. What will you be requiring by way of dress?"

"Just jeans, shirt and my sneakers. I've got a lot of work to do, and I don't need to wear a tux."

"Very good, my lord."

Thirty minutes later Brant walked with a rather lagging step into the breakfast room. Only Aunt Cloe was there, waiting for him, he quickly realized.

"Good morning," he said.

She gave him a long look. "Handsome is as handsome does," she said.

"I didn't sleep with Lucilla."

"Didn't you? Lucilla didn't give that impression."

"I told her I had a headache."

Cloe wanted to be furious with him, but that calm, rueful string of bluntness made her break out in laughter. "You didn't!" she gasped. "How marvelous! That's called turning the tables, I'd say!"

"Am I forgiven?"

Cloe was shaking her head. "If only Mr. Sparks—my late husband, you know—if only he'd had your sense of humor! When he didn't want to make...well, that is...Yes, my boy, you're quite forgiven. Sit down. Mrs. Mulroy left your breakfast on the sideboard. I," she added handsomely, "will be delighted to serve you."

She was still chuckling when she handed him a plate loaded with scrambled eggs, several strips of crispy bacon and something else he couldn't identify. "What is this?"

"Oh, those are bloaters. Smoked herring, you know."

Brant gingerly tried one and nodded in approval. "Tell me about Mr. Sparks," he said, giving Cloe a boyish, teasing grin.

"Don't be impertinent, laddie. Now, tell me, Brant, what are you going to do?"

"I'm going to hang new wallpaper in this room today. I selected it myself."

"That," she said, frowning, "isn't what I meant! What color wallpaper? Something light, I hope. I always hated this grimy stuff. So depressing, but father wouldn't ever listen to me. Wouldn't listen to Daphne, either."

"It's light yellow, with white and pale blues in it. I hope it will make the room look nice and airy, a perfect setting for bloaters. Where's Daphne?"

Cloe didn't miss a beat. "Out riding. And it should make the room look very livable."

"She couldn't stand the heat, huh?"

"If you mean by that nonsensical American slang, was she upset, yes, she was. She's used to going off by herself when she's upset. She must be broken of that habit."

"And, of course," Brant said blandly, crunching down on a bite of bacon, "you want me to do the breaking."

"Certainly, my boy. You aren't stupid; at least, you don't give me the impression of stupidity. Of course, I could be wrong, I suppose. I remember what I thought of Mr. Sparks when he was courting me. Well, I changed my mind on our wedding night. Do you know what he did...? No, you aren't stupid. I want you to marry her. She'll make you a grand wife. And she loves this house. It was only her Uncle Clarence she detested, and with excellent reason."

Brant said very slowly and calmly, "Cloe, I don't even know Daphne, nor she me. What's more, she's very English and I'm very American. She's also—"

"Opposites attract, I always say," Cloe interrupted serenely. "You'd be good for each other. You would help her grow, and she would do you proud. She's quite the lady, gentle, kind, and she does have a sense of fun. Most pronounced, really, when she's not...what do you Yanks say? Oh yes, not...in heat."

Brant choked on his eggs and quickly downed half a glass of orange juice. "No, not quite that, Cloe. It's called can't stand the heat. Incidentally, Daphne informed me quite plainly last night that she thought I was a conceited jerk and she wanted nothing to do with me. I think if she could, she would have punched me out. She wants me to refuse to marry her so she can get five hundred pounds rather than just one hundred."

"Such passion from my little egg. I'm very pleased."

Brant could only stare at her. "Where," he asked, "is that place you Britishers call Bedlam?"

* * *

The wallpaper was hung and the breakfast room looked fantastic, at least it did in Brant's modest opinion. He'd been left alone all morning to do the job, and he supposed he'd been pleased about it. Where was Daphne? he wondered for the dozenth time.

She wasn't present at lunch. Lucilla and Cloe complimented him at least as many times as he wondered where Daphne was. He finally made his escape and went to the stables. Her horse was back in its stall.

There was a chill wind, and he zipped his sheepskin jacket all the way up. He called her name. She wasn't in or around the stables.

He wandered to the back of the Hall to her garden. She was there, on her hands and knees, digging furiously in the hard ground. She was wearing a brown knit stocking cap pulled down nearly to her eyebrows, an old pair of slacks and a thick short coat.

"Coward," he said, standing over her, his legs spread.

She spun about and tumbled back on her bottom. Brant dropped to his haunches in front of her. "Coward," he repeated.

"Go to hell," Daphne said.

"Good grief!" He slapped his hand over his head. "The Victorian maiden has uttered a profanity. What is the world coming to?"

"Go to hell in a handbasket."

"I didn't know you Britishers had that phrase."

"We don't. I heard it in an American movie."

"Really? Which one?"

"I don't remember. Would you please leave?"

"No. And you are a coward."

"I had no intention of watching you and Lucilla making obscene faces at each other!"

"Obscene? Goodness, I've never tried that."

"It isn't funny! I had it up to here—" She poked at her eyebrows and dislodged her knit cap. "Well, anyway, you can do just as you please. I don't care."

"Thank you for your permission. It means everything to me. And I didn't sleep with Lucilla." At her incredulous look, he continued blandly, "Cloe believed me. Isn't your bottom wet from the cold?" He rose and stretched out his hand to her.

She took it, and he pulled her to her feet. "If Cloe believed you, it's because she likes men, young men. She'll believe anything they say, if they're slick enough."

"I guess I was slick enough, then." He studied her closely for several silent moments. "How bad are your eyes without your contacts?" he asked finally.

"Without them you'd be a pleasant blur, which, I might add, wouldn't be at all a bad thing!"

"Can you sleep in them?"

"Yes. I can wear them an entire week. Why?"

Because when I make love to you I want you to see my face very clearly.

"Just wondered, that's all. Would you help me sand down some of the molding in the library?"

"Why not?" She sighed, swiped off her bottom and fell easily into step beside him.

"I promise you a reward for your help."

"What kind of a reward?"

He grinned at her suspicious tone. "Here's a down payment." He leaned down and quickly kissed her. He gave her no time to react, merely began walking again. "First we need to drive into the village. I need a special fine sort of sandpaper."

Chapter Nine

Brant and Daphne worked in companionable harmony for several hours in the library.

"You're quite good at this," he said. "Just be careful that you don't scratch up your hands."

"Aunt Cloe isn't going to be pleased about my fingernails," Daphne said. "I can't seem to keep them as long as she would like. Maybe it's a lack of calcium or something."

"Let me see," Brant said, sitting on the floor and holding out his hand.

She shot him another one of her patented suspicious looks and tentatively placed her hand in his.

"No ridges on the nails. They look good to me." He gave her a wicked grin. "Personally, I prefer short nails on a woman; it's safer."

"It's true," she said on a sigh. "I'm always scratching myself."

"My point exactly."

"It probably isn't, but I dread to know just what your point is."

"Perhaps you'll find out. Oh, the film of one of my better football games came this morning. You wanna watch it with me?"

Her eyes sparkled. "Oh yes, that would be great sport."

"Let's do it now. We'll finish up in here tomorrow."

The rented projector and screen were in Brant's bedroom. "Safe from interruption, I hope," he said when she gave him another suspicious look. He got the film threaded and turned up the volume. Soon the big screen was filled with his teammates.

"My God! They're so big! Is that you, Brant? You look so different!"

"Yes, now pay attention. You see me calling the toss? I won and chose to receive the football. That means that we're on the offense. You can only score when you have the ball."

"Like ping pong," Daphne said.

"Exactly, but not really."

To Brant's surprise and delight, Daphne's eyes were glued to the set. Suddenly she jumped and clapped her hands. "That was great! So graceful. How can you throw the ball so far?"

"That's not so far," he said modestly. "Only about thirty yards. My prime receiver—a player whose main job is to run down the field to receive or catch a pass—is Lloyd Nolan. You'd like him, I think."

There was a touchdown pass a few plays later, and Daphne clapped her hands, as excited as any Astro fan. "Marvelous! Such precision. I never imagined—wait a second, Brant. They knocked you down. Are you all right?"

"Sure. I didn't get creamed too many times in this game. The Patriots' defense couldn't get to me. Just once or twice. Now you see the score is 6-0. Watch Guy Richardson kick the extra point. It's good. That is, it goes between the goalposts. That gives us another point. We're winning now, 7 to 0."

They got through nearly to halftime.

"Well, hello. What is this?"

Daphne's hands curled into fists. She was shocked at the degree of disappointment and downright jealousy she felt.

"It's a film, Lucilla, of one of Brant's football games."

"How delightful! Do you mind if I join you?"

She did, but Lucilla stayed anyway, and the third quarter passed in stiff discomfort. Brant's explanations grew shorter and shorter, and Daphne's questions fewer and fewer.

"Goodness," Lucilla said, "it's time for tea. Can we watch the rest of the game some other time, Brant?"

"Daph?" Brant asked.

"Sure. I'll join you downstairs soon. I have to wash off my dirt."

"Yes, please do, dear."

Daphne left them to go to her room. "How is your headache, Brant?" Lucilla inquired, shooting him a smile.

"It's under control. How do you like the new wallpaper in the breakfast room?"

"It's lovely." She slanted him a questioning look. "But didn't I tell you I like it? Well, never mind. I was thinking, how would you like to drive down to London? We could take in a play and have a superb dinner. We could even stay the night, if it got too late.''

Brant's first thought was why not? It just might make Daphne jealous. He drew up short, appalled at his devious reasoning.

"I don't think it would be a good idea, Lucilla," he said.

"Why not?" she asked, taking the bull by the horns.

"Lucilla," he said, drawing her to a halt beside him on the stairs, "how well off are you financially?"

"Very well," she said; then, realizing the import of her words, she quickly added, "That is, I doubt I'll starve. But taxes in England, you know. They're dreadful. I try very hard to live off my limited income, of course, but—"

"But you were offering to bankroll Daphne."

"Bankroll? Oh, you mean loan her money?"

"No, give her money."

"I could afford it, of course, and I will when I receive my inheritance."

"I see," he said. "Ah, Cloe. Have you been in the library?"

"Yes, Brant. A marvelous job you and Daphne are doing. Where is she?"

"Washing off her dirt," Lucilla said, in such a tone as to imply that Daphne was covered with muck.

"Well, she'll be here in just a moment, then. Cook has made some marvelous scones. They're biscuits, Brant, flaky and not too sweet. You spread them with butter and jam."

He knew well enough what scones were, but he said nothing. Thank God for Cloe, he was thinking, and her timely appearance. Of course, he realized, she had probably been on the lookout for him and Lucilla.

After an appallingly stiff tea time, with honeyed salvos flying back and forth between Lucilla and Cloe, Brant set down his tea cup and rose. "Daphne and I are going for a ride. Come along."

She hesitated, and he added, "I need to discuss our plan of action for the library tomorrow."

"All right," she said, the first two words she'd uttered since tea had begun.

Lucilla looked as if she'd object, but Cloe said quickly, placing a hand on Lucilla's arm, "Did I ever tell you about the lovely Greek hairdresser I met in Crete? Let me tell you, Lucilla, he was utterly magnificent! And those dark, snapping eyes!"

Brant escaped. "Where are you going?" he barked when Daphne turned to go up the stairs.

"To rub on some dirt."

He grinned. "Why is it you only find your acid tongue for me?"

She smiled back, unable to help herself. "You," she said, suppressing a giggle, "are a wretched man!"

"And you," he said softly, the words coming out before his mind approved, "are an adorable woman."

"But my fingernails are too long."

"I'll make sure they're trimmed when the time comes."

"And I'm stupid."

"Only around Lucilla."

"Aunt Cloe calls me her little egg."

He considered that for a moment, stroking his fingertips over his jaw. "I'll have to ask her what she means by that. I don't think she can mean you're hard boiled. Now, come along."

It was very cold, and the wind was blowing strong from the east. There wasn't an ounce of sun to provide any warmth.

Brant knew it was too cold, but he didn't want to return to the house. Their jackets were no match for the wind. He remembered an abandoned, tiny house toward the back of the property, and smiled to himself.

Daphne said nothing as he guided his horse directly toward the house. When it was in sight, he said, shivering dramatically, "Lord, it's cold. I think I'm coming down with pneumonia. Hey, Daph, see that house over there? Do you think the people would mind if we came in for a moment and warmed up?"

"No one lives there. We could stop there, I suppose, and warm up."

Ah, he thought, such innocence.

They tethered their horses outside, and Brant pushed open the wobbling front door. There were only two rooms, a small kitchen of ancient vintage, and a living/sleeping room. "How long has the place been abandoned?" he asked.

"For as long as I can remember," Daphne said, moving to the center of the living room. "I guess we could light a fire if you're really cold."

"Let's."

Daphne proved more adept then he, and soon there was a blaze in the fireplace, and a goodly amount of smoke puffing out into the room.

"You know, we could have gone back to the Hall. It was just as close as this place."

"I didn't want to see you turn into a defensive madonna again," Brant said smoothly. "Come on, let's sit down."

They sat cross-legged on the floor in front of the fire.

"Are you still angry at me for last night?" he asked after a few moments.

"No, not really," she said, keeping her profile toward him.

"I didn't mean to sound like a conceited jerk."

"Probably not. It just comes naturally?"

He grinned. "Maybe. Would you have been upset if I'd slept with Lucilla?"

She slewed her head around and blinked at him. "No! It has nothing to do with me!"

"Not even a little bit upset?"

"Well, maybe a little bit."

"But not more than just a tad?"

"If a tad is an American thimble, then you've got it about right! Oh damn. Lucilla's so lovely, I don't know how you could resist, particularly when she turns on that sexy look of hers."

"You ain't so bad yourself, lady. And I was noble as hell."

"And profane as well."

"Lord, are your ears going to turn red when you meet all the jocks on my team. It isn't really cursing, you know. It's just part of the general idiom."

She gave him a long, thoughtful stare, then said very quietly, "I don't know how I'd ever meet your jock teammates, Brant."

Brant jumped to his feet, thrust his hands into his jacket pockets, scowled at her and said, "Oh, hell, Daph, let's get married."

He took a step back, but his eyes remained on her face. She'd flushed a deep red.

"I don't appreciate your notion of a joke, Brant," she said in a voice so cold it could have rivaled the outdoors.

"It isn't a joke, damn it! How can you think that? You're blushing."

Daphne pressed her palms to her cheeks. "Why?" she asked in a bewildered tone.

"Why not?" he snapped.

"But I can't *do* anything!"

"You can be my wife." He removed his hands from his pockets, his body as well as his mind beginning to warm to the idea. Why not indeed? he thought. She was beautiful, witty, not at all shy with him, and he wanted to take her to bed. "I think you could do that quite well."

"Do you really think so? Despite everything?"

He dropped to his knees in front of her and cupped her face between his hands. "Yes," he said, smiling into her eyes. "Despite everything. I think it would benefit both of us equally."

"A marriage of convenience," she said slowly, pursing her lips, and he swooped down and kissed her.

He pulled her up to her knees and enfolded her in his arms. "Part your lips," he said, and she did.

Brant felt her arms tentatively clutch at his shoulders. He deepened his kiss, but kept a firm control on himself. She tasted so sweet; and so surprised. He raised his head and smiled gently down at her. "You've got to breathe through your nose. Then you can kiss until the cows come home."

"Show me," she said.

He did.

"Are the cows here yet?" Her voice was shaky, her eyes somewhat dazed.

"I thought I heard a moo just a second ago. I'm very fond of you, Daph. Do you think you could become a bit fond of me?"

"As in a tad?"

"As in whole bunches. As in let's get married. We'll spend the greater part of the year in the U.S., and the remainder here, at Asherwood. There's so much we can do together.''

She scooted away from him, for his nearness made her mind shift into reverse. She said more to herself than to him, ''I guess what I feel about Lucilla is jealousy, at least when she monopolizes you. And I do like for you to kiss me. That's very nice.''

She paused a moment, and he said, ''Continue thinking out loud. That way, there won't be any unanswered questions between us.''

''We've not known each other very long. And I'm not entirely a dolt. Your proposal just now, it popped out, didn't it? You didn't mean to ask me to marry you.''

''That's true. I do know that I wanted to bring you here so we could be assured of being alone. I also know that I want to make love to you so badly I hurt. I've never felt that way about a woman before.''

''You don't love me. You're talking only about sex.''

''I don't think fondness and sex are a bad start, do you?''

She rubbed the end of her nose, her expression a combination of bewilderment and confusion. ''I might not be any good at sex, Brant. Then you'd be stuck with me.''

''I'm willing to take my chances. You're looking ferocious. What are you thinking now?''

''I'm thinking that if Uncle Clarence hadn't written his will the way he did, you wouldn't look at me twice.''

Brant looked away from her into the leaping flames, clasping his arms around his knees. ''I thought you were gorgeous when you stepped out of that taxi and I looked at every inch of you I could manage before I knew who you really were. But that's not really the point, is it? I think, Daph, that it's impossible to answer that objectively. In any case, I can't. The will does exist, and I wouldn't be honest if I assured you that I didn't give a damn about it, because I do. I love Asherwood, and the money that comes with it will enable me—us—to fix it up exactly as we wish." He sighed. "I just don't know about that. But I do know that we have a good shot at making it work. What do you say?"

He'd said he thought she was gorgeous, Daphne thought, gazing into his eyes. She couldn't imagine a man more lovely than Brant. "Would you teach me how to use a checkbook?" she asked.

"I'll teach you everything you want to know."

But it all sounded so wretchedly lopsided, she thought. She supposed that her dowry of the house and money was something of worth, but it wasn't from her, it was from Uncle Clarence.

"If Lucilla were me, would you have proposed to her instead?"

"No," he said emphatically, with no hesitation. "That I can be quite certain about. I think I would have taken to my heels and been on the first plane back to the U.S."

She chewed over his words, and believed him. She'd always thought of herself as plain and dowdy. It was difficult to adjust to his image of her. She said slowly, "I've never been to America. I realize we'd live there—"

"And you feel like you'd be traveling to another planet?"

"Something like that. What if your friends don't...like me? What if your mother thinks I'm an adventuress?"

Brant leaned toward her and cupped her face between his hands. "I love it when you talk nineteenth-century to me. An adventuress. I like the sound of that, but everyone will think I'm an adventurer. My friends will love you. And I'll tell you something else, Daph. We're going to take a nice long honeymoon. By the time we return to

New York, you're not going to have an unself-confident bone left in your body."

"Just how do you imagine you'll achieve that?"

"You'll see, sweetheart. You'll see. Now, say yes, then we can neck for a while."

She pursed her lips and tilted up her face. "Yes."

Chapter Ten

Brant pulled Daphne into a close embrace behind a thick yew hedge that bordered the drive. He kissed her quickly and said, "I want you to wear something gorgeous tonight. I want you to smile, look at me like I'm the living hunk of your life, and not fall apart when Lucilla blows a fit. Okay?"

She gave him a smart salute and a forced smile.

He patted her bottom. "Good girl. Go get 'em, tiger."

But I'm a woman, not a girl, she thought briefly, then quickly forgot it, trying to match his stride to the house. He left her at her bedroom door with another quick kiss.

"I want you to look gorgeous, too," she called after him.

"Winterspoon will see to it, I promise."

Forty-five minutes later Winterspoon was admiring his handiwork. "Excellent, my lord. Just excellent." He lightly brushed a speck of lint from Brant's tuxedoed shoulder.

"Miss Daphne and I are going to get married," Brant said.

Winterspoon didn't look even remotely surprised. "Congratulations, my lord. His old lordship would be so pleased, indeed he would. Miss Daphne is a most charming young lady."

Brant gave him a wide grin. "My sentiments exactly."

"When is the happy occasion, my lord?"

"As soon as I can manage it. You'll have to tell me how I go about things."

"It will be my pleasure, my lord."

Brant added on a rueful note at the door, "Wish me luck, Winterspoon. I have the distinct feeling that this evening won't be entirely pleasant."

"You will do just fine, my lord. As my father used to say, 'keep your back to the wall'."

I've just been advised by a pro, Brant thought as he strode down the stairs. Winterspoon had probably seen just about everything. He paused a moment before entering the Golden Salon, squared his shoulders, and walked in. His eyes immediately met Daphne's. She looked remarkably beautiful in a gown of obvious French design. It was floor length, of a pale green silky looking material, and accentuated her narrow waist and beautiful full breasts. She'd piled her hair on top of her head, and several tendrils curled about her face. He felt very proud of her, and assured himself again that he was doing the right thing. Yes, everything would work out just fine.

"Good evening," he said. "Cloe, Lucilla, you're both looking great. Shall we go in to dinner?" He took Cloe's arm and winked at Daphne.

When Mrs. Mulroy had finished serving the soup, he called her over a moment and requested a bottle of champagne.

"Eyuh," she said, "so that be how it is."

"That be how it is, yes," Brant said.

When Mrs. Mulroy left the room, Aunt Cloe asked brightly, "Where did you and Daphne ride this afternoon?"

"It got a bit chilly, so we warmed up at that abandoned house at the north end of the property."

"Oh?" Lucilla asked, her soup spoon pausing in mid air.

"Daphne makes a great fire," Brant added blandly.

As for Daphne, she was studying the contents of her soup bowl with intense concentration. Little coward, Brant thought.

"My little egg has so many talents," Cloe said.

"Aunt," Daphne asked suddenly, "why do you call me your little egg?"

"I say, love, I'm not entirely certain. Mr. Sparks used to call me that when we were...well, in moments of fondness."

"I'm going to London tomorrow," Lucilla said. "Would you like to come with me, Brant?"

"First, here's the champagne. Thank you, Mrs. Mulroy." Brant rose and filled everyone's glass. He was aware that Cloe was regarding him with fascinated eyes, that Daphne still had her eyes trained on her plate, and that Lucilla was clutching her fork.

"I have an announcement to make," he said, holding up his glass. "Daphne has agreed to marry me."

"Oh, how marvelous! Congratulations, Brant, Daphne."

The silence that followed Aunt Cloe's excitement was deafening.

"Well," Lucilla said, sitting back in her chair and folding her arms over her breasts, "you're willing to marry a man who doesn't love you, Daphne. I'd thought you'd have more pride."

"Thank you, Lucilla, for your kindness." Daphne's chin was up, and her eyes gleamed bright lime green.

"And as for you, Brant, I would have thought that if you'd wanted money, you could have found a woman who was a bit more—"

"In addition to everything else," Brant interrupted her smoothly, "Daphne and I have discovered that we are quite fond of each other. I trust both of you ladies will come to the wedding. It will be as soon as possible."

Lucilla wanted to howl in fury and disappointment. How the hell could he want Daphne, for God's sake! I will not make a spectacle of myself, she thought. She rose from her chair, carefully placing her napkin beside her plate. "I hope everything works out for both of you as I think it will." With that obscure parting shot, she left the room.

"That wasn't so terrible, was it?" Brant asked Daphne quietly.

"No, it wasn't. It's odd, but I feel bad for her."

"Lucilla won't starve, sweetheart. Cloe, you'll stand up with us?"

"With the greatest pleasure, my boy. We should go to London and see Reggie. Mr. Hucksley, that is. He'll want to get everything in order."

Daphne had the funniest feeling that she'd just been filed away under All Went According to Plan. She heard Aunt Cloe ask Brant if he intended to have a civil service and wondered why she wasn't the one being asked. Because you're a stupid twit and nobody cares what you have to say. She said aloud, her voice shrill, "I want to be married again in the United States. It's not fair to Brant's mother not to be at her son's wedding."

Brant shot her a surprised look. "That would be fine," he said slowly. "My mom would appreciate that, I'm sure."

"And your sister and her husband and children."

"Okay. We should be able to work that out."

"Where are you planning to honeymoon, Brant?" Aunt Cloe asked.

"Hawaii . . . if that's okay with Daphne," he added.

Her eyes sparkled. "Hawaii!"

"Yes, the island of Kauai, to be exact. I own a condo there. I think you'll enjoy it, sweetheart."

"Goodness!" Cloe exclaimed, rising from her chair. "There's so much to be done! I must make a list. Come along, Daphne."

Every last item on Cloe's list was marked through by the time Brant and Daphne were married in the office of the Registrar General. The ceremony lasted only five minutes.

Daphne was in a daze.

Brant was quite pleased with himself.

Cloe wanted to shout her triumph, and did, to Reggie Hucksley.

Lucilla had left for Italy three days earlier.

Both the Old Man and Harlow rode in the limousine with Daphne, Brant and Cloe to Heathrow airport.

"Yes, indeed, my lord," the Old Man said for the third time, "everything is in order. There are funds in the bank for the work on Asherwood Hall to continue on schedule."

Harlow, who had never seen Daphne before, continued to stare at her in unabashed admiration. "Lovely wedding ring, Mrs. Asher," he said.

"Yes, thank you," Daphne said, staring for a moment at the huge diamond surrounded with sparkling emeralds.

"Hawaii," Aunt Cloe said. "That's an awfully long trip, isn't it, Brant?"

"We'll fly to New York, take a connecting flight to Los Angeles, then fly to Honolulu." He didn't add that there was another connecting flight of forty minutes to be made to Kauai. He hadn't thought about stopping; he always slept on airplanes. Now he realized that he hadn't asked Daphne her opinion. Well, it was too late now. All the arrangements were made. He wanted his wedding night to be in Hawaii. It satisfied his imagination. The balmy weather, the sound of the waves washing onto the beach, Daphne wearing a see-through something.

My God, Daphne was thinking, staring out the window, what have I done? I'm leaving my home. I'm married to a man I scarcely know. She was nearly incoherent with anxiety when Aunt Cloe kissed her goodbye. "I'll come see you in New York, little egg," she assured Daphne. "But I'll give you two time to yourselves first."

"Yes, that's marvelous. Please, Aunt Cloe...yes, do come."

Brant shot a look of indulgent surprise at his bride. He shook hands with the Hucksleys, kissed and hugged Aunt Cloe, clasped his bride around her waist and led her through the tunnel to the plane.

They were flying first class. Suddenly, Daphne paled and said, "I forgot my Dramamine!"

"You get airsick?" Brant asked with awful foreboding. At her mute nod, he jumped from his seat and collared a flight attendant. He had ten minutes until the plane took off. He made it back with three minutes to spare. He watched Daphne swallow the pill, and prayed that it would be effective so close to take-off.

His prayer was answered. She was in a drugged sleep within thirty minutes.

Nearly twenty hours later, they landed at the Lihue airport on Kauai, the time change making it not too many hours after they'd left London. Daphne was in a state of numb exhaustion, and so doped up from all the Dramamine Brant had forced down her that she could barely put one foot in front of the other. As for Brant, he'd gotten his second wind and was raring to go. He breathed in the sweet, clean air, then directed Daphne to a seat inside the small terminal. Thirty minutes later he helped her into a rental car. He loved Kauai and kept up a nonstop monologue about everything they would see and do as he drove down Highway 50 to the southern end of the island. Daphne was asleep when they finally arrived at the Kiahuna Planation on Poipu Beach.

He pulled the Datsun into the space in front of the condo and turned to look at his wife. She was slouched down in the seat, her eyes closed, her face pale with exhaustion. He felt a pang of guilt. Damn, he should have stopped over in New York, or Los Angeles.

So much for your romantic wedding night, old buddy.

"Daphne." He gently shook her shoulder. "Come on, sweetheart, wake up."

"No," she said quite clearly, her eyes remaining tightly closed.

He looked bemused for a moment, then shrugged. He took their luggage upstairs, unlocked the door and turned on the overhead fans. He shot a wistful look at the big queen-size bed in the single bedroom. Forget it, old man, he told himself.

He carried Daphne upstairs and gently eased her down on the bed. Her hair was tangled, her lovely cream-colored dress wrinkled to death. He tried again to wake her, but she didn't budge. He took a quick shower, changed into shorts and a golf shirt, and went out to forage for some dinner.

When he returned nearly an hour later with some carryout Chinese, the first thing he heard was the shower. Her clothes lay in a trail from the bedroom to the bath-room. He looked at her panties and bra, and felt a flood of desire. She was in the shower, naked, and she was his wife.

The bathroom was divided into two small rooms. The door to the shower and toilet was closed. "Daphne," he called, lightly tapping on the door. "Are you all right?"

Daphne raised her head at the sound of his voice and stared dumbly through the glass shower door. She'd come suddenly awake thirty minutes before, aware that some-thing was wrong. It took her a good five minutes to dis-cover it was the sound of the ocean and an overhead fan. She felt dirty, rumpled, and her head ached. She had stared around the bedroom at the rattan furniture and looked up at the whirling fan overhead. I'm in Hawaii, she thought, bemused, and I'm married.

She'd called Brant's name, but there had been no an-swer, which was an enormous relief. She had dragged herself out of bed and begun to strip off her clothes, her only thought of drowning herself in the shower.

She heard him call her name again and forced herself to call out, "Yes, I'm fine. I'll be out in just a bit."

"I've brought us some dinner."

"Okay."

She sounded as if he'd said he'd brought worms, he thought, staring at the closed bathroom door a few minutes longer. It was dark, but the third floor condo faced the ocean, and the half-moon cast a romantic light, making the ocean waves silvery. He carried the food, plates and forks to the small table on the deck. He opened a beer, sat down, and let the warm air and the sweet smell from all the flowers flood his senses.

"Hi. Here I am."

He slewed his head about and smiled at his wife. Her thick hair was damp from her shower, falling about her shoulders. She wore a sexless cotton robe.

"How do you feel, Daph?"

"More alive now, thank you."

She still looked awfully pale, her movements sluggish. He said, as he served her some sweet and sour pork, "We'll hit the sack after we eat. A good twelve hours will put you to rights again."

Daphne found she was starving. She consumed at least half the three Chinese dishes nonstop, and a half-dozen fortune cookies. "Life in this body still exists," she said, and sat back in her deck chair. "I love Chinese food. This place must be heaven, Brant. I never imagined anything so beautiful." She stretched, drawing his eyes to her breasts, then rose to lean over the balcony.

Doesn't she know that I want to rip her clothes off and make love to her until she... Stop it, you fool! Brant drew a deep breath, and said, "Do you like the condo? I bought it about two years ago. Most of the year it's rented out to tourists. We really lucked out. We've got it for two uninterrupted weeks."

She mumbled something, and Brant continued, "The kitchen's fully stocked; we've got color TV; and the beach is at our back door. Do you snorkel, Daph?"

"Yes," she said, turning. "I learned in Greece."

The soft moonlight behind her made her look like a fairy princess, Brant thought, somewhat dazed. Her hair was dry now, and looked like spun silk. "That's good," he said. "Why don't you come here a moment, Daph? Then we'll go to bed."

She cocked her head at him, watched him lightly pat his bare thighs, and said, "When you told me to bring all my summer things, I really couldn't imagine wearing them. You look nice in those shorts, Brant."

"Thank you. Come here, just for a minute."

"Yes, it's so warm," she mumbled and took several slow steps, coming to a halt in front of him. He gently pulled her down on his lap.

"Just relax, sweetheart." He pressed her head against his shoulder, then settled his hands around her waist. "Listen, I'm not going to make love to you tonight. You're too tired, and jet lag is beginning to hit me, too. We'll start our official honeymoon tomorrow, okay?"

She nodded her head, her soft hair sliding over his chin. She felt enormous relief and, she admitted to herself, just a hint of disappointment. Brant didn't seem at all crazed with desire for her.

"I'm going to take very good care of you, sweetheart. Will you trust me?"

He held her quietly for some minutes, the only sound the lapping waves beneath them, splashing against the shore. He smiled, realizing that she was fast asleep. Just as well, he thought. Less temptation. He rose, clutching her in his arms, and took her into the bedroom. He gently slipped off her robe and pulled the sheet over her.

My wife, he thought again, staring down at her. He took off his own clothes and got into bed beside her. His last thought before he fell asleep was that he'd never before just *slept* with a woman.

Chapter Eleven

Daphne awoke at dawn, a bemused smile on her lips and smooth male skin under her palm. She became even more bemused when she realized that she was pressed tightly against Brant, facing him, one of his legs between hers, one of his arms thrown over her back. Her nightgown was up around her waist, and she could feel his belly pressed against hers.

She didn't budge. He felt so different from her, and very nice. Oh dear, she thought, jerking slightly, did he make love to me and I don't remember? Was I too sleepy to know what was happening? She frowned against his shoulder and lightly stroked her fingers down his back. He moved in his sleep, and his hairy leg moved upward between her thighs.

How dreadful! She hadn't lived through her wedding night, so to speak. But she didn't feel any change in herself. Surely she should feel *different*.

She thought about this for a while as she listened to her husband's even breathing and the steady thudding of his heart. From the books she'd read, the films she'd seen, she knew that she couldn't possibly be lying naked against him and he not have done anything. No, that was impossible. She'd been made love to, but she'd been too drugged to be aware of it. She groaned softly. I must look different, she thought. Slowly she eased herself away from him and came up on her knees on her side of the bed. He mumbled something in his sleep, flung one arm above his head and fell onto his back. The single sheet was around his knees. Daphne gulped. She'd never before seen a naked man. She'd seen a couple of pictures in a racy magazine once, but not *everything*.

Well, I'm seeing everything now. Lord, was he gorgeous. He wasn't covered with hair like many of the men she'd seen on the beach. Just enough, she thought, her hand tingling to touch him. Her inquisitive eyes followed the lovely line of hair down his belly to his . . . She pressed her palms against her cheeks in pleased embarrassment. She even loved the tuft of hair under his raised arm.

It must have happened, she thought again, and quietly scooted off the bed. She trailed to the bathroom and stared at herself in the mirror. Her hair looked like a bird's nest, her nightgown rumpled and ratty. But she looked like that most mornings, she thought. She touched her breasts, wondering if he'd felt her there.

She remembered the feel of his muscled leg between hers and gave a delicious shudder. It had certainly felt nice when she'd awakened.

She turned and looked back toward the bed. There was no door to the bedroom. In fact, the only door in the entire condo was the one to the shower. He'd moved slightly again, spreading his legs. She gulped, turned quickly away and pulled off her nightgown.

After a quick shower and shampoo, she crept out of the bathroom and looked at him again. He hadn't moved. Maybe, she thought, smiling slightly, she'd exhausted him. Weren't men supposed to be exhausted after making passionate love? That made her feel pleased.

Why don't I feel exhausted? But she didn't; she felt marvelous. Completely rested and full of her usual morning energy. She dried her hair and quickly dressed in a pair of shorts and a matching top. She wandered onto the deck and sucked in her breath at the sight of the rising sun over the ocean. It was every bit as beautiful as Crete. A balmy breeze caressed her cheek and ruffled her hair. And all the flowers! Plumeria, bird of paradise, bougainvillae in whites, bright reds and pinks. She wondered if she'd be able to grow these beautiful flowers in her new home. Brant had told her he lived primarily in New York City. She wondered if he had a good-sized garden. She hoped so.

"Good morning."

She whirled around. Her husband gave her a sleepy smile and ran his hand through his rumpled hair. He'd put on a pair of running shorts.

"Hi," she said, her breathing quickening a bit.

"You're a morning person?"

"Yes, disgusting, isn't it?" Was he looking at her intimately? She hunched her shoulders just a bit.

Brant yawned. Nothing intimate about that, she thought, somewhat disappointed. She straightened again.

"Do you like Kauai so far?"

"It's beautiful. I like it; truly. It's still awfully early. Would you like to go back to bed?"

He gave her a slow, wicked smile. "I can't think of a better way to wake up."

"Oh!"

He watched her turn various shades of red. She jerked her head up from looking down at her bare feet and blurted out, "I don't remember anything!"

He cocked his head at her, wondering what the devil she was talking about. He wasn't at his best in the mornings.

"I'm sorry," she said, flushing more deeply. "I was hoping I would remember something, but I don't. I even thought I'd look different, but I can't see any changes."

He scratched his hand over his stomach. Finally he understood. At least, he thought he did. He grinned at her. "You were great," he said, his voice a deep caress. "You cried out and held onto me and told me you loved it."

She heard only the intimacy, missing the teasing in his voice. "It isn't fair," she said. "Why didn't you pour coffee down me or something?"

"I didn't think about it. You seemed to be having such fun. Did you enjoy the . . . view this morning?"

"Yes," she said. She suddenly felt inordinately relieved that it was over and she'd responded so well. "You looked very nice."

"Sprawled on my back with my legs apart?"

"That, too. But you see, Brant, I wasn't sure anything had happened, so I didn't look at you all that long. That would have been like invading your privacy."

It was on the tip of his tongue to tell her that nothing at all had happened, but he laughed instead. "Tell you what, sweetheart, why don't we have some coffee and go back to bed? Now that you know everything, it will be even more fun for you. And you can look at me as long as you like. I'd definitely love to invade your privacy. Will you make me some coffee while I shower? I bought some stuff last night for breakfast.''

She gazed at him somewhat somberly for a long moment. She said slowly, thoughtfully, ''I won't be embarrassed now, will I? There's no need to, is there?''

''None at all,'' he said. He hugged her briefly; and kissed her lightly against her temple. ''No, none at all.''

''Well, that's a relief,'' she said, and smiled up at him.

In between arias in the shower, Brant found himself grinning inanely and wondering if he should tell her the truth. No, he decided. Now he wouldn't have to fight her inherent modesty. He felt a leap of desire and quickly soaped himself, then turned on the cold water for a moment.

After drying his hair, he wrapped the towel around his waist and joined Daphne on the deck. She smiled at him and handed him a cup of coffee. ''It's thick and black and very American,'' she said. ''Winterspoon told me that was the way you liked it.''

''Did Winterspoon tell you anything else about me?''

She sipped her own very blond coffee. ''Just that you were, in his opinion, a nice man, despite your being American. He even admitted that you had some wit.''

''Quite an accolade.'' His gaze flitted from her soft hair downward. ''You have a very nice figure, Daph. Yes, very nice.''

''Did you tell me that last night?''

''I must have. Now, why don't we go back to bed and I'll tell you again?''

He looped his arm around her shoulders, leaning down to nibble her ear. ''I'll kiss every inch of you . . . just like I did last night. You loved that, Daph. Every inch.''

She turned in his embrace, wrapping her arms about his back. "I must have," she said against his shoulder. "It sure sounds nice right now."

He grinned over her head and said lightly, "Have I created a monster? A sex fiend?"

"Well, I do have some of Aunt Cloe's blood, and she, I think, adores sex, or at least she must have when Mr. Sparks was alive."

Brant found that the few steps to the bed had made him so taut with downright lust that he was breathing hard. His wife, he thought. She was his wife. For life, not just a brief fling. He realized how important it was to make everything nice for her. He couldn't imagine his life without sexual satisfaction, both for himself and for his partner. Go slowly, old man, he told himself.

He tumbled her onto her back and came down over her, balancing himself on one elbow. "Hi, wife," he said, and leaned down to kiss her. "Open your mouth. How could you forget so soon?"

"You must have short-circuited me," she said, and parted her lips.

He didn't touch her below her shoulders for a good ten minutes. It felt strange to be so methodical and, in a sense, Machiavellian, but he held himself in check and continued his slow assault. He felt her ease, then respond to him. "That's it, sweetheart," he whispered into her mouth. "Just relax with me. Nothing new, you know."

Daphne wriggled beneath him. She wanted him to touch her, but she was embarrassed to ask him. What had she done the previous night? "Brant," she said finally, her voice ragged, "please." She thrust her hips upward; and gasped at the hard feel of him.

Brant eased off her and quickly pulled off her top. "Good God," he said, staring down at her. "You are so bloody beautiful." Tentatively, he touched her full breasts. So white they were, her breasts appearing almost too large for her slender torso. Her nipples were already taut and darkened to a dusky peach. He began kissing her again as he gently stroked and caressed her breasts. He laid his palm flat for a moment and felt her heart pounding. Slowly he kissed his way down her throat to her shoulders, then took her nipple into his mouth. She cried out, arching her back upward.

He felt her hands frantically kneading his back. Her breasts were very sensitive, and it delighted him. So much more of her to go, so much to anticipate, to appreciate.

"What do you want me to do?" she gasped.

He was gently stroking his tongue over her. "Just lie still and enjoy. This is what a man likes best to do."

He covered her belly with his leg and gently pressed. Daphne was beginning to feel frantic. She wanted to feel him, all of him, and began to wriggle to face him so she could jerk down his shorts.

"Slow down, sweetheart. You first." He pulled off her shorts and panties, then raised himself up on his elbow. She was very fair complexioned. Her waist was narrow, her belly flat. His eyes locked on the tuft of dark blond hair, and he felt himself begin to tremble with need. Slowly he stroked his hand from her breasts downward until he was lightly cupping his palm over her. He looked into her eyes, watching every expression, as his fingers gently probed. He sucked in his breath. She was damp, her delicate woman's flesh swelled and beautifully warm.

He began to rhythmically stroke her. "You like that," he said softly. "Remember?"

"I—I feel urgent. It almost hurts, Brant."

He eased his fingers away and stroked them down her slender thighs.

He eased himself up and pulled off his shorts. Daphne stared at him, her eyes growing wider. "Oh dear," she managed. "I liked *that*?"

It took him a moment to gather his wits. He looked briefly down at himself. Asleep this morning, he imagined he'd looked nothing like this. "Yes," he said, "you did. Very much." He slid his hands between her legs and eased them apart. Slowly he eased down on top of her. He made no move to enter her, though he felt himself straining against her. Hey down there, you've got no brain and no sense! Cool it!

He pressed against her, and she responded. He felt a rippling shudder go through her body. He covered her and began to kiss her, his tongue thrusting into her mouth. He felt her arms tighten almost painfully around his back. All the way, he thought. Yes, all the way. He eased himself down her body, pausing to enjoy her breasts, then her belly. She stiffened, and he raised his head.

"Listen, sweetheart. You wanted to know what you could do for me. I want to kiss you and love you, and I want you to relax and enjoy it. You did . . . last night."

When his mouth closed over her, Daphne lurched upward. She felt no embarrassment now, assuming that all her embarrassment had happened last night. It felt so good. "I like that," she gasped, tangling her fingers in his thick hair.

Brant did too. She tasted fresh and sweet and . . . Suddenly she gave a deep shudder, crying out. He felt the tension in her legs, and her release. Her breathing was ragged, and he felt her uncontrollable trembling. He loved the convulsive little shudders, the soft sounds from her throat. He eased his rhythm, then began again.

Daphne felt dazed. She felt as though she'd been on a roller coaster. It came down, finally. Then it started upward again. She was stunned, but eager. Brant felt it and used every ounce of his expertise to bring her up again. He felt her tense, heard her moaning softly. He quickly reared over her, and with one single thrust, entered her. There was no maidenhead, thank God, but she was very small. He felt her stiffen and press her hands against his shoulders. "Easy, sweetheart," he said. He buried himself deeply within her, then eased down over her, his eyes on her face. "It's okay, Daph. Just a little while longer and any discomfort will be gone. I won't move. Get used to me."

"All right," she whispered. She buried her face against his shoulder. Slowly he felt the tension drain from her, and he began to move within her. He bit down on his lower lip, hoping the brief pain he'd given her would tighten his control. He'd never made love to a virgin before, and it was a heady experience. He could feel her muscles clutching him, and he groaned. "Daphne," he gasped, "no!"

She didn't know what he was talking about. "Brant, please," she said, her voice high and urgent. He slipped his fingers between them and found her.

To his delight and near insanity, she arched upward, drawing him deeper. She yelled his name and nearly bucked him off in her frenzy.

He gritted his teeth and gave her release before he allowed himself to let go. He felt swamped with feeling, feeling so strong that he shook with it.

He collapsed on top of her, his face next to hers on the pillows.

"I'm going to die," she moaned.

He managed to gather enough energy to raise himself on his elbows and look into her dazed eyes. He stroked her hair off her forehead. "You were marvelous," he said. "And you aren't going to die, although I can just see the headline: Sex-Starved Bride Succumbs."

"How about: Bride Buried Smiling?"

She closed her arms about his back and squeezed. "I'm glad we got married. This is such fun."

"You think so, huh? Not bad, I'd say, for your first..."

Her eyes flew open and narrowed on his face. "My first what, Brant?"

He kissed her very seductively, but she was sated and tenacious. "What, Brant?"

He gave her a lopsided grin. "We didn't make love last night, Daph. I'm not into unconscious women."

"You...you crook!"

"Why did you think we had?"

"I woke up all tangled together with you and my nightgown...well, it was up, and not down where it should have been. And you are a crook, and dishonest, and a dreadful tease—"

"Yes, but you weren't embarrassed, were you?"

She chewed a moment on her lower lip, and he quickly kissed her again.

"Still..." she began.

He kissed her once more. "The very pleasurable result," he said with a disarming grin, "justified the means, as the Prince is supposed to have been taught."

She lowered her thick lashes. "Well," she said finally, "maybe. Just maybe. Brant, did I react normally? I mean, I didn't disappoint you, did I?"

"If you'd reacted any more, I'd be dead." He paused a moment, enjoying the feel of her soft body beneath his, "I don't think you could ever disappoint me, sweetheart, not in a thousand and one nights."

"What about a thousand and one days?"

He moaned loudly and collapsed on his back.

Chapter Twelve

"Do you remember the song, 'Puff the Magic Dragon'?"

"Oh yes, it was quite popular in England."

"Well, old Puff was from Hanalei, and that's a town on the northern shore of Kauai. We'll go swimming up there and do some snorkeling."

Daphne sat back, sated from a delicious bacon cheeseburger, and patted her stomach. "Is the drive long enough so I won't sink like a fat whale when I hit the water?"

"Finish your planter's punch and you'll go down happy."

Brant leaned back in his chair and looked out over the Kiahuna Golf Club course. The back part of the restaurant was a roofed patio, and the air was redolent with the sweet scent of flowers and freshly cut grass. He felt good. He'd discovered that he enjoyed the freedom of being married, enjoyed the growing intimacy between him and Daphne. He sent her a sleepy glance, watching her slurp up the final bit of planter's punch. He'd made sure she was well-coated with sunscreen and in the past two days she'd just gotten a bit red, but no sunburn. She'd french-braided her hair this morning, and the plait lay heavy and lustrous between her shoulder blades. She looked fresh, sweet, and so inviting that he felt his body react yet again. He closed his eyes a moment, picturing her in that outrageous orange bikini Cloe had bought her. It was a wonder, he thought, that she hadn't been attacked on the beach in Crete. His presence was the only thing that saved her here.

"When do we take the helicopter ride? You did tell me that a lot of the *Thorn Birds* was filmed here. I want to see the beach where Father Ralph made love to Meggie."

"Inspiration?"

"That," she said, "I don't need"

"I like being married to you," he said, stretching lazily.

"Me too."

"I guess it's time we did something. That is, I guess it's time to show you the island." His eyes fell to her breasts, and his gaze was so intent that Daphne quivered.

"I'll never see it if you keep doing that," she said, her voice shaky. "You, Brant, are very addictive."

"So are you. Maybe I'll leave you alone in fifty years or so."

"So soon? I can just picture you, a little old man, placing your cane carefully by the bed, then creaking in between the sheets."

"And drooling all over you." He looked up to see the waitress grinning down at him. "Our check, please," he said. Out of habit, he watched her walk away and cataloged her finer points.

"You are a dirty young man!"

"Old habits are hard to break."

They left the golf club and walked the quarter of a mile back to the Kiahuna Plantation. "Do you want to learn how to play golf?" he asked.

"It seems rather a silly game, but I'll give it a try. What are we doing this afternoon?"

He gave her a long look. "Why don't we discuss it in bed?"

But they didn't. Her back was arched, the thick braid hanging over her shoulder. Brant let her control the depth of his penetration, let her determine the pace. It drove him wild to see the lightly tanned parts of her and the utter white of her breasts and belly. He felt her thighs hug him, and he gasped. He pulled her down on top of him. "Lie still," he said, gritting his teeth.

Daphne couldn't hold still. She cupped his face between her hands and kissed him deeply. "I love the way you feel inside me," she said between gasping breaths into his mouth. She felt him tighten his grip on her hips, holding her still.

"Sweetheart, I—"

She straddled him again, drawing him deep, and it drove him crazy. He closed his fingers over her and watched the surprised look in her eyes when the building sensations swamped her. Her muscles tightened convulsively, and he let himself go.

He drew her down against him and stroked her nape and back, reveling in the sheet of perspiration on her smooth flesh. "You're so bloody sexy," he whispered in her ear. "And I love the way you look so incredulous just before you start making all those cute little noises."

She was incapable of answering him for several minutes. Slowly she came back to life as she used to know it. It seemed the past two days that she'd been in a kind of dazed fog. "If," she said finally, arching up a bit so she could see his face, "you ever get a headache, I'll never forgive you. It just keeps getting wilder and wilder." She lowered her lashes a moment. "I like being on top. You were so deep."

He felt himself swelling again and groaned. "Let's eat some Macadamia nuts; they're supposed to help."

She giggled and kissed his chin. "They've got such a sweet taste, and such a crisp bite...roasted to perfection, dipped in rich creamy...ouch!"

He rubbed the hip he'd just smacked. "You, Daphne Asher, are a smart-mouthed...creamy...."

She moved over him, and he couldn't have found another word if his life depended on it.

At four o'clock they finally strolled to the beach and fell asleep in the sun.

"Below are the Wailua Falls. If they look familiar it's because they're in the opening scene of *Fantasy Island*."

Daphne snapped three pictures as the helicopter swooped down over the double waterfalls.

"Below is the Huleia National Wildlife Refuge. It's gotta look familiar; it's where part of *Raiders of the Lost Ark* was filmed. Everyone, even you mainlanders, has seen that."

"Damn," Daphne muttered. "I'm out of film."

Brant patted her knee in commiseration, the sound of the helicopter blades made it hard to talk and be heard.

"We'll go up again if you like," Brant said when they'd landed. "Did you like seeing the nurses' beach from *South Pacific*?"

She bubbled with excitement. She skipped beside Brant. "Oh yes. And I can't get over Waimea Canyon. Just like the pictures I've seen of the Grand Canyon! And all the waterfalls, Brant! And the wettest spot in the entire world!"

He smiled down at her, enjoying her enthusiasm. When she'd finally completed giving him a rundown on what they'd seen, he said, "Tonight, Daph, we're going to the Sheraton for a luau. Are you into pig?"

"Just as long as I don't have to watch it being roasted."

"You don't. The entertainment isn't bad, either. And, I swear, there's plenty of planter's punch to keep you afloat."

Brant stopped in Koloa on their way back to Poipu Beach and parked in front of a line of shops. They picked her out several muumuus, not the shapeless ones, but exquisitely fashioned fitted ones. He left her to pay while he went to another shop, and for the first time since their arrival in Kauai she felt an unwelcome jolt of reality.

"I'm sorry, ma'am, but I'll need your husband's signature on those traveler's checks."

Daphne realized that she didn't have a cent. And all the checks were in Brant's name. "But I have the same name," she said

"I'm sorry, ma'am," the sales person repeated, "but I can't break the rules."

"I understand," Daphne said. She left her packages on the counter and wandered outside to sit on the steps to the store. It wasn't that she was used to having her own money, because she wasn't. It just felt odd and somehow embarrassing that she, a married woman, was utterly dependent on her husband for everything.

"Hi, gorgeous," Brant said, sporting a new straw hat. "What's up, sweetheart? Where are your clothes?"

She looked up at his handsome face, so deeply tanned that his eyes looked even bluer. "I couldn't sign your traveler's checks," she said evenly.

"Oh, that, I'll be back in a minute."

He pulled off his straw hat and flipped it to her, frisbee style.

Daphne didn't go back into the store. She was looking at postcards of Spouting Horn when Brant came out carrying several big shopping bags. "You're going to look gorgeous, lady. I like the gold one that's got the thin straps best."

It's not his fault, she thought, forcing a smile. She said formally, "Thank you, Brant. The dresses are lovely. I appreciate them."

He cocked a dark eyebrow at her. "That sounded like a recording. What's up, sweetheart? You change your mind about the dresses?"

She didn't reply until they were seated in the car. She turned slightly and asked, "Brant, there's something I don't understand. The inheritance from Uncle Clarence, is it yours or mine?"

He sent her a startled look. "It's ours, of course. We're married, you know."

"That isn't quite true. Did you inherit the money, or did I?"

"I did. But what difference does it make? What's mine is yours, Daph."

"And what's mine is yours, only I don't have anything to share with you. Nothing."

Brant pulled the car off the road and switched off the motor. "Okay, what's the matter? And don't give me any runaround bull."

She gnawed on her lower lip and shook her head.

"Daph, were you bothered because the traveler's checks were all in my name? If you were, I'm sorry. I just didn't think. Tomorrow I'll flip over to the Waiohai and have some made in your name."

"Thank you."

"Your enthusiasm is deadening," he said, his eyes narrowing on her face. He shrugged. "Look, I guess I'm just used to being on my own, and," he added on a wicked grin, "even when I wasn't on my own, no one ever complained when I picked up the tab. When we get home to New York, I'll set up a checking account for you, in your name, okay?"

"It's still your money, not mine. It's like an allowance that you'd give to a child."

His hands clutched the steering wheel, and he said acidly, "Don't be an ass. You're my wife, my responsibility—"

"An encumbrance, a parasite, a—a dependent."

He cursed softly, started the engine and screeched back onto the narrow highway.

Brant parked the car in their parking space, and they walked up to the third floor in silence. Brant unlocked the door, then stepped back for her to enter first.

"Come here and sit down," he said. "I want to get a few things straight."

She wanted to tell him to go to hell, but the habit of obedience was strong, the habit of bending her will to the stronger. And, after all, what had he done wrong? Nothing, she thought, her shoulders slumping in depression. She sat down.

"I thought," Brant said, standing in front of her, crossing his arms over his chest, "that we understood and agreed on our respective roles. That is, I would bring home the proverbial bacon and you would be responsible for our home. However, if not having your own money bothers you, I'll sign over half the money from the inheritance. Is that what you want? It will make you independent. You can have all the bloody traveler's checks you want in your name."

"I didn't earn that money," she said, thrusting up her chin just a bit.

"Like hell you didn't! You were the old man's slave for how many years? Did he pay you a salary for all the work you did? Let's consider your half of the inheritance as back pay. You can spend it; you can invest it; you can stuff it under your mattress."

"You're very... kind."

He shot her an exasperated frown. "Daph, for God's sake, I want you to be happy. You're my wife. You will have our children."

She stared at him, her face paling under her tan. "Children?"

"I haven't been using any birth control. Have you?"

She paled even more. "I didn't think about it." She rose jerkily to her feet, clasping and unclasping her hands in front of her.

Every bit of irritation disappeared in an instant. He grasped her shoulders and gently drew her against him. "I'm sorry, sweetheart. I was making decisions for you. I just assumed... well, I'll be responsible for birth control. When we get home, we can discuss what you'd like to do. All right?"

She wished for just a brief instant that he would yell and holler and call her an idiot, just like Uncle Clarence had with great regularity. But he was so reasonable, so kind. He was really trying to be nice to her. It was almost depressing. She felt like a fool, an overreactive ass.

She felt in the wrong. "All right," she whispered against his shoulder. "I'm sorry. Please forgive me."

"It's not for you to apologize, turkey. It appears that our conversations haven't hit on some very important issues. And that's your fault, of course, for being so delectable that my mouth is kissing you all the time and not talking." He kissed the tip of her nose. "Is that a band of freckles I see?"

She smiled and wrinkled her nose. "I don't know about a band. I think I'd prefer a sprinkle."

"Or a gaggle or a herd?"

She punched him in the stomach, and he obligingly grunted. He cupped her hips and lifted her against him. "We've got a couple of hours before we need to go to our luau," he said, nuzzling her neck. "You got any ideas on how to spend them?"

"How about the beach? Maybe I can get a herd of freckles."

"Forget it," Brant said.

The luau was a major production, Daphne realized as they pulled into the special parking lot at the Sheraton. There were a good one hundred people, much laughter and high spirits. There were no individual tables, so they sat with two other couples. One older man from Ohio recognized Brant, and Daphne sat back and watched her husband wrap everyone at the table in his own special brand of charm.

"Are you newlyweds, dear?" the older man's wife asked Daphne while the men were discussing the Astros' chances for the Superbowl in the upcoming season.

"Yes, we are."

"You're English, aren't you?"

"Yes, ma'am, I am."

"Call me Agnes. Is this your first trip to Hawaii?"

The other woman, a stunning brunette from Seattle, soon joined in, and Daphne forgot her shyness.

"What a wonderful evening," Daphne said later to Brant, her voice just a bit fuzzy from the mai tais.

"I was proud of you, Daph," he said, hugging her against his side. He'd been a bit concerned that she'd clam up meeting strangers, but she hadn't, much to his delight.

"Brant," she said when they were sitting out on the deck a few minutes later, "have you called your mother?"

He was glad it was dark and she couldn't see the flush on his face. "Yes," he said. "I called her a couple of days ago when I was over at the Waiohai."

She felt herself stiffen a bit, wondering why he hadn't called her from the condo. "What did she say?"

He caressed the nape of her neck. "After she got over the shock she started singing hallelujahs." It wasn't precisely the truth, but close enough. Actually, he had been able to see her mind working, wondering just why he'd married an English girl so quickly. He'd ended up telling her the terms of the will. "She can't wait to meet you, sweetheart, and is delighted that you want another ceremony for her and the family. You wanna marry me next month?"

She gave him such a sweet, radiant smile that he froze for a moment, taken aback at the odd, twisting emotions that smile evoked. "Yes," she said, "I think I've compromised you enough without a minister's blessing."

"Are you certain that you weren't a Victorian maiden in your past life? Compromised? I love it."

There were no more snakes in the garden for the remainder of their stay in Kauai. Brant told her about every one of his teammates, his intention being to ease her shyness when she met them. They discussed Asherwood Hall, coming to agreement on all the renovations. Three days before they left Daphne discovered she had no worries about being pregnant, and Brant, groaning, told her he was going to have to live in the shower, under a steady stream of icy water. His joking eased her embarrassment, as he intended it to.

It started as a joke on their return flight to Los Angeles. "Why not have Winterspoon come to New York and be our majordomo?" And it ended up as a plan. "I can't wait for Marcie to get hold of that item," Brant said. "An English valet in residence with a football player!"

"Who's Marcie?" Daphne asked, latching immediately on this heretofore unmentioned name.

"Marcie?" Brant repeated carefully. "Just a friend, sweetheart. She's a reporter for a newspaper in New York."

Ah, Daphne thought, a woman who's done something with her life other than live it at the orders of someone else. But that wasn't true, she chided herself. She would do something. She wouldn't sit around Brant's house doing nothing.

Their arrival in New York's Kennedy Airport was a nightmare. Brant's mother was there, along with a group from the press. A flashbulb went off in Daphne's face, and she shrank against him. "Damn," he muttered, then forced a smile to his lips. He knew she was practically insensible from all the Dramamine. How the hell had the press found out when he was returning?

The afternoon paper turned her into a silent ghost.

''Football Pro Gains Title and Rich Bride.'' The by-line was Marcie's.

Chapter Thirteen

"How is she, Brant?" asked Alice Asher when her son came back into the living room.

"Asleep. She was so doped up to begin with and this—" he flung a disgusted arm toward the newspaper "—this didn't help. How did the press find out, Mom? Do you know?"

"Marcie called me last week and, fool that I am, I told her you'd gotten married in England and were in Hawaii. That's all."

"Of course all she had to do was call the airlines and find out which flight we were coming back on." Brant sat back, pulling a thick sofa cushion behind his head. "And, of course, she called some of her buddies in England. Well, it's done. I'll call Marcie later; you can be sure of that."

"I like Daphne, Brant," said Alice. "She seems unlike all the other women in your life, so—"

"Sweet? Guileless? Innocent as a lamb?"

"Perhaps. We'll get her over this...this nastiness."

Alice went into the kitchen and made some coffee. When she returned to Brant's very modern living room, she saw him standing in front of the large glass window, staring down on Central Park. "May I ask you something personal, honey?"

"Sure, Mom, everyone else does without even asking my permission." He turned to face her, and she saw the weariness on his handsome face.

"Did you marry her because of the will?"

"In part," he said honestly. "As she did me. But I'm fond of her, as she is of me. We both love Asherwood. We both want it restored to what it was years ago. By marrying, we got the house and ensured there'd be enough money to fix it up. She's guileless as hell, it's true. And young and inexperienced." He gave her a lopsided grin. "Well, maybe not so inexperienced about some things now."

"I gather," Alice said dryly, "that you handled that quite well."

"I guess there's something to be said about raising a girl in the bowels of the country. She'd had no chance to learn everything she shouldn't like or shouldn't do."

"Is that your oblique way of telling me that Daphne enjoys the physical side of marriage?"

"Yeah." He grinned. "She's very natural and loving."

Alice was silently relieved about that. She said, "Incidentally, Lily and Dusty are ready to fly up from Houston whenever you give them the word."

"Good. Give me some time to get Daph back in shape, then we can arrange everything. Just family and a few friends, okay, Mom?"

"No problem, honey. I've already talked to Reverend Oakes."

"Mom, I don't want you ever to think that I would marry just for money. But you know that's what the press is going to continue pushing."

"I know you would never do such a thing. I was thinking, Brant, once Daphne gets out and meets people, everyone will see what a lovely person she is. And, of course, she's very beautiful."

Brant drank some of his coffee, but didn't sit down. He began pacing and Alice watched him, a question in her eyes.

"Mom," he said abruptly, "I don't know much about birth control. That is, I know about it, and Lord knows I've been very careful in the past. I just don't want Daphne taking anything that could possibly hurt her. What do you think?"

"I would suggest that you call the medical society and ask for a woman gynecologist."

"Woman?"

"I think it would make Daphne feel more comfortable, don't you?"

"Yeah, probably. Thanks for coming, Mom. It's late. Are you ready to turn in?"

"Yes." She rose and hugged Brant. "Everything will work out, honey, don't worry."

"I'll try not to." He grinned down at her. "Would you be willing to make breakfast tomorrow morning? I'll help you. Daphne isn't too much of a marvel in the kitchen."

"Sure thing. After all, I spoiled you rotten for thirty-one years. Why stop now?"

Brant didn't turn on the bedroom light. He could see Daphne's outline in his large brass bed, and it gave him a warm feeling. He'd sleep next to her every night and wake up next to her every morning. It added a completeness that he'd never really realized wasn't there until he had it.

She murmured softly in her sleep when he eased in beside her. He kissed her lightly on her ear and pulled her into his arms.

"Brant?" Her voice was fuzzy and blurred.

"Shush, sweetheart. Go back to sleep."

"Can we go see the Spouting Horn again tomorrow?"

She was still in Kauai. "Sure thing." He stroked her hair lightly and pressed her cheek against his shoulder. "We'll do whatever you want."

Daphne was a morning person, awake and alert the moment she opened her eyes. But this morning she woke up slowly. She was aware that she was in a strange place, and she reached for Brant. He wasn't there. Slowly she sat up and stared at the expanse of bed. Brant's bedroom, she thought, shaking her head clear of confusion. Brant's home, no, she corrected herself, his condo. What a strange word! She remembered the events of the previous evening and cringed. She'd acted like Daphne the shy, insecure, dowdy, double bagger, and fallen apart in front of Brant's mother.

"You're full of rubbish," she said aloud to the empty room. "How odd," she added softly. Unlike the living room, which was a study in modern glass, chrome and stark furnishings, the bedroom was a study in elegant antiques. She quickly recognized an original eighteenth-century French armoire, and several heavy Spanish chairs. There was a scroll-armed sofa that reminded her of the Regency period, but she wasn't sure. The rug was a thick rich coffee color and covered the center of the polished hardwood floor. She climbed out of bed, pausing a moment to touch the beautiful brass headboard. She found herself wondering how many women had slept in that bed with Brant.

She giggled. With the lights off, it would take two people a good deal of time to find each other in that huge bed. She trooped into the bathroom and stood a moment, gaping at the incredible, utterly decadent tub. It was circular and deep, and there was some kind of a motor settled against one side. She hadn't the foggiest notion of what to do with that, and was thankful there was a separate shower stall. She quickly showered, then set about drying her hair and putting her face to rights.

Forty-five minutes later, dressed in wool slacks and a fitted long sweater with a gold belt at the waist, Daphne opened the bedroom door and peered out. She heard voices and laughter. Brant's mother was there, she thought, squaring her shoulders. She stepped into the small dining room.

"Hi," she said. "Forgive me for being so late. It took me quite a while to get my engine started."

Brant rose and came to her, smiling. "Morning, sweetheart. We've kept breakfast warm for you. You hungry?"

She nodded, flushing when he lightly kissed her in front of his mother.

"Sit down and get acquainted with your dragon mother-in-law, and I'll get you some eggs and bacon."

"Good morning, Daphne," Alice said. "Just ignore the Son of the Dragon and his big mouth. Are you feeling better today?"

"Yes, ma'am. Oh! I hadn't realized it yesterday, but Brant looks so much like you!"

"I'll take that as a compliment if it doesn't include huge shoulders and five-o'clock shadow. Now, tell me how you liked Kauai."

Brant stayed a bit longer in the kitchen than necessary, giving the two women time alone together. He heard the tension ease in Daphne's voice, heard her laugh. Such a sweet, clear sound. It made him feel good.

"Service from the chef," he said, setting her plate in front of her. "There's even tea, Daph."

She grinned up at him. "You the chef? I have this terrible feeling that we're going to starve."

Under Alice's skillful handling Daphne found herself talking about her life in England, Aunt Cloe, Lucilla and the minions at Asherwood. "Did Brant tell you we're going to invite Winterspoon to come over?" she asked, shyly smiling at her husband.

"Talk about culture, honey," his mother said, laughing at him. "I remember reading that all English valets were born with taste and snobbery."

"True enough," Brant said. "Even though you're a dowager something, he'll probably politely turn up his nose at you."

Alice encouraged Daphne to talk more about Hawaii, listening to her guileless enthusiasm and watching her closely when she referred something to Brant. They'll be quite good for each other, she thought. If Daphne wasn't yet in love with her husband, it would be just a matter of time. As for Brant, he seemed so...indulgent, gentle, protective.

Oddly enough, Alice felt herself wanting to protect this charming girl. No, Alice, she told herself sternly. She can't remain a girl. To live in Brant's world, she's going to have to be a woman and stand on her own two feet.

"Now," she said, when there was a lapse in the conversation, "let's talk about your Connecticut wedding."

Later Brant escorted the two women on a brief tour of New York. To avoid any vulturous press, they ate dinner at one of Brant's favorite Spanish restaurants down in the Village. Unfortunately, when they returned home, there were two men waiting for them in the underground garage. There was no way they could escape them.

"Glad you're home, Brant," one of the men said good-naturedly, easing his way carefully forward. "Is this the heiress? Hey, Mrs. Asher, give us a big smile!"

Daphne froze as a flashing light went off in her face. Suddenly she felt Alice Asher squeeze her hand. I am not Daphne the double bagger, she told herself fiercely, but somehow she couldn't make her muscles move into a smile. Alice said quickly, "My new daughter is very much enjoying New York and her new home. Everyone has been so, so... kind, haven't they, dear?"

Daphne nodded mutely. Why did her hair all of a sudden feel so stringy?

Brant tucked Daphne's hand through the crook of his arm. "Anything else, gentlemen?"

"Yeah. Mrs. Asher, Brant here got a real good deal when he married you, right? Would you like to comment on that, ma'am?"

Brant wanted to smash the man's face in, but he said calmly enough, "We both got a great deal, boys, but you're right. I don't think I've ever seen a prettier lady, have you?"

"Sure, Brant," one of the men said. He said in a carrying voice as he and his partner walked off. "If you like rich girls who are mutes."

Daphne felt tears sting her eyes. She'd let Brant down. Again. She'd acted like a stupid parrot who couldn't talk.

I might not look like a double bagger, she thought, her shoulders slumped, but I still act like one.

"It's all right, dear," Alice said, patting her shoulder. "It will just take a bit more time for you to get used to things."

"She's right, Daph. Don't worry about the grubby bastards."

"I'm sorry," she mumbled.

"Don't be an ass," Brant said, ignoring his mother's gasp. "You're shy, Daph. I'll protect you. Just don't get depressed about it. Okay?"

She blinked back tears and nodded. Damn, she wasn't shy around Brant. Why did she have to be such a fool with strangers?

The ride up the elevator was a silent one. When they entered the condo Brant said in a too-hearty voice, "You haven't told me how much you like my house, Daph."

"I like your house a lot," she said.

"What I meant was our house, Daph. If you'd like to change anything, just let me know."

"I just wish there was a garden," she said, walking over to the huge picture window that looked out over Central Park. She gave a self-conscious laugh. "I'd been picturing acres of land. I didn't realize that New York was all buildings. Stupid of me, after all the pictures I've seen."

He frowned at the back of her head. "I suppose we could get a house in the country," he said.

It was a generous offer, but Daphne quickly shook her head. They already had a house in the country, in England.

"Well, my dears," Alice said, smiling at them. "I think I'm ready for bed. I'll see you both in the morning."

Brant kissed his mother good night, then turned toward his wife, who was still standing, staring out the window.

"The lights are beautiful, aren't they?" he said.

She nodded. He pulled her against him, gently kneading her shoulders. "Are you ready for bed, sweetheart?" He leaned down and began nibbling at her ear lobe.

She felt a surge of desire, but it was quickly dashed by her own feelings of inferiority. Was he just humoring her in bed? Was she as much of a failure making love as she was dealing with people? Angry at herself, and anxious to prove to herself that she could do something right, she turned in his arms and crushed herself against him. She stood on her tiptoes, cupped his face between her hands and kissed him.

Good Lord, Brant thought, a bit dazed by her enthusiastic attack. He locked his arms around her, cupping her hips in his hands to draw her closer. He felt her move her hips against him, and moaned into her mouth. "I want you now," he said. He picked her up in his arms and carried her into the bedroom, casting one eye toward his mother's room, thankful that the door was shut.

When he set her on her feet, she didn't let him go, but pulled him down on top of her on the bed. He didn't understand her urgency, but he was feeling near desperation himself, so it didn't matter. He pulled up her skirt, jerked off her panty hose and panties, and gave her what she needed. When she was trembling in the aftershock of pleasure, he jerked down his zipper and entered her warm body.

He lay heavily on top of her, rather stunned at his own violent reaction. He nuzzled her throat and said, "Will you let me go long enough to take my clothes off now?"

"All right," she said. Suddenly she hugged him tightly to her. "I was so afraid."

He eased up on his elbows so he could see her face. "Don't be afraid of those stupid media people. They're not worth it."

"No, not them," she said, biting down on her lower lip.

"Of what, sweetheart?"

"I was afraid that I would fail at everything. I did give you pleasure, didn't I?"

He felt a wave of pity for her, but forced himself to grin at her. "You wanna feel my heart? It's still galloping fast enough to be in the Kentucky Derby."

"So is mine," she said. "You are so nice, Brant."

"Don't forget it, Mrs. Asher. Now, how about taking a shower with me?"

"I think I'd prefer the tub with that engine in it."

Alice Asher left for Connecticut the following day to set the wedding plans into motion. Brant and Daphne would come the following weekend, as would Lily and Dusty. "To do the Deed," Brant said. "Again."

That evening, Brant and Daphne went to a formal dinner party given by a vice president of the ad agency doing Brant's sporting goods commercial. Daphne was wearing a new long gown of soft white chiffon and an emerald pendant Brant had bought her at Tiffany's. Mr. Morrison's house was on Long Island, and as Brant drove his Porsche out of Manhattan, he told Daphne about the people they would meet.

"Morrison's a short, balding, very nice man," he said. "The president of the sporting goods company is named Dicks, and the man's a shark. I just met him once, but not, thank God, in an alley or at the Stock Exchange.

Speaking of the Stock Exchange,'' he continued non-stop, looking briefly toward his silent wife, ''we'll go to the bank tomorrow and get your checking account set up. And you'll need credit cards in your name. Then we'll talk to my lawyer about transferring half the inheritance to you. Did I tell you how gorgeous you look tonight?''

''Yes,'' she said, turning slightly to give him a tentative smile. Like a damned puppy who's just wet on the carpet, he thought.

''Look, Daph, I know Max the doorman showed you the damned paper. Would you please just forget those toads? You'll like most of the people you'll meet tonight, I promise. Just be yourself, but don't treat any of the men like you do me, okay?''

That made her smile real. ''None of them could look nearly as lovely as you do. In fact, I sometimes have fantasies that you're starkers under your coat.''

''Sometimes...'' He laughed. ''I like that. You're going to be changing the New York idiom, sweetheart. Will you promise me one thing?''

I'd promise you anything you wanted, she thought. ''What?''

No, he thought quickly, don't caution her any more. He gave her a leering smile. ''Don't fall out of your gown. Your beautiful breasts are only for me.''

She flushed, laughed, and moved closer, sliding her hand up his thigh. She felt his muscles tighten under her fingers.

''Watch what you're doing lady, or we might find ourselves arrested for doing indecent things on the freeway.''

Forty-five minutes later they pulled into the large circular drive of the Morrisons' East Hampton home. They stepped through the front door and were inundated with noise from close to fifty guests. "Just remember," Brant whispered in her ear, as their host and hostess approached them, "you're the most beautiful woman here, and you're my wife."

Daphne was reserved, but Mrs. Morrison decided that quality was typically English, and she smiled her approval. All that garbage in the newspapers was just that, she thought. Brant stuck to Daphne through all the introductions, and was relieved when she smiled up at him, completely at ease, and told him she was going to the loo.

Brant patted her arm and watched her walk gracefully to a maid and speak to her. She was doing so well. Her natural sense of humor was coming out, and the women as well as the men were warming to her. He began to look around for Marcie. He'd seen her earlier, and he wanted to talk to her. He couldn't find her.

Daphne was repairing her makeup in the large bathroom off the master suite when she heard a woman's cold voice say, "Well, if it isn't the little English flower. Alone at last."

Her hand jerked, and the lipstick ended up on her cheek. She turned slowly to face a gorgeous redheaded woman, gowned in silver lamé that accentuated every beautiful curve of her body.

"Hello," Daphne said as she wiped off the lipstick.

She's so damned young and pretty, Marcie thought, feeling a stab of jealousy, disappointment and fury. But what had she expected? A troll? "My name is Marcie Ellis. I'm a very close friend of Brant's."

"A pleasure, ma'am. My name is Daphne."

"Ma'am? I'm not that much older than you are. Daphne. What a . . . clever name, so unused nowadays." Marcie tossed her hair, a studied movement that showed off her long, graceful neck. "Oh yes, I know who you are. You're the stud's little bride."

Daphne felt every muscle in her body stiffen alarmingly. Marcie must be one of Brant's lovers. No, ex-lovers.

"So odd," Marcie continued, wishing she could toss a bottle of pink paint on Daphne's hair. "Brant marrying you so quickly. But then again, he always moves quickly when he wants something, whether it's a new car, a new woman or a good financial deal."

"If you'll excuse me, Miss Ellis," Daphne said, clutching her purse and inching toward the door.

"Tell me, Mrs. Asher, what do you do...professionally?"

"Nothing," Daphne said flatly.

"Ah, the little house *frau*." She laughed. Her lower teeth weren't very straight, and it made Daphne feel better. There was a flaw. "I'll give Brant three months, and then, my dear, you'll be just like any of Brant's other possessions, and you can sit around with his silly antiques and gather dust."

"His antiques are lovely!"

"His lovely brass bed as well? Have you played in his Jacuzzi yet? He enjoys that."

She's treating me like Lucilla does, Daphne thought; she's nasty and condescending. She wanted to rage at the woman, but she could easily picture her in that awesome tub with Brant, frolicking about, and that wiped out any smart retort she could have made. How could he possibly want anything from her except the money? She felt flat-chested, dumpy and stupid. "I don't think you're very nice," she said, and fled from the bathroom, Marcie's laughter ringing in her ears.

Brant was in close conversation with two men, and she didn't consider interrupting him. She slipped onto the lighted patio and cursed herself silently. It was frigidly cold, but she didn't notice.

"Here now, Mrs. Asher. Don't want you to take a cold."

Mr. Morrison gently drew her back inside. "Someone has upset you," he said, eyeing her pale face. He caught a glimpse of Marcie Ellis and heaved a deep sigh. He wanted to comfort Daphne and tell her everything would be all right, but he wasn't stupid, and knew that was the last thing she needed. He said matter-of-factly, "You know, Mrs. Asher, your husband is in a high visibility position. And you, Brant told me, have lived all your life in the country. Most people, you know, are kind, and those who aren't usually have a reason. For example, take Marcie Ellis." She gave a start, but he continued blandly. "She is really a nice woman, but Brant's marriage gave her a nasty start. She and your husband were close, I suppose, but that has nothing to do with anything now. You have two choices, ma'am. Either you turn the other cheek and let her exhaust her venom, or you make a fist and punch her out. If you choose the latter, I hope you won't do it here," he added, giving her a wide grin. "I have high blood pressure, and such a sight just might topple me into the hereafter."

Daphne laughed, unable to keep it in. "Brant told me how kind you were, Mr. Morrison, but he didn't tell me how funny you were!"

"Call me Dan."

"I think you're safe tonight, Dan. I shan't punch her over."

"Out, Mrs. Asher. American slang."

"I'll remember that. You're very kind, sir. The habits of a lifetime are difficult to break, I think." She drew a deep breath and straightened her shoulders. "It's time I stopped hiding behind Brant. I am, after all, a grown woman."

"Quite grown, I'd say," Dan Morrison agreed.

Brant looked up to see his wife in close conversation with Dan Morrison.

"Well, Brant, is your wife that desperate?"

"Hello, Marcie. I tried to get you yesterday, but you were out. How's the news business?"

"All right, I suppose. You haven't given me that exclusive you promised, Brant."

"How badly do you want it?"

She looked at him closely. He was tense, and his eyes glittered brightly. "A knight in football armor, Brant? My, how ferocious you are! I gather you want to make a deal?"

"Yes, you could say that. No more crap, Marcie, and no more ridiculous attacks on my wife, or innuendos about the circumstances of our marriage. The straightforward, unvarnished truth. That's my deal."

Marcie flinched when he said wife. "I'll think about it," she said finally. "You sure you want the unvarnished truth? As I understand it, unvarnished, it makes little green eyes a gold digger, and you, well..." She turned to go, but couldn't resist saying over her shoulder, "I personally found your *wife* about as interesting as a head of cabbage."

Brant didn't ask Daphne about her conversation with Dan Morrison, and she didn't mention her scene with Marcie Ellis.

The next afternoon Brant was busily showing Daphne how to write a check and maintain a checkbook. He looked up at the sound of the doorbell, and frowned. "Who the hell—" he began.

When he opened the door, he took a step back at the sight of most of the Astros football team, complete with wives and champagne.

"Surprise!"

Chapter Fourteen

"Have another glass of champagne, Daph."

She smiled up at Tiny Phipps and thrust out her glass.

"I've always thought Brant's condo was huge," she said in some bewilderment. "Now, with all of you, it looks like a Liliputian's house bursting with Gulliver's."

"Yeah," said Lloyd Nolan, "we can't even run plays in here. You should see the place when all the players drop in."

"There are more of you?"

"Oh sure. It's the off-season now, and we couldn't round everybody up. So, Daph, what do you think of New York?"

"And football?"

"Yeah, you gotta see Dancer strut his stuff. We brought some tapes over for you"

She nodded enthusiastically. "I'd love it. Brant showed me just one back home."

"Lloyd wants you to admire *him*, too," said a lovely black woman, as she poked Lloyd in the ribs. "I'm Beatrice, his better half, but you don't have to remember it this time. You've got name overload, right?"

"Oh yes," Daphne said happily. "He's really called Dancer? He never told me that, although he was quite graceful when we danced a bit in Kauai—"

There was a hoot of laughter. Daphne felt a huge arm go around her shoulders and hug. "Ignore the fools, Daph," said "Choosy" Williams, a defensive lineman. "Your old man is called Dancer because he can scramble out of the pocket as well as Fran Tarkington. He doesn't want to get his beautiful body wrecked."

"I see," said Daphne with wide-eyed seriousness. "He does have a splendid body."

This guileless observation brought on fresh gales of laughter. Brant, in conversation with his coach, Sam Carverelli, looked over at the group surrounding his wife.

"You look like a fatuous bull," said Sam. "Lovely girl, Brant. And so at ease with everyone. I think Tiny is smitten."

She was at ease, completely at ease, Brant thought, and with a bunch of football players. And their wives, he added to himself, as he watched Cindy Williams lean over to whisper something in Daphne's ear. He couldn't believe it. He heard more champagne corks popping.

He blinked when his wife and a dozen or so players and wives left the living room.

"We're going to show her one of your famous plays, Brant!" Guy Richardson shouted across the room. "You know, the one where you tried a quarterback sneak and got creamed."

When Brant entered the den nearly a half an hour later he saw his wife sitting cross-legged on the floor in front of the TV, surrounded by the women. The men were draped over every piece of furniture in the room.

"Watch this pass, Daph," Lloyd was saying. "Sixty yards and right into my arms."

There was loud cheering when Lloyd trotted across into the end zone for a score, with Daphne's voice one of the loudest.

"How does he keep the ball from wobbling when he throws it so far?" she asked.

"Technique, darlin', technique," Lloyd said.

"He's got lots of that!"

"He sure seems to," said Daphne.

"Come on now, Nolan," Sam Carverelli scolded. "Look, Daphne," he said, showing her a football he'd pulled from the closet. "You have to handle the ball like this. See the seam? Look how I'm holding it. Here, you try it."

"Right over here, Daph," called Lloyd, backing to the far corner of the den.

She flung the ball at him, and he caught it against his chest. He gave a mighty "Ummph," and staggered backward.

"If he hadn't caught it, it would have ended up in Central Park," said Tiny, the self-appointed champagne pourer.

"Talented lady," Beatrice said to Brant.

He grinned. "Small hands, but yes, very talented."

"I love it when you talk dirty, Brant," Tiffy Richardson giggled.

Brant looked over her very pregnant stomach and said blandly, "Talk is cheap, by the looks of it."

"Look at that sweep around the right end!"

Brant blinked. The words had come from his English wife's mouth, and her eyes were glued to the TV screen.

"Oh, Brant, watch out!"

"Sorry, old buddy," Ted Hartland, the center, said, wincing as Brant was tackled by three of the Patriots' players.

"What a mess that play was," said Sam. "You nearly got a cracked rib out of that one, Brant."

Daphne turned to stare up at him. Brant dropped to his haunches. "I wasn't hurt, love. Just a bit black and blue. It's all part of the game, particularly when these idiots turn blind and clumsy on me."

"She doesn't want you to hurt your splendid body, Brant," said Nolan.

"All of you have splendid bodies," Daphne said. "You must be more careful, every one of you. Don't you agree, Beatrice?"

"I sure do. I can't count the times Lloyd comes home looking like a reject from a bruise factory."

"I bet he moans a lot to get sympathy," said Sam.

A good-natured argument between the men and women ensued about machoness and how it lasted only until the players got home. "Then he dissolves like a little boy," said Tiffy. "And Guy hardly ever gets tackled, 'cause he's the kicker."

"But the pain, watching the rest of the guys taking blows," Guy said, rubbing his ribs.

Brant sat on the floor beside Daphne, but he let the other guys tell her about the plays. She's like a sponge, he thought, seeing first confusion in her eyes at an explanation, then understanding. And if she didn't understand, she asked. This is my family, he thought, and she fits right in.

"Hey, Brant, you got a chalkboard?"

He looked up at Lloyd Nolan. "Sorry," he said. "Why?"

"Daph wants to see a double reverse."

"We'll wait for a nice day, then show her everything she wants to see in the park. Would you like to learn touch football, Daph?"

Tiny beamed at her when she nodded enthusiastically.

"You really lucked out," Tiffy Richardson said in a lowered voice to Brant. "We were all so worried."

Brant cocked an eyebrow at her. "Show of support? Or did all of you want to see if I'd married a cretin for money?"

"Well, the most obnoxious innuendoes were from Marcie, of course, and everybody figured she would slant things in the worst possible light. Daphne is..." Tiffy paused, then continued thoughtfully. "She brings out the protective instincts in one, doesn't she? I've never seen the guys so, well...careful. She seems like a lovely girl, Brant."

"Yes," he said, "she is."

"I love listening to her talk. I guess most Americans get off on an English accent."

"Particularly when she talks about a sweep around the right end?" He tried to mimic her accent, and they burst into laughter.

"Oh, Sam," they heard her call out to the coach, "you shouldn't pull your hair like that! It's just one play that went awry."

Guy Richardson showed her the final few minutes of the play-off game they'd lost to the Steelers, all the while explaining to her how their...darned kicker had missed two field goals before this.

She was indignant, hissing with the rest of them at the loss. "That's disgusting! You're the much better kicker, Guy. I'm so sorry." She turned to her husband and hugged him fiercely, surprising him. "Next season you'll demolish them. I promise."

The Astros didn't leave until nearly midnight. Tiny ordered in a dozen pizzas, and Brant watched with the fondness of a proud parent as Daphne laughed when they teased her mercilessly about the anchovies.

Nor did they leave until the wreckage was cleaned up. Daphne was hugged until her ribs ached. When the door closed for the last time she turned to Brant and flung her arms around his waist. "I'm so happy! I've never met so many nice people."

"You're tipsy," he said, running his hands up and down her back.

"Not that tipsy," she said, raising her face, her lips parting.

He kissed the tip of her nose and led her into the bedroom. When she was naked, her turned her onto her stomach, smiling when she looked at him questioningly over her shoulder. "Trust me," he said, leaning down to nip the nape of her neck. He moved deeply into her, and she moaned softly, wriggling beneath him as his hands stroked her breasts and belly. He realized vaguely that she didn't have her doctor's appointment until the following day, but when he tried to pull out of her, she twisted onto her back and held him deep within her.

"Sweetheart," he said desperately, "don't move." But his fingers found her, caressed her, and she jerked upward. "I can't stop," he said, his voice ragged.

"I can feel it," she gasped. "I'm filled with you."

Rippling, wild feelings surged through him, making him oblivious of everything except the warmth of her and the mindless depth of his pleasure.

"Only with you," he said. "Only with you."

In the next instant he was asleep.

What, Daphne wondered, dazed by her own passion, had he meant by that? She curled against him, listened to her galloping heart slow to normal, and fell asleep, replete with happiness.

"I would like to write you a check," Daphne said to the clerk in Lord and Taylor. She and Brant had just come from her doctor, and he had told her they should celebrate. The diaphragm would be ready in two days. The boots on sale in the display window drew them both in. Daphne's were a wreck.

"Certainly, ma'am," the saleswoman said. "Wouldn't you like to have a Lord and Taylor credit card? It's much easier, you know."

Daphne wondered where Brant was. He'd quickly approved her selection of the new leather boots, then wandered off.

"A credit card," she repeated. She'd never owned a credit card in her life. Suddenly it seemed the most important thing in the world. "Yes," she said, "I would like one."

"Excellent. Ah, Mrs. Asher, I'm certain your credit will be approved." She directed Daphne to the sixth floor. That was where Brant found her some twenty minutes later.

She was sitting very straight in the chair opposite a rather tired-looking man whose glasses kept slipping down his nose. He heard the man say, "You will need your husband's approval, Mrs. Asher, and, as I said, his signature."

"But all you have to do is speak to Mr. Edward Caufield, the broker. The card is for me, as I told you, not for my husband."

"Mrs. Asher..." The man was beginning to sound out of patience. "Ma'am, it's policy. You have no income of your own."

"Is there a problem?" Brant asked, stepping into Daphne's line of vision.

The man looked ready to embrace Brant with relief. "Mr. Asher? You're the football player, aren't you? A pleasure, sir." He quickly rose and shook Brant's hand. "We just need your signature, and some information for the application form."

Brant had two major credit cards, and had no wish for another one, but he saw the strained look in Daphne's eyes and quickly succumbed. "Of course," he said, seating himself beside his wife.

He realized that he'd totally misunderstood the situation when she said abruptly, "I want the credit card in my name, not his."

Mr. Reeves sighed and tried again. "Mrs. Asher, I can't imagine that credit is handled that differently in England. Of course you can have a card in your name; it is just that the major account will be in your husband's name. It is his responsibility—"

"No, Mr. Asher doesn't want a Lord and Taylor card. Only I do! *I* will be writing you checks to pay for purchases, not him."

"Ma'am, you have no major, steady source of income." He sent a pleading look at Brant. "You have no job and no credit record."

Damnation, Brant thought, what the hell was he supposed to do now? Daphne looked ready to spit nails. He said as calmly as he could, "My wife does have an income of her own. A thousand dollars a month is deposited into her account. Now, let's get this bloody application filled out."

She was back to an allowance. Although she had over two hundred thousand dollars in investments, arranged two days previously by Brant's broker, all she could prove was that she had quarterly incoming interest from the investments. She bit her tongue, rage flowing through her. Rage at herself for being so utterly worthless. She rose jerkily to her feet, clutching her purse in front of her like a weapon. "I don't want your credit card, Mr. Reeves. I am going to go downstairs and write a check for my purchase."

"Daphne, wait," Brant began, but she was marching out of the office, her shoulders squared like a militant...whatever.

He looked back at Mr. Reeves. "Maybe some other time," he said, and left. The man's commiserating look made Brant want to strangle Daphne.

Daphne wished she had never even seen the damned boots, but she wrote out the check, her very first with elaborate care, and thumped it next to the saleswoman's cash register.

"May I please see your driver's license and a major credit card, Mrs. Asher?"

Daphne looked at her blankly. "What?"

"Since you don't have an account with us, ma'am, I need to see ID with your check. It's store policy."

Brant arrived in time for this exchange. He closed his eyes a moment, wishing he were playing football in California. Hell, he'd even settle for Alaska. It was his own fault. It hadn't occurred to him that she would need ID to write checks.

"I don't have any ID," Daphne said through gritted teeth.

The saleswoman looked at her helplessly. "I understand, ma'am, that you're new in this country. Let me speak to the manager, unless, of course, your husband could provide—'' She broke off at Daphne's furious glare and fled.

She was smart enough to escape the impending eruption, Brant thought. He gently laid his hand on Daphne's arm. He could feel her trembling through her coat sleeve. ''I forgot,'' he said. ''I'm sorry. We'll get you ID this week.''

Her contacts itched with the wretched tears welling up, and she dashed her hand across her eyes, inevitably dislodging a contact. A lime green dot of plastic fell on the counter. She cursed, and Brant was so surprised that he laughed.

''I hate you,'' she said, her voice low and trembling. ''I don't want these damned boots. I don't want anything, do you hear?'' She managed to pick up the contact, then left him standing at the counter, feeling like an utter fool. He was aware of pitying glances from other customers.

''I'm sorry, Mr. Asher,'' the saleswoman said, ''but I will have to have your check instead. Or a credit card?''

Brant silently wrote out a check. When the boots were packaged, he went to stand outside the women's room. His wait was a long one, and he was beginning to think that Daphne had left before he'd gotten there. Five minutes later she emerged, her head down, her knitted hat pulled low over her forehead.

''Let's go ice-skating,'' he said, taking her arm in a firm grasp.

''You have an appointment, don't you?'' she asked, not looking up at him.

''The appointment can wait. I'll make a phone call.''

They went ice-skating at Rockefeller Center, and Brant watched her take all her frustration out on the ice. She was a very good skater, very graceful, and he was thankful. On the taxi ride back to their building he said calmly, "Tomorrow we're going to get you a New York driver's license."

"I'm sure you won't mind my taking the test in your Porsche?" she said sarcastically.

The thought of anyone but himself driving the Porsche in New York traffic chilled him, but he said nothing.

"What if I wreck your bloody car? I don't have any ID. I don't have any auto insurance. And they won't even accept my check!"

Thank heaven the cab pulled up in front of their building at that moment, and he was saved by having to search for the cab fare.

He said nothing until they were safely inside the condo. He tossed the package containing the infamous boots on the sofa. "All right, we're going to talk, Daph. No more snide remarks from you, no more infantile behavior."

She had the utter nerve to walk away from him into the kitchen. How anticlimactic to argue in front of the sink, he thought, glaring at the back of her head. He watched her drink a glass of water.

"Are you quite through now?" he asked.

"No. I want to go to the bathroom."

"Convenient cause and effect," he muttered. He followed her through the bedroom and stopped abruptly when the bathroom door was slammed in his face.

A wife, he thought, striding back into the living room, is a pain in the butt. He was trying to smooth things out for her, and all he got in return was childish anger and scenes. He was well lathered up when she came into the living room some ten minutes later.

"I'm fed up with you," he said, erupting. "I should have married a woman, not some naive, silly girl whose only claim to anything is her performance in bed." Unfair, he raged at himself once the words were out, but he wouldn't take them back. He'd finally gotten her attention.

Daphne stared at him, her eyes darkening with anger.

"If you start on me again, I'm leaving. Now, do you want to talk like two reasoning adults or continue to carry on? And don't you shake your head at me!" He grasped her shoulders and shook her slightly. "Well?" he demanded.

"I should go get dinner started," she said.

"Oh? Burned tuna casserole? Cold scrambled eggs?" He plowed distracted fingers through his hair. "Damn it, I'm sorry, I didn't mean that. Come here and sit down. Now."

She curled up at one end of the long sofa and looked straight ahead at a pink marble sculpture of a naked woman on a side table.

"Daph," he said, drawing on his patience, "what happened today was unfortunate. There was no reason for you to freak out like that. It's no big deal. We'll get your ID, and you'll be free to shop anywhere you want to and write a zillion checks. What else do you want?"

"I want to go home," she said, then realized how stupid it all was, and gave a nervous laugh. "No, that's not true. I just feel so...useless."

"Useless! You're my wife! Or are you beginning to regret marrying me now?"

"No, it's not that," she said unhappily, feeling stupid and inarticulate, and guilty. It wasn't his fault, after all, that she couldn't do what any normal adult person could. How could he ever think that she'd regret having married him? He was the one with the cross to bear. She licked her dry lips. "It's just—" Just what? she wanted to yell at herself.

"Please spare me any psychological crap about not knowing who you are and wanting to search out your identity in the scheme of life."

"All right, but it's not psychological! I'll spare you everything. Don't you have an appointment soon?"

"Yes," he said, rising abruptly. "I do. When I get back, we'll go out to dinner."

She watched him helplessly as he shrugged into his beautiful leather coat and slammed out the front door.

She wandered around the house before settling in the den. She turned on the VCR and put in a video of one of Brant's football games. She felt pleasure begin to flow through her at the excitement of the plays. "That," she said to the empty room, "was a draw play. It didn't work, but it was a good call."

Chapter Fifteen

"Welcome, my dears," said Alice Asher, embracing first Daphne, then Brant. "The house is filled to bursting! Come in quickly, it's so cold outside. Isn't the snow lovely? Here, let me take your coats. And, Daphne, I have quite a surprise for you."

Surprise wasn't the word for it. Daphne stared first at Winterspoon, then at Aunt Cloe, and burst into tears.

"Little egg!" Cloe exclaimed. "What is all this nonsense? Come here and let me give you a big hug. I brought you a reminder of England, that's all. Hush now." She held the slender body tightly against her, meeting Brant's eyes over Daphne's head. He shrugged and said, "Welcome, Aunt Cloe, and you, Winterspoon. I hope your trip wasn't too tiring?"

"Very tolerable, my lord," Winterspoon said.

"Actually, Brant," Cloe said, a pronounced twinkle in her eyes, "Mr. Winterspoon and I inbibed freely across the Atlantic and arrived with vacuous smiles on our faces! Thank you so much for sending the tickets.''

Daphne turned in Cloe's arms to look at her husband. "You arranged for them to come?"

"Yes," he said, his eyes intent on her face. "I thought it would please you."

All she could do for the moment was gape at him. In the next instant she hurled herself against him, burying her face against his throat. "That's more like it," he whispered against her temple. The past three days had been tense and strained, except when they were in bed, and Brant had decided the more time in bed, the better. He'd held off since they were married, giving her time to adjust to him sexually. But not during the past three days. To his delight and relief, she'd responded enthusiastically, even though he knew she must be sore. When he'd pointed out that fact she'd moaned softly, telling him she didn't care.

"I don't hate you anymore," she whispered back. "I think you are a very nice man."

"Thank you, love. You've ravished my poor body at least ten times during the past few days. Maybe you should continue hating me. I like the result."

"I'll ravish you even more now, I promise."

"All right, you two love birds," Alice Asher said. "In an hour we're going to have Lily, Dusty and the kids invading us from Houston."

"How are they getting here from New York, Mom?"

Alice laughed. "Silly question, Brant. By limo, of course. Now, I would suggest that you and Daphne get unpacked and prepare yourselves. Cloe, Mr. Winterspoon, why don't we have a cup of tea?"

"Oscar, ma'am."

"Good heavens, Mr. Winterspoon," Cloe said exuberantly, "what a bloody noble name!"

"Thank you, Mrs. Sparks."

"Cloe, sir. After all, we are in America now."

Brant nibbled Daphne's ear as they walked upstairs to his old bedroom. "You didn't forget your diaphragm, did you?"

She slanted him a look that made him instantly horny. "I think," she said primly, "that it's going to be worn out by next week."

"Lord, wouldn't that be a trip! Just think of the look on your doctor's face. I'd have to fight her off with a two-by-four."

"She's fifty-five, Brant."

"With a stick, then?"

"Conceited jerk."

"Just think of it—I'd probably be written up in medical journals. How's this for a title of the article?" He leaned over and whispered in her ear.

"Ten hard what?" she said.

Alice, downstairs in the living room, smiled at the sound of her son's hearty laughter.

The dining room was crammed with food and laughter, adults and boisterous children.

"You're much more beautiful than Brant led me to believe," Lily said after she'd spooned a good helping of green beans on her daughter's plate.

"What a thing to say, darlin'," Dusty said. "I think the good ole boys in Houston would go stark raving mad at the sight of her."

"Well, I didn't mean it the way it came out," Lily said.

"You never do," said Brant. "Lily's got an uncensored brain," he added to Daphne.

But Daphne was gazing at Dusty, fascinated by his accent. "Could you say something else, please, Dusty?"

"After dinner I'll sing y'all a western song, how's that, ma'am?"

"His favorite is 'Flushed Down the Toilet of her Heart' or something exquisitely literate like that."

"This gal ain't got no taste," Dusty said, drawling even more to please his English audience.

"I'd love to hear you sing anything," Daphne said.

"Have some more chicken, dear," Alice said. "You've scarcely touched your dinner."

"I agree," Brant said. "You've got to keep up your strength, sweetheart."

She smiled at him happily, but turned to Cloe. "You must go to Hawaii, to Kauai! It's so beautiful, and everyone is so nice!"

"I bet you wrung their withers in that orange bikini," Cloe said.

"Lord," Brant said, "I had to hire an armed guard to keep the men away."

"Did you really, Uncle Brant?" eight-year-old Keith asked, his fork suspended between plate and mouth.

"Sure I did. All women."

"Brant, don't lie to him," Lily said. "Only half the guard were women, Keith."

"I say, madam," Winterspoon said politely, "this is a very tasty dish. I trust you will give me your recipe."

"Certainly, Oscar," said Alice Asher. "You plan to cook for Brant and Daphne?"

"Of course. Her ladyship was rarely allowed near the kitchen at Asherwood."

"Now, Winterspoon," Brant said firmly, "no more lordships or ladyships. This is America. Plus, it's damned embarrassing."

"I love it," said Lily. "Oh dear, I forgot to curtsey!"

"When does training begin, Brant?" Dusty asked.

"Too soon, I'm afraid. In about four months. We'll be training in upstate New York, and the humidity is enough to knock your socks off."

"How 'bout that commercial, brother?"

"You'll be seeing my handsome puss on TV next week, I think. And, Lily, it's sporting goods, not underwear or shaving cream."

"Well, underwear might be okay. What do you think, Daphne? Would you mind millions of women seeing Brant in his European boxers?"

"Oh no," Daphne burst out. "He's so beautiful—" She skidded to a stop, color flooding her cheeks.

Brant leaned over and whispered in her ear, "But, love, you've rarely seen me in underwear."

"What are you saying, Uncle Brant?" asked Patricia.

"I was just telling your Aunt Daphne that she's got great taste."

"Daphne sure is a funny name," said Danny.

"You can call me Daph. Your uncle does."

"That sounds like Daffy Duck," said Keith.

"Who's Daffy Duck?" asked Daphne.

The English contingent listened with great interest to Keith's convoluted description before Dusty interrupted, chuckling, "Let's keep your new aunt out of cartoons, okay son?"

"Are you and Uncle Brant going to have kids soon?" Patricia asked.

The green beans suddenly lodged in Daphne's throat, and she grabbed at her glass of water. Brant lightly thumped her on the back.

"Yeah," Keith said, adding his two cents. "We'd like some cousins."

"You all right, sweetheart?" Brant asked. At her strangled nod, he turned to his nephew and nieces. "Hey, you guys, it's hard work. What do you think, Daph?"

The ball's in your court, his wicked look told her. He loved her scarlet flush, the curse of all blondes. To his surprise she said, "Actually, I'd love some kids. But your uncle is a very busy man, you know. You'll have to be patient with him."

Brant was so surprised, he blurted out, "But I didn't think that you wanted . . . that is, you seem to . . ."

"He did the same thing on the first ten takes for the commercial," Daphne said, lying fluently as she patted his arm. "When he gets nervous, or excited, or surprised, he can't cope with words."

"Good grief, boy," Dusty said. "I never knew that. Always thought you were as slick as a pair of wet boots."

"I did, too," said Brant. His voice held humor, but there was none in his eyes as they searched his wife's face.

Alice cleared her throat. "Tell me, Cloe, how long do you plan to stay with us?"

"Well, I simply must meet all those lovely football players. If they all look like your son . . ." She gave a delighted shudder, her eyes sparkling.

"They are all marvelous, Aunt Cloe," Daphne said.

"As in huge with great . . . physiques?"

"Yes, ma'am. But I'm not sure you should meet them all at once."

"Yeah, we don't want you to have cardiac arrest, Cloe," Brant said.

"Dead right, sir," said Oscar.

Reverend Oakes's wedding ceremoney, held in the ultramodern presbyterian church in Stamford the following morning, was simple, elegant and blessedly short.

Daphne wore a pale yellow wool dress, and Brant a dark suit. "Do you feel doubly married now?" he asked as he lightly brushed her lips at the close of the service.

"I feel scared to death," Daphne said.

"Why? You know what I'm going to do to that gorgeous body of yours." She didn't laugh as he'd expected her to, but he didn't have time to ask her what was going on in her lovely head.

The children, on their best behavior up to this point, could no longer contain themselves, and clutched at their uncle's arms.

"Mom said you'd never get married, Uncle Brant," Keith said. "Now you've done it twice."

"And to the same lady," said Patricia.

"Yeah, Mom said you like to play the field, but I told her you had to 'cause you're a football player."

"Out of the mouths of little heathens," said Lily. "Congratulations, Daphne," she said, hugging her sister-in-law. "Are you going to drag Brant back to Hawaii?"

"Actually," Brant said, "I'm going to drag her back to England. We've got lots of work to do on Asherwood. What do you think, sweetheart?"

"Yes," she said quietly, not meeting his eyes.

"You and I are going to have a nice, long talk," Brant said firmly. He turned away to speak to Reverend Oakes.

Because they weren't, strictly speaking, newlyweds, Brant spent the afternoon showing Cloe and Winterspoon over Stamford and the surrounding area. He and his bride had no time alone until late that evening.

"No," he said, watching her from the bed, "no nightgown. You won't need it. I'll keep you warm." He patted the bed beside him. "Come here, Daph."

She started to slip off her bra, then leaned over to flip off the bedroom lamp. "No," Brant said, "leave it on. I want to see you."

She hesitated perceptibly, and he frowned. "Daph, I know your body almost as well as my own. What's the matter, sweetheart?"

She shook her head, and turned her back to slip out of her underwear.

"Nice view," he said. "I love those long legs of yours and that cute little—"

"Brant!" She quickly moved into the bed and pulled the covers to her chin.

He was balanced on his elbow, studying her profile. "All right," he said seriously, "enough. No more jokes. Tell me what's wrong."

She shook her head, not looking at him.

"Daph, I'm not going to ravish you until you tell me what's in that mind of yours."

Without warning she threw herself against him, burying her face in his shoulder. He felt her trembling, felt her hands clutching at his back.

"Sweetheart," he said quietly against her hair. "What's all this? Please, talk to me."

She whispered against his throat, "You went through the ceremony today like . . . like you really wanted to."

He became very still, his hands halting their stroking down her back. "Of course," he said. "What did you expect? That I'd take one look at you and call a screeching halt? We're already married, Daph. This was for my mother."

"You're making the best of a bad bargain."

His hands cupped her buttocks, drawing her closer. "If this is a bad bargain, then certainly pigs will fly, quite soon."

"You'd enjoy sex with any woman, and you know it. You'll be bored with me soon enough."

"Why?"

She raised her head at his bald question. His eyes were resting intently on her face, his eyebrow arched upward. "Because I'm stupid, and make you furious and you're stuck with me."

"You're anything but stupid, yes, and like glue."

"You want to go back to Asherwood because I embarrass you here."

He whistled softly. "So that's what's going on. You're such an idiot, Daphne. Sexy, sweet, but an idiot. I want to go back to Asherwood because I love the place, and I thought you did, too. It's our other home now, and I don't want to neglect it. I never did get to refinish the wainscotting in the library."

"But I'm useless! You don't want to have children with me because that would mean you'd have to stay married to me!"

He didn't say anything. She felt his fingers stroking down her belly to between her thighs.

"What are you doing?" she gasped.

She felt his finger easing inside her, and she tried to jerk away, confused.

"Hold still," he said sharply. "Ah, just a bit further. Here we go. A pity, now we won't have the chance to wear out your diaphragm. I was kinda looking forward to being a new entry in the *Guinness Book of Records*."

She heard it thump onto the floor.

"I don't understand! Why did you do that?"

"We're going to make a baby so I'll be stuck with you forever."

"But you don't want to! You're just doing this because... you're honorable!"

"God, you're warm and soft." She squirmed as his fingers moved downward again, gently probing, stroking, driving her crazy. "Brant!"

"Stop bleating and kiss me. I love to feel you, and in just a few minutes, after you calm down, I'm going to kiss every inch of you."

"You make me sound like a goat," she giggled.

"I'm definitely the goat. I've wanted you all day, Mrs. Asher."

She felt him hard and velvet soft against her thighs. "What was it you said about ten hard—"

He kissed her deeply, easing between her legs and pressing upward.

"You," she gasped, feeling the swamping sensations build in her belly, "are an oversexed man."

"Lord yes," he said. "Aren't you glad?"

Her soft moan was her answer, and he smiled, loving the glazed look in her eyes. "There's quite a bit to be said about awakening a sleeping beauty."

He moved inside her, and felt her muscles tighten convulsively around him. He cursed softly and withdrew from her, his breathing ragged. She tried to bring him into her again, but he whispered, "No, love, not yet. You've blasted my control. I'll leave you if I'm inside you."

"But—"

"Hush, let me make you feel as I do." She opened to him as he caressed her with his mouth, knowing that the marvelous feelings would build and build until she wanted to die with the force of them. When her whimpers became cries, she felt his hand gently covering her mouth. Then his mouth replaced his hand as he eased over her, and she was frantic with the feel of him deep inside her. She moaned into his mouth, whispering brokenly.

Daphne thought the world a most perfect place when she stared up into her husband's face as his own pleasure overtook him. He moaned through his gritted teeth, his head thrown back, his body arched upward.

Brent knew his weight was too much for her, but he didn't have the strength to move. "You are my wife," he said, the simple words mirroring the warm, incredibly tender feelings welling up within him. "My wife."

"Yes," she said, pulling him down to kiss him again.

They listened to each other's breathing slow and even out. Brant said, "I've never made love to another woman in this bedroom."

"I trust not," she said dryly.

He rolled off her onto his back, and turned off the light. When he felt her head on his shoulder, he said, aloud, "No."

"No what?" she asked on a satisfied yawn, snuggling closer against him.

"No, we can't leave for England right away. Aunt Cloe's got to meet the Astros."

"Do you think they'll survive her?"

"I can't wait to find out."

Chapter Sixteen

Tiny Phipps looked shell shocked. He grabbed a beer and threw back his head. Daphne stared at his massive neck, fascinated by the play of muscles as he downed the entire can.

After he lowered the bottle and swiped his mouth with the back of his hand, Daphne asked, her expression deadpan, "Did you enjoy meeting my Aunt Cloe, Tiny?"

"Daph, she patted my butt and told me I was really a cute hunk!" He looked like a little boy who couldn't quite grasp the complexities of the adult world.

Daphne laughed heartily. "Well, you are, Tiny. My aunt has excellent taste. She just learned the word 'hunk' and is simply practicing it on all appropriate males."

"But she's old enough to be my mother. My grandmother!"

"The term 'dirty old man' applying here, guys?" Brant asked.

"With a change in gender," Daphne said. She looked over at her aunt, who was now in avid conversation with Lloyd Nolan and Sam Carverelli. "They'll all survive," she said. "In fact, Sam is giving her the same look he gave Gus Colima after you guys beat the Rams."

"What a game that was," Tiny said. "Brant passed for over three hundred yards."

"I know," Daphne said. "And a seventy-two yarder for a touchdown."

"How 'bout another drink, Daph?" Beatrice asked.

"Not for me or I'll fall asleep before everyone even gets here. Wonderful party, Beatrice. I love your house. It's so rustic and homey and huge."

"Thank you. Lloyd has always had this thing for rocks and glass. It was close, but I managed to talk him out of a rock bathtub." She rolled her eyes. "But the glass, well, have you seen the bedroom?"

"I thought I'd haul Daphne in there in a little while and give her a demonstration," Brant said.

"What kind of demonstration would you do with glass?" Daphne asked. "You mean glass blowing?"

There was a spate of laughter, and Brant moaned.

"Little egg," Cloe said, "what's all this about mirrors in bedrooms?"

"Well," Daphne said, "I'm not really sure. I'm being laughed at; that's the only thing I'm really certain of."

Cloe said to Tiny, "Why don't you show me? Come, my boy, let's do it now." She thrust her arm through Tiny's and dragged him away. "What lovely, monstrous muscles, my dear," Daphne heard her say fondly to her captive.

The doorbell rang. "More folk," Beatrice said. "Excuse me, guys."

Daphne was admiring the beautiful view through the French doors when she felt Brant stiffen beside her.

"What the hell!" he said softly. She turned to see Marcie Ellis come into the living room on the arm of a man she'd never seen before.

"Who is he?" she asked, but her eyes were on the beautiful woman at his side, who looked both flamboyant and elegant in a moss-green jump suit. She felt her hair begin to turn stringy, and her front teeth turn crooked.

"Matt Orson, the defensive coach. It looks like Marcie is really doing a number this time. Oh...damn! They've brought along a photographer."

He shot Daphne a worried look, and she knew he was concerned that she'd shatter again under pressure. And make him look like a fool. And make her look like a moron.

"Well, it looks like old home week," she heard Marcie say to Beatrice.

"We've got a couple of new faces," said Lloyd. "Have you met Daphne? And her aunt, Mrs. Sparks, here from England to visit?"

"Immigration seems to be getting out of hand," Marcie said in a carrying voice as her eyes met Daphne's. "I suspect all things foreign will return home soon enough. Perhaps I'd best do my interview with Brant here, before he's turned loose on New York's women again."

Oh God, Lloyd thought, so that's the lay of the land, is it? Spare me a cat fight. He shot a look at Matt Orson, who merely shrugged. Lloyd wondered if Matt knew he was being used. Probably so, he wasn't a fool.

"Little egg, how very fascinating, to be sure," said Cloe, coming up behind Daphne. "She's quite lovely, of course, but nothing compared to you," she added, not missing a beat.

"I agree," said Brant easily, but he looked as tense as a man facing a firing squad.

"I can't wait to talk to her," Cloe remarked. "Perhaps she'll be more of a challenge than Lucilla. More wit, I think. Buck up, Daphne! It's about time you realized you had my outrageous blood in your veins."

"She was Brant's lover before he came to England," Daphne said in a low voice to Cloe.

"So! Dear boy, please fetch me a glass of white wine. Thank you." After Brant moved away reluctantly, Cloe continued, "I never thought Brant would bed a woman who wasn't a looker. If you'd but realize it, little egg, this could be most amusing. You are the wife, you know."

"Yes," Daphne said slowly, her eyes widening, "I am, aren't I? And I can also write checks and balance a checkbook. I'll have my driver's license soon. And a Lord and Taylor credit card."

"Sounds like the top of the heap to me," said Cloe.

"Well, well, so the wolf left the little shepherd unprotected."

"Hello, Marcie," Daphne said. "This is my Aunt Cloe, from England."

"Scotland, actually," said Cloe. "You're a journalist, aren't you, Marcie?"

How did Aunt Cloe know that? Daphne wondered.

Fluttering old lady, Marcie thought. She smiled. "Yes, and I hope to get the true story from Brant today. His being suddenly a lord, a husband, and a castle owner."

"I dare say Daphne here can tell you all about it," said Cloe, her voice utterly complacent. "I can't say exactly what Brant thinks of being a lord, but he adores being a husband and a castle owner." Cloe shook her head and patted Marcie's hand in a fond, maternal gesture. "I've never before seen a man so smitten. Of course, he had to cut out all her admirers first."

Daphne did her best not to drop her jaw in surprise at her aunt's words.

"I suppose it's natural enough for an heiress to have many men around," Marcie said. She didn't want to revise her opinion of the old lady, but . . .

Daphne laughed. "An heiress! That's one thing Brant should have corrected immediately. I'm surprised, Marcie, that Brant didn't tell *you*, of all people. I didn't have a *sou*, a dime even."

Marcie, who had pulled a pencil and pad out of her purse, looked as if she'd just swallowed the eraser. "What do you mean?"

"Why, just what I said, of course." Daphne gave her what she hoped was an evil smile. Her pulse was racing, but not with fear.

"But Brant told me before he left for England that he'd inherited only the title and a moldering old house."

Maybe a bit of fear, then. She shrugged. "English solicitors are notorious for keeping little tidbits of information back until they meet their clients face to face. Brant didn't know about me, either."

"I see," said Marcie, who didn't see at all. She watched Brant approach, a glass of wine in his hand.

Cloe laughed indulgently. "It took him little time to rectify that situation. Ah, my boy, thank you for the wine. Daphne here was just telling the journalist lady that she was poor as a beggar, and not the heiress everyone thought. Love at first sight it was when Brant laid eyes on her. I really didn't believe such a thing existed. Of course, when I met Mr. Sparks, and he took me for a drive in the moonlight, well . . ."

"Very nearly," Brant said easily. "Remember, Daph? I was working on the roof and turned to see your gorgeous legs coming out of a cab? I nearly expired in the gutter."

Marcie, who was endowed with a pair of the nicest legs in New York, said tightly, "But you always were a leg man, weren't you, darling?"

Brant grinned. "That and other things." He wrapped his arm around Daphne's shoulders. "All of which my beautiful wife has, in abundance."

Marcie was aware of the old lady's eyes resting on her face and started. The old bird was looking at her with pity! Marcie wanted to spit. "What do you intend doing now that you're in America?" she asked Daphne.

"Get a driver's license and run Brant's Porsche into the ground."

There was a crack of laughter behind Marcie. Matt Orson said, "What's this, Brant? You never let anyone drive the Porsche."

Brant, who had no great enthusiasm for Daphne's plans, merely shrugged. "You should see her behind the wheel. She stops traffic." He looked thoughtfully at his wife. "Perhaps I should get you your own car."

"A station wagon to cart around all the kiddies?" Marcie said, wishing that she could leave this wretched party and forget that she ever decided to marry Brant herself. Could he really have fallen in love with this vacuous girl? Well, she had seemed vacuous, she amended to herself. Now she seemed to sparkle with confidence. Was one born with those unbelievable green eyes?

"No," Daphne said with great decisiveness, "that will be the third car."

"Come along, love," Brant said. "It's time I showed you all that glass in the bedroom, particularly since I'm beginning to envision myself in the country, surrounded with infants and autos.''

Matt took himself off to the bar, and Marcie was left with Mrs. Sparks, the devious old lady.

''My dear Daphne is getting quite good at launching smart retorts, don't you think? Brant calls them salvos. I'd hoped you'd be a bit more up to snuff, Marcie. Your insults dwindled into catty nothings.''

Marcie said ruefully, ''She didn't have a word to say for herself when I saw her the first time. Damn it, she was a dolt, and I couldn't imagine Brant putting up with that.''

''Things change, I've always found.'' Cloe patted Marcie's shoulder. ''Buck up, my dear. Forget and forgive. You're a bright girl; don't continue swimming upstream with the salmon.''

Marcie uttered an obscenity under her breath.

''I know. Did that help?''

''You're a wicked woman, do you know that, Aunt Cloe?''

''Me? Ah, I remember how Mr. Sparks used to say that...well, that's neither here nor there, is it? There's that gorgeous boy, Tiny. What an odd name, to be sure. Excuse me, Marcie. And remember, you're too smart a girl to keep plowing in a field that's no longer fallow.''

Brant watched his wife lying on her back, staring up at the mirrored ceiling. ''Getting any lascivious ideas, sweetheart?''

''Oh yes,'' Daphne said enthusiastically. ''I could see all of you while you—'' She broke off and gave him a come hither smile.

He shuddered slightly, easily picturing himself covering her, her white legs wrapped around him, her arms clutching his back. To distract himself he said, "You handled Marcie quite nicely."

"Yes," she said, her voice surprised. "Yes, I did."

"You didn't need me at all."

Daphne cocked an eyebrow at him. "I thought you were tired of playing knight errant to my damsel in tongue-tied distress?"

Brant ran his fingers through his hair. "I'm crazy. Ignore what I say."

Daphne came up on her knees on the bed. "I think I hear Lloyd shouting about a videotape of one of your games. Let's go see it, okay?"

He cocked his head at her. "You really like football, don't you?"

"I can't wait until August for the exhibition games. I'll be cheering myself hoarse for you. But there's still so much to learn. I've got to talk to Matt Orson. There's lots I need to understand about the defense, particularly how they know what to do when the quarterback does an audible." She continued talking as she walked out of the bedroom, assuming that he was following her.

Brant shook his head. She was changing so quickly that he was having trouble keeping up. He remembered the girl he'd met not two months ago and shook his head again, bemused. Who the hell had told her about audibles? He pictured her driving his Porsche and shuddered.

The following evening, as they left a French restaurant on the east side, a flashbulb went off in their faces. Brant's arm immediately went around his wife's waist, to bring her protectively close. It was the same two men who had trapped them in the garage some time before.

"Hey, Mrs. Asher, you got anything to say this time?" one of them called out.

Brant felt a surge of anger, and his hand clenched. He had no time to do or say anything. Daphne, a snide smile on her face, said, "Hi, guys. Nice to see you again. You've stopped lurking in garages?"

The man ignored that. "Everyone's gotta eat," he said. "I suppose you heiresses are used to dining in the best spots?"

"Tomorrow night Brant is going to take me to a Mexican restaurant. I love tacos. What's your favorite food?"

Ah ha, she thought when he had no answer, satisfied that she'd taken him totally aback. The man's partner snapped another picture.

"What do you think of all your husband's women, Mrs. Asher?"

"He has excellent taste," she said blandly. "I've been meaning to send out letters of condolence."

"Gentlemen," Brant broke in, "I think you've shot your wad. Daph, let's go home."

"All one has to do is feel good about oneself," Daphne said, trying to snuggle closer to Brant, but unable to in the Porsche.

He revved the engine, saying nothing as the Porsche screeched around a corner in Central Park. She'd handled the men like a pro. You want her to fit in, not to be afraid and tongue-tied around people, he chided himself. But somehow he felt as though he'd lost control. Stop it, you're acting like a dog who's lost his own private bone.

When they finally got home they found that Winterspoon and Aunt Cloe were still out. Brant turned to his wife, "Let's go to bed."

"All right," she said, her eyes twinkling up at him.

Brant didn't wait for her to undress. He stripped her, tossed her onto the bed and turned every bit of his uncertainty into wild passion and, he realized vaguely as he thrust into her, a show of complete control and dominance. His savage moan of release filled the silent bedroom.

"Damn," he muttered as his breathing eased. He hadn't given a damn about her feelings, and now he felt like a complete and utter bastard. Her eyes were closed. "Daph," he said softly. "Sweetheart, forgive me." He pulled away from her and yanked off the rest of his clothes. Gently he eased her under the covers and pulled her against him. "I won't let you retreat from me," he said, anger at himself in his voice.

"I don't understand," she said finally against his shoulder.

"I don't either," he admitted. "But I'm going to try my damndest to see that you forget what a jerk I just was. Did I hurt you?"

"No, but it wasn't fun, either."

That's certainly the unvarnished truth, he thought. He called on every ounce of expertise he possessed to bring her to pleasure, and when he succeeded, he again felt that odd combination of power and control. He loved the way she shuddered in her climax, the way her eyes blurred over, the way she burrowed against him as if she wanted to get inside him.

As for Daphne, she was in a daze. She felt like a limp dishcloth, wrung out and used up. She hadn't understood his wildman performance, or the gleam of satisfaction in his eyes when she'd arched and whimpered in her release.

"Are you all right, sweetheart?" she heard him whisper softly against her temple. His hand, big and warm, was still cupped over her, lightly pressing and stroking, as if he wanted more from her. She could feel the wetness from both of them on his fingers.

But she didn't have anything more to give him. She wondered if she'd ever understand men, this one man in particular. She managed to nod against his shoulder before she fell into an exhausted sleep.

Chapter Seventeen

"Damnation! Hold it! I want the tree thinned, not denuded!"

The tree man turned off his electric saw and stared down at Lord Asherwood. "What did you say, sir?"

Brant lowered his voice. "I'll point to the branches I want you to take off, okay?"

Daphne, who was coming around from her now-budding rose garden, stopped and grinned. The tree man, Tommy Orville, had a wounded look on his round face. She stood quietly, watching Brant point patiently to a particular dried up branch. He looked so bloody handsome, she thought, her eyes roving over his body. He was wearing a red-and-white Astros sweatshirt, and a pair of very well worn and tight jeans. His thick dark hair shone in the bright afternoon sunlight. Passion was such a nice thing, she reflected, glad she'd discovered it before she'd gotten too much older. She'd asked Brant once after recovering from what she termed bouts of marriage, if it was always like this, and if it was, why people ever got divorced. He'd given her a long, lazy look and assured her that she was the luckiest woman he knew.

"Because you're the world greatest lover?" she'd said with laughing sarcasm.

"You'd give me your vote, wouldn't you?"

When she'd paused, trying to come up with a retort, he had gently begun to caress her breast and nibble on that very sensitive spot just below her right ear. "I give up," she'd giggled. "You're the world's greatest everything!"

"You ain't so bad yourself, cookie," he'd said.

She wondered, though, gazing at him now, if he were as pleased with her as she was with him. Shut away at Asherwood as they had been for three months now, he certainly seemed to be contented. The restoration of the Hall took up a great deal of their time, but they had taken off days at a time to travel, once to Glasgow to visit Aunt Cloe, another up to York, another to the Lake District to stay on Lake Widemere. He seemed fascinated with Daphne's historical tales of all the sites they visited. Stonehenge had been his favorite. "Like huge football players in a huddle," he'd announced. It was like the continuation of their honeymoon.

The electric saw died once again, for the last time. Tommy climbed carefully down and cocked a faded brown eyebrow at Brant.

"That'll be all, thank you," Brant said. "Great job. Hey, Daph, what do you think?"

"Magnificent. Say hello to your sister for me, Tommy."

"Sure thing, Daphne," Tommy said.

"I'm so glad you're using local talent," Daphne said to her husband.

"It was a close thing. I'm glad I came out in time to save the tree from getting a flat top. How's your rose garden coming?"

"Come and see." She tucked her hand in his and lengthened her stride to match his. "Can we afford a gardener to keep things in shape after we go home?"

Home, he thought, smiling down at her. So New York was now home to her, was it? "Yes," he said, "I think we can manage it. I'll probably have to sell the condo and the Porsche, but roses are important, I know, and I wouldn't—"

She poked him in the ribs. "I'll pay for it once I liquidate some of my investments. Hmmm," she added, running her hands over his ribs, "nice."

In the next instant she was squealing. Brant's hand was under her loose top, inching around to cup her breast. "Brant, stop it! What if someone—"

"Just returning the favor, ma'am. You're not bad yourself, and no bra." He felt her quicken and grinned wickedly down at her. "You sure you want to show me the roses now? There's that other lovely garden you just might invite me to play in."

"You're terrible! So you did read some Greek plays in college. All right, I've decided it's time to have my way with you."

She did, to Brant's exhausted delight.

Daphne eased out of bed, leaving Brant sprawled on his back, beautifully naked and asleep. Just like in Hawaii, she thought, studying him in the dying afternoon light. I sure know a lot more about things than I did then, she thought, smiling. Well, she was no longer a naive twit, she thought as she climbed back onto the bed, leaned down on her hands and knees, and rained light kisses over his belly. He mumbled something in his sleep, and she kept kissing, lower. She was totally absorbed in her explorations when she heard him say softly, "Lovely view," and felt his hand lightly stroke over her bottom. He moaned suddenly, his body jerking, and she forgot her temporary embarrassment at him gazing at her backside, her legs slightly parted.

"Daph, sweetheart, you'd better stop before it's too late." He tangled his fingers in the veil of hair that covered her face, and tugged, but she wouldn't release him. "Daph," he managed once again, then gave up, expelling a sigh of pure pleasure.

"What's Winterspoon making for dinner?" he asked her sometime later. He'd wondered for a while if he'd ever be able to talk again.

"I haven't the vaguest idea," Daphne said, burrowing closer. "Sex and food. Is that all you jocks think about?"

"Just food, for the moment. I'll eat anything that doesn't bounce around on my plate. Woman, you wore me out."

"You deserved it," she said, her voice complacent. "I didn't want you to get the idea that only you could initiate ... things."

"I swear that's the kind of idea men hate. Anytime you want to ravish my poor body, you go right ahead." She ran her palm down his chest to his belly. "But not right at this moment," he added. "The spirit is willing, but nothing else, I'm afraid."

"I love your spirit," she giggled. "And everything else."

"Good. We're leaving for Paris tomorrow. Say for a week?"

"Brant!" She threw herself on top of him and planted a wet kiss on his mouth.

His hand gently cupped her. "There are so many beautiful gardens in Paris, after all."

"Jerk."

Daphne's feelings were mixed when they returned to New York in mid-June. It was the real world, and she wasn't at all sure that she was ready for it. They flew back on the Concorde, a special treat for both of them, and arrived shortly after they'd left London.

"Sir, ma'am," Winterspoon greeted them, flourishing a silver tray of canapés for their welcome home. He'd flown back a week earlier to "set everything to rights," he'd told Brant.

"And champagne, Winterspoon?" Brant asked.

"Champagne!" Daphne exclaimed. "Is this going to be an orgy or something?"

"Well, almost," Brant said, smiling down at her. "One glass and I've got a something to show you."

"Oh?" she asked, slanting him a provocative look.

The something was a new Mercedes 380 SL, silver body with black leather interior. Daphne stared at it, then at her husband. "So that's what your mysterious phone calls were all about."

"Yep."

"And all your ever-so-subtle questions about my preferences about this and that?"

"Yep. If you'll remember, I always asked after we'd made love. I knew your mind would be well beyond suspicious thoughts."

"Very low, Brant, very low."

"That too. You've got to name her and take me for a ride."

By the time Brant left for training camp in upstate New York, nearly every member of the Astros and their spouses had ridden in Gwendolyn, and the car and Daphne were a well-known sight to the doorman, Max.

"I wish," Daphne said on a small sigh to Tiffy Richardson one afternoon as she was cruising Gwendolyn toward Tiffy's home in Westchester, "that we could go up to the training camp."

"I used to wish the same thing," said Tiffy, patting Daphne's knee, "but Guy assured me, as I'm sure Brant did you, that there's absolutely nothing to do, since they're stuck out in the middle of nowhere, and after practice they're all dead."

"Still..." Daphne began.

"You miss him, I know. But it won't be much longer now. The first exhibition game is August 14, against the Lions."

"We'll butcher them," Daphne said with relish. "Their offense relies primarily on the running game, and their defense stinks against the pass. Tiny was telling me—"

"Good grief, Daph! You've really gotten into football, haven't you?"

"I love the game, it's true, and I bought lots of books on football at Barnes and Noble, and Brant's got a huge video collection of games. I'm talking too much, aren't I?"

Tiffy laughed. "No, not at all. I love to hear your starchy English accent when you talk about football. Tell me," she continued without a pause, "how do you like marriage to Brant Asher?"

"Former playboy of the western world?"

"I believe former is the operative world," said Tiffy.

Daphne looked straight ahead at the highway and chewed a moment on her lower lip. "I think the question should be how does he like marriage to me? He's a gentleman, you know. Always says and does the right thing, sticks to his bargain and all that.''

"No," Tiffy repeated, "how do you like marriage to him?" Bargain? she wondered silently. What bargain?

"I guess," Daphne said on a long sigh, "that I love him dearly."

"I'm glad to hear it. Brant deserves the best, and I think you're it, Daph."

"The best? Me? I'm really not sure of that, Tiffy. As I said, Brant's a gentleman." And he's never told me he loves me. She thought of all his love words, sometimes slurred when his need for her was great, but never a simple declaration over dinner, say, with Winterspoon in the kitchen. *Well, you haven't said anything either, idiot!* But she'd wanted to. Coward, that's what she was. He was such a gentleman that he'd probably say it back to her out of politeness and concern for her feelings.

"You're not still worried about Marcie, are you?"

"Oh no. I saw her last week at the theatre—I was with Brant's mother—and she was really quite nice. She's been a real brick. Brant's mother, that is."

"You're lucky. My mother-in-law is the martyr type. Drives me nuts. And, of course, whenever she visits us, she treats Guy like he's God's gift to the universe. He's impossible for a good two weeks after she leaves."

They spoke of Tiffy's two children and her interior decorating business, a growing concern in the past year.

"Will you be flying to Detroit for the game?" Daphne asked.

"Oh no. It's just an exhibition game. Guy shouldn't play more than two quarters at most. Sam'll want to give the new guys a chance to perform. Even Brant shouldn't play all that much. Evan Murphy has got to have some practice quarterbacking."

"Yes, I know." *In case Brant ever gets injured.* "But I'm going. I think even Winterspoon wants to give it a try. 'Bloody barbaric,' he calls it, but I've seen him reading some of my books."

"An English butler!" Tiffy laughed.

"It does boggle the mind, doesn't it?"

Daphne spent the final week before Brant's return from training camp with Alice Asher in Connecticut. And on a side street in Stamford one hot afternoon she nearly met her Waterloo, as she later told Alice in the hospital.

"Broadsided by a truck carrying Miller beer as I tried to avoid that boy on his bike. There must be some irony in there somewhere. It's not fair. What will Brant say?" She turned alarmed eyes to her mother-in-law. "I'm okay, Alice, really. You won't call Brant, will you?"

"Hush now, honey. You're very lucky, only a couple of bruised ribs and a mild concussion. And of course I called Brant. You were dead to the world for quite a long time."

"Oh, I wish you hadn't. This is the last thing he needs. He's got to concentrate on football, not get sidetracked by me and Gwen."

"If Gwen looks as good as you do, sweetheart, I won't say a single word."

"Brant!"

He walked over to her bed, leaned down and carefully studied her face. "You all right, woman driver?"

"It wasn't my fault," she said indignantly. "I did everything right, and if it hadn't been for that stupid beer—" He kissed her pursed lips. "And Alice said that Gwen is an awful mess."

"I'll have a look at her later. Not to worry." He picked up her hand and absently began to stroke her fingers. "What's all this nonsense about sidetracking me from football? Don't be an idiot. You're my wife."

"But the game plan for the Lions!" she wailed. "Watching their tapes, strategy..."

"Shush. I left Evan Murphy chomping at the bit. I like that little bruise over your right eye. Gives you a rakish look." His voice was light, because he'd spoken to her doctor briefly before coming into her room and knew she was all right. "You scared the hell out of me, you know."

Daphne gave Alice a reproachful look. "You shouldn't have worried him," she said.

"That's what husbands are for, honey," Alice said. "Now, I'm going to leave you two alone for a little while. Not too long, Brant; she still has the remains of a concussion."

"You make it sound like the leftovers from a meal," Daphne said.

Brant waited until his mother had closed the hospital door behind her, then seated himself on the bed beside his wife. He pulled back the covers and eased up her hospital gown.

"Whatever are you doing?" Daphne asked, wondering crazily if he wanted to make love to her, here in the hospital, with the nurses clustered not ten feet away at their station.

"Your ribs," he said, and bared them. "Pretty impressive," he said finally, staring at the dark purple and yellow streaks below her left breast. Actually, he tried to keep from swallowing convulsively, even though he knew they weren't broken. His mother's telephone call had done more than scare the hell out of him. He'd felt cold, clammy and seared with fear until she'd finally managed to convince him that Daphne was all right.

"I'll be able to make the exhibition game, I promise," she said. "I won't let you down again, Brant."

He looked briefly at her flat stomach before he carefully eased her hospital gown down over her ribs and pulled the starchy sheet and light blanket back up.

"We'll see about the game," he said, briefly closing his eyes. He wondered if he should tell her that she'd miscarried. No, it wouldn't make any difference, and it would likely make her feel guilty. Early days, the doctor had told him. Barely seven weeks, if that. He shook his head, reaffirming his silent decision.

He felt her fingers tighten over his. "What's the matter, Brant? I'll bet you're very tired from your trip."

"I wish you'd think only about yourself for once. Who the hell cares if I'm tired or not?"

She started at his harsh tone, but her head had begun to ache with a vengeance. "I care," she said quietly. "I care very much."

He saw the brief look of pain in her eyes and rose. "Is it time for a pain pill?"

"Probably," she said, turning her head very slowly to look at him. "I'm feeling completely sober, and they don't seem to like that."

"I'll talk to the nurse. You rest now, love, and I'll see you this evening."

"Will you go look at Gwen?"

"I'll even make sure she gets a pain pill."

Daph had been lucky, very lucky, he thought later as he eyed her Mercedes. The beer truck had hit the passenger side. He started to sweat again, and the humid Connecticut weather had nothing to do with it. He rubbed his hand over his forehead, and the ignoble thought occurred to him that he wouldn't be able to make love to her for a good three weeks. How to convince her not to, he wondered. He shook his head to clear it when he saw the bodyshop owner walking toward him.

Brant flew back to training camp three days later with Daphne's promise that she would remain with his mother and take it easy.

"You can't do anything else anyway," he told her. "Gwendolyn won't be ready to hit the road again for another week."

She hugged him exuberantly and promptly winced from the pain in her ribs. He stroked his fingertips over her smooth cheek. "I'll call you tonight, sweetheart, okay?"

Winterspoon closed up the condo and arrived in Connecticut that afternoon. "You will take care of Miss Daphne," he told Alice Asher, "and I'll see to the meals."

"It beats me how he only had to say that and I folded my tent and retired from the field," Alice said later to Daphne.

"Winterspoon is an autocrat, but a benign one," Daphne said, smiling. She knew not to laugh; it still hurt.

During the next week Alice was to shake her head several times. Daphne had been so unsure of herself, but the constant stream of visitors, all wives of the football players, made Alice realize soon enough that her daughter-in-law was very well-liked indeed.

On August 13, she blinked in surprise upon entering Daphne's bedroom. Daphne was packing.

"I'm going to Detroit to see Brant play," Daphne said firmly.

"Shouldn't you talk to the doctor—"

"Winterstoon is driving me over in about thirty minutes for a final checkup. I'm fine, Alice, really."

"But what will Brant say?"

Daphne twinkled at her. "He doesn't know. It's a surprise."

Chapter Eighteen

Dr. Lowery was running late, and Daphne fidgeted in the waiting room, thumbing through one magazine, then another. Not one sports magazine, she thought, disgruntled.

"Mrs. Asher?"

"Yes," Daphne said, rising to face the nurse.

"Dr. Lowery will be with you in just a few minutes. Why don't you come with me to the examining room?"

Daphne dutifully followed the nurse into a small, sterile room and sat down on the single chair. The nurse handed her a paper gown and fiddled with instruments while Daphne stripped.

"Why do I have to change into this thing?" Daphne asked, looking askance at the paper gown. "It's just my ribs and head."

"Dr. Lowery will want to do a quick internal exam," said the nurse.

"Why?" Daphne asked, frowning. "I had a complete exam just about six months ago."

"I'm sure she'll want to check that you're all right after the miscarriage."

Daphne stared at her. "Miscarriage?" Her voice was thin and high.

The nurse turned and smiled at her. "Not to worry, Mrs. Asher. It's standard procedure, you know, and you were only about seven weeks along. I'm certain you're just fine."

She gave Daphne a reassuring pat on the shoulder and left the small room. Like an automaton, Daphne changed into the ridiculously embarrassing paper gown and perched on the edge of the examining table. *I lost a baby and nobody bothered to tell me about it. Dear God, I didn't even know I was pregnant.* She reviewed the previous weeks before the accident in her mind, realizing that she had missed a period. But she hadn't really thought about it. And she'd never felt ill. She stared at the white walls, her eyes widening. Did Brant know?

"Good afternoon, Mrs. Asher. My, but you're looking lovely and tiptop again."

Daphne said, without preamble, "Why didn't you tell me I'd miscarried, Dr. Lowery?"

Lorraine Lowery knew it had been a mistake to keep that information from Daphne. She should never have let Brant Asher talk her into it. And Jane Coggins, her talkative nurse, must have inadvertently spilled the beans. She sighed and sat down, gathering words together. "You were out of things for quite a while," she said finally, deciding she'd assume the responsibility for the omission. "We asked your mother-in-law if you were pregnant, and she said no, of course. That's standard procedure before we order any x-rays. The accident caused you to miscarry, but we would have had to abort in any case after the series of x-rays were completed. There was nothing anyone could have done. I'm sorry, Mrs. Asher.''

Daphne nodded, mute. *You caused it, you fool, in that damned accident!*

Daphne knew about x-rays and pregnant women. She silently endured the examination, answering Dr. Lowery's questions in terse monosyllables.

''Why don't you get dressed and come into my office?'' Dr. Lowery said when she was done. Daphne nodded, waiting until she was alone to scoot off the table and change.

When she was sitting across from the doctor, she wanted desperately to ask if Brant knew of the miscarriage, but she was afraid to hear the answer. Of course he didn't know, or else he would have said something to her.

''Your ribs are just fine. You no longer look like a foreign flag. You said you no longer have any headaches, so we can safely assume everything is back to normal there.'' She paused a moment, tapping her pen on her desktop. ''If you wish to become pregnant again, Mrs. Asher, I would advise that you wait for another three months or so. We want your body to have time to heal itself.''

''It will be longer than that,'' Daphne said. ''Football season starts in a couple of weeks. I don't want to be pregnant and traveling all over the country at the same time.''

''You had no idea you were pregnant?''

Daphne shook her head, her eyes on her fingernails.

''Well, these things happen. Be thankful you weren't farther along. As to sexual relations with your husband, I suggest you wait another week or so.'' Dr. Lowery rose and extended her hand. Daphne shook it silently. "Have a visit with Dr. Mason in New York in three months, okay? She'll just doublecheck for you. Good luck to your husband and the Astros, Mrs. Asher."

Sure, Daphne thought as she left the doctor's office. Easy for her to say. Good luck to the football team. Case closed. Too bad, but it was all for the best. Daphne closed her eyes against the bright sunlight. She wouldn't tell Brant. She couldn't. She didn't know how he would react. Did her mother-in-law know? She wouldn't ask her. She wouldn't mention it to anyone. It was done, over with. She would forget it, in time.

"Are you all right, ma'am?" Winterspoon asked as he opened the passenger door for her.

"What? Oh yes, Winterspoon, I'm fine. Just fine."

The game wasn't even a contest, Daphne thought in disgust as the final seconds ticked off. The Astros won 35 to 7, the Lions' only score coming on a thirty-yard run in the third quarter. Brant had played magnificently, his body agile, the announcers applauding his talent and throwing arm. She'd yelled herself hoarse. She hadn't sat with the few wives present, most of them rookies' wives, not wanting to chance any of the players looking at their special section and telling Brant she was there.

She walked down the stadium steps and positioned herself outside the Astros' locker room. A smile tugged at her lips as she thought of the look on Brant's face when he saw her. She couldn't wait to tell him that no pro football player could be better than number 12, or more handsome in the white uniform with its red lettering.

A man asked, "Are you a wife of one of the players, ma'am?"

She turned and her radiant smile encompassed him. "Yes. I'm Mrs. Asher."

"Ah, the English heiress," the man said, enthusiasm over his surprise discovery raising his voice a half octave.

"No, the English *wife*. Wasn't that Lions' fumble crazy? It looked like that game—hot potato—for a few minutes." Her eyes began to shine. "Brant is in excellent shape, isn't he? So graceful. It's as if the ball is an extension of his arm. And he runs as swiftly as any of the backs. Lloyd's three touchdown catches—he must have jumped a good three feet to bring the ball in." She continued speaking to her increasingly appreciative audience of one, recounting points of strategy, the performance of the different players in exquisite detail, the obvious outcome. "We're going to the Superbowl this year. Yes, we are."

Mac Dreyfus wrote as quickly as he could. The girl was a natural. She knew the game. And she was English. It was amazing. Absolutely amazing. He waved to his partner, Tim Maloney. Neither of them had wanted to cover the exhibition game. Lord, what a great break! When Brant finally emerged from the locker room he was met by a brilliantly smiling wife who threw herself into his arms. He kissed her and heard the flashbulb go off.

"Great game, Brant," Mac said jovially. "And a great wife. Nice to have met you, ma'am."

Other players gathered around Daphne, and Brant heard her giving them all a rundown on the health, current moods and thoughts of their wives, children and pets. He saw Mac Dreyfus turn in his tracks, an arrested look in his eyes. Brant found himself wondering if she ever forgot anything as he listened to her compliment each player on a specific play in which he had been the key. They basked in her praise.

It was close to thirty minutes before they were alone. Daphne hugged him again. "I love Detroit," she said. "I want to stay a day or two and visit one of the automobile places."

"This is quite a surprise," he said once he could get in a word edgewise.

"Yes, isn't it?" Her smile was sunny, guileless.

"Are you sure you're all right?"

"Winterspoon gave me his stamp of approval," she said. "You were truly brilliant, Brant. It was such a thrill to watch you play in person. I've already arranged for us to get our own tape of the game in less than a week. You know, though, that new pass interference rule is going to cause some problems for a while, I think. You must remind the guys to be sure to *look* back toward the ball before they cream the receiver. Danny looked so furious when he got called, but it was legitimate."

He stopped a moment and gazed down at her. "You're something else, you know that?"

"Just don't squeeze me too hard for a while, okay?" She grinned, wrapping her arms around his waist and hugging.

To her surprise, his eyes darkened with worry.

"My ribs are fine," she said. "Please, there's nothing more to worry about, Brant."

He wasn't thinking about her ribs, but, of course, she couldn't know that. How, he wondered, am I going to keep her from lovemaking tonight? He was certain he shouldn't touch her for another week or so. She had to have time to heal.

"God, I'm happy to see you," he said, and kissed her deeply. "Now, wife, you're going to get your first dose

of after-the-game aches and pains from your husband."
He flexed his throwing arm.

"I'll rub you all over, I promise," Daphne said. "You
only got sacked once. You hurt from that?"

"Nothing a little wifely tender loving care won't cure.
You wanna play in the Jacuzzi, little girl?"

"We don't even have to go to California."

It was, of course, a mistake, but Brant figured the only
obvious part of him was underwater, if Daphne would
only keep her hands to herself. She did for a while, gently massaging his shoulders, but when she climbed into
the swirling water with him, gorgeously naked, he
groaned mentally. Distract her and yourself, you idiot, he
thought, aware only of her beautiful breasts pressing
against his chest.

"Mom's okay?"

"Humm? Oh yes, she's just fine and sends her love.
Cloe called and wished you luck, and Winterspoon
watched the game on TV."

I don't feel sore at all, Daphne was thinking. And I
haven't for days now. No, not sore at all. Dr. Lowery's
instruction had just been a suggestion, at least that was
how she now chose to interpret it. She wanted her husband, very much, and made no attempt to stem her rising desire for him. She also had a supply of pills, so there
was no danger of her getting pregnant until it was safe to
do so. Her palm glided down her husband's chest to his
belly, paused just a moment, and found him. Ah, she
thought, smiling, he wasn't at all indifferent.

"Daph, don't," Brant said, his teeth gritted.

"Why? Haven't you missed me?"

"I'm tired and sore, and only interested locally. Please,
sweetheart, not tonight. I feel like I'm an old man."

"I understand," she said, but he saw the confusion in her eyes.

He cursed fluently in his mind. Deception led to ridiculous problems. Here he was, ready to ravish her, yet he couldn't but she didn't know he couldn't. Damn.

"I'm glad you came," he said, drawing a deep breath. "Mac Dreyfus is probably half in love with you. I saw him staring at you in the most fascinated way."

"He just wanted to talk about the game after he got over that stupid English heiress bit. So we did. I probably bored him silly. Is he a sports writer?"

"Yeah, with the Chicago *Sun*. Let's get out of this thing before we turn into prunes."

She insisted on drying him, trying him to the limit. And she wore no nightgown to bed. He groaned when she wrapped herself around him. He could feel her heartbeat, erratic and fast. At least he could ease her, he thought, smiling into the darkness. He pressed her onto her back, balancing himself on his elbow beside her. "Just hold still," he said, and kissed her mouth at the same time his fingers found her. Her quick, surprised intake of breath delighted him. Lord but she was responsive. He wished the light was on when he felt her body begin to quiver. He wanted to see her face. She clutched at him frantically, her last rational thought being that if he was too tired to make love to her, where was he getting the energy for this?

She cried out, and he covered her, taking her moans into his mouth.

"You are the most perfect husband in the whole world," she murmured vaguely as she nestled against him.

He grinned, a bit painfully, and kissed her temple. "You're right," he said.

He awoke from the most intense erotic dream he'd ever experienced, only to realize that it was all too real. Early morning sunlight was filtering through the shades of their hotel room, but it took a moment for him to focus on his wife, who was covering his lower body with her own, her soft mouth caressing him. He couldn't hold back, and his moan of raw pleasure filled the silent room.

"Now, Brant, aren't I the most perfect wife in the whole world?" she asked, grinning up the length of his body.

"I'll let you know when and if I come back from the dead."

She giggled. "You only have about thirty minutes. I ordered breakfast from room service."

It was closer to fifteen minutes later when they were sitting on the bed, breakfast trays on their laps. Brant drank some of the hot black coffee and absently turned the pages of the Detroit paper to the sports section. He set down his coffee cup, very slowly and very carefully. There was a good-sized picture of Daphne kissing him enthusiastically, the caption beneath: "English Wife All-American."

"Good grief," he said, and handed Daphne the paper.

"That's a pun, isn't it? That All-American bit?" she asked in the most pleased voice he'd ever heard.

"Yes," he said, "it is. Mac likes that sort of thing."

"Listen to this, Brant. 'Daphne Asher is probably giving tips to her quarterback husband as well as all the other Astros players. Her understanding of the game is astounding, given the fact she only heard of football six months ago. Take this in, coaches—'" Daphne paused, quickly scanning the rest of the article. "I don't believe this, Brant, he's practically quoted me! It's crazy."

She handed the paper back. Brant read quickly, feeling somewhat dazed. He laid the paper on the bed and asked, "I knew you were learning at a great rate, but this—"

"I've been doing quite a bit of reading," she interrupted him, her voice demure, "and watching lots of films."

"It looks like the world is changing fast. My world, that is."

"Yes," she said, forking down a bite of scrambled eggs, "you're a married man. It's gotta change."

Gotta he thought. How long before she lost her English accent?

He enjoyed her growing popularity with the press until after the game with the Cowboys.

Chapter Nineteen

Brant, sore, bruised and bone-weary from the hard game with the Cowboys, a game they'd lost, stood staring at Daphne, unable to take in what she was saying. He wondered vaguely if Winterspoon, cooking something very English in the kitchen, was listening.

"...so first I'd be doing straight interviews, then by season, if everything goes well, I'll actually be involved in the halftime talks."

Daphne, so excited she could barely talk straight, continued after a tiny pause, "And you'll not believe this, Brant! Maybe, just maybe, I'll be the first woman to actually do the play-by-play. Actually cover the games while they're happening! Joe Namath. Frank Gifford. O.J.—"

"Good God, Daph, hold it a minute." He shook his head, trying to get his mental bearings. "What the hell are you talking about? A network has offered you a sports job?''

''Yes, and they want me to interview my husband, Brant the Dancer, first! Oh, Brant, can you just imagine it? Interviewing you, and we can talk about all the players and your going to the Superbowl! Mr. Irving said that—''

''I don't believe this,'' he interrupted her in a stunned, incredulous voice. ''Why the hell would they offer you a job like that?''

''A Scotch, neat, sir.''

''What? Oh, Winterspoon. Thanks.'' Thank the Lord he'd made it a double.

''Just the thing, sir, to clear away confusion.''

''A start, in any case.'' Brant downed the Scotch and wiped the back of his hand across his mouth. ''I'm going to the Jacuzzi,'' he said. ''To clear away more confusion.''

Daphne blinked at his back and opened her mouth, only to be forestalled by Winterspoon's calm reflections. ''You know how he is after a game, Miss Daphne, and that sack in the third quarter by that brute probably shook his insides.''

''But this is important, Winterspoon!'' She rushed toward the bedroom after her husband. She saw a trail of clothes leading to the bathroom and grinned, momentarily diverted. His socks were always the last item to go, the left one specifically. He was standing in front of the mirror, slowly and carefully flexing his throwing arm. Daphne bit down on her enthusiasm.

''I've got to talk to the guys on the line, Brant,'' she said, pursing her lips. ''It was Phil, mainly. He left a hole as wide as the Lincoln Tunnel. That's why they made a sandwich of you.''

"Daphne," he said, and she started at the use of her full name. "You won't talk to Phil or anyone. You got that?"

"You're just tired and…cranky," she said, giving him a maternal pat on his shoulder. "Come on into the Jacuzzi."

"I am tired, but I'm not a damned five-year-old! Now, why don't you exit and go flutter around Winterspoon? You can offer to threaten the potatoes for him."

She stiffened, watching him with quickly narrowing eyes as he climbed into the swirling hot water. "You don't have to be nasty," she said, her voice as stiff as her back. "And I wasn't *fluttering*; I was trying to be nice and understanding."

Brant closed his eyes and leaned his head back against the tub. "Well, from the sound of it, I won't have to endure your niceness much longer, will I?"

"Just what is that supposed to mean?"

He cocked an eye open to see her standing, hands on hips, beside the tub. "It means that you'll cease being a wife when and if you accept this TV deal."

"What a stupid, mean thing to say! Of course I'm your wife. If I weren't, I doubt anyone would be interested in anything I had to say, regardless of whether I knew a smidgeon about football or not."

"A smidgeon is about all you do know, and I'm glad you finally realize why anyone would offer you anything!"

"Oh, I see now," she said, fury rising to the boiling point. "If it weren't for the great Brant Asher, shortened from Asherwood—the way you Americans shorten and change and butcher everything—I'd still be counting eggs and pruning roses at the Hall, afraid of my own shadow!"

"You got it, lady. Now, will you please just leave me alone?"

Daphne grabbed a washcloth and flung it at him, striking his face. Brant peeled it off and tossed it to the bathroom floor. "Talk about five-year-olds," he muttered.

"I'm not leaving," Daphne said between gritted teeth. "And I'm beginning to think that it would be just great if I didn't have to put up with your wretched aches and pains after every bloody game!"

"You won't, if you take that job. That kind of thing is demanding as hell. You'd barely have time to send me mailgrams."

"I'd be earning a lot of money, Brant. I could even afford to call you once in a while."

"I got it now. How many more credit cards do you want? How many more little pieces of paper that prove you're worth something?"

"I am worth something, you . . . you cad!"

"Back to the 19th century again." He sighed. "Why does it bother you so much that I'm the breadwinner in this family? We have a very comfortable life; Gwen will be back on her wheels in no time—"

"I don't understand why you're not thrilled about all this. And this has nothing to do with you making all the money. What do you want, a—a stick in the dirt?"

"Mud," he said. "You've been about as much a stick as I've been a hockey player."

He rose, reaching for a towel. "You wanna be a good little wife and dry my back for me?"

"I'd rather cut your throat!"

"So much for pleasant married life."

"I'm leaving," Daphne said, her body rigid with anger.

"As I recall, I asked you to several times." He continued drying himself, then tossed the towel on the floor and strode back to the bedroom. He eased onto the bed and stretched his arms above his head. "You still here?" he asked.

"Is this how you treated Marcie and all your other women?" she asked, her voice trembling with an effort at sarcasm.

"No. If you weren't here and Marcie were, she'd be doing all sorts of marvelous things to make me forget my aches and pains."

Daphne sucked in her breath. "I can do those things, too."

"Then why aren't you? Why are you harping on that ludicrous plan of yours to gain fame and fortune off your husband's name?"

It was cruel, and he knew it, but her next words made him forget every conciliatory word he'd ever considered saying.

"Damn you, Brant Asher! I don't need your name! I can and will do it all myself!"

"How can you be so damned stupid?" He jerked upright, anger and frustration churning in him. "If I hadn't agreed to marry you, you'd be whatever Lucilla told you to be, a wretched little file clerk, probably, in a dingy London office. That, or you'd be buried away in Glasgow with Aunt Cloe while she, poor lady, would be trying to marry you off to some unsuspecting soul with credit cards and a profession you'd try to dominate."

"I could marry anyone I wanted to! Dominate! God, I just don't believe you. Ha! You begged me to marry you."

"Begged, hell. It did, I'll admit, seem like quite a good idea at the time. Here was poor little Daphne, helpless, insecure, with about as much confidence as a drowned rat—"

"Stop it!"

"Why should I? It's the truth, isn't it?"

"I'm not insecure anymore! I'm competent now, and I can do anything, and—"

"Damn it, you couldn't even manage to drive competently enough to keep from losing the baby!"

She froze, her eyes glazing in shock and pain.

Brant cursed himself royally. He rose quickly from the bed, and, to his shock, she backed away from him. He stretched out his hand toward her. "Daph, I'm sorry. I didn't mean that. I've got a big mouth and—"

"You knew," she said dully, turning away from him, her arms clutched about her chest. "And you didn't tell me. I had to find out from a big-mouthed nurse."

He went after her and pulled her rigid body against him. "It was my decision not to tell you, love. The doctor thought you should know, but I insisted. I didn't want you to feel guilty or anything. I'm sorry, but when I get mad I shoot my mouth off. Please, Daph, forgive me."

"That's why you didn't make love with me in Detroit."

"You had to heal. Besides, I did give you pleasure, and I thought you enjoyed it."

He felt her hands flutter against her chest, but she said nothing.

"We can have kids, love, whenever you want."

"Don't call me *love*," she said, her voice steely. "Ours was an old-fashioned marriage of convenience; you know it as well as I do. You saved me from a wretched life; you don't have to remind me of that fact. And you're right. It's not proper of me to take advantage of you and your profession, to dominate, to stick myself in where I obviously don't belong.''

He'd rather have her mad and spitting at him, he realized, listening to her emotionless voice against his shoulder. He felt like a prize jerk, a 19th-century cad, and he wished he had another Scotch, neat. What to say to her, what to do? Why had he flown off the handle at her like that? Dumb bastard! He stroked his hands down her arms.

''Daph, about that offer from the network, forget all that nonsense I spouted, please. It's your decision. Really.''

She felt his hands move from her arms to begin gently massaging her shoulders, then rove down her back, hugging her more tightly against him. How stupid she'd been to believe he'd be as excited as she was over the offer. He'd kept to his part of the bargain, treating her well, staying faithful to her even when she'd acted like a total twit and nitwit. Why isn't it nit-twit? she thought crazily. But she'd seen what he really thought of her, despite his reassurances now. She understood. Slowly she eased away from him.

''Thank you,'' she said, not meeting his eyes. ''Would you like to rest before dinner? I'll tell Winterspoon to hold it back for as long as you want. I think it's a pot roast, so it shouldn't be a problem. He's . . . teaching me how to cook, a bit. I'll call you in an hour?''

He let her go, watched her walk to the bedroom door. He stared after her, feeling utterly helpless. ''An hour,'' he repeated. She didn't slam the bedroom door. He wished she had. No, she just slipped through it like a lifeless ghost. He threw himself back down on the bed and stared at the ceiling. Why don't you just admit the truth, at least to yourself, you idiot? Your overblown reaction was because you're afraid of losing her. You want all of her—her zest, her excitement, her caring, her *presence*—you want to know that she's cheering or booing in the stands while you're playing. You don't want her leaving you. You love her, fool. The admission made his guts churn. He'd believed he was immune, and he'd been more or less content to have that vague emptiness in his life. Until Daphne. He wondered now how long he'd loved her. This love business was sneaky, consuming him before he'd realized he'd been had. Oh yes, he'd loved her a long time, but had just been too blind and insensitive to realize it. He started to jump out of bed, to yell it to her, hell, to yell it to all New York. He stopped cold, falling back. She'd never believe him now.

She probably believed now that he was so small-minded, so much a male chauvinist, that he couldn't bear the thought of his wife having a life apart from him. Dog-in-the-manger syndrome, one of his shrink friends had tagged such behavior. No, he was certain he wasn't guilty of that. It wasn't that he was at all threatened by the notion of her success. He remembered Jayne, a professional model who at the time had earned more money than he had. It hadn't bothered him a bit. And Lisa Cormanth, a computer genius. And Marcie Ellis, a very successful journalist. No, boiled down to a proper pulp, he simply wanted his wife with him. He wanted to wallow in his good fortune. Some good fortune his mouth had provided him with now. She was probably ready to toss him out the door and good riddance to him.

And he'd thrown up her miscarriage at her. It occurred to him to wonder why she hadn't told him about it—unless, of course, she'd already known that he'd known. He saw again the pain in her eyes. She'd been carrying around that damned misery by herself, never letting on to him, not worrying him, protecting him, not wanting him to feel pain. And guilt? No, that was ridiculous. The accident hadn't been her fault.

Maybe she's still insecure enough to think you'd hate her if you knew about the miscarriage. That's why she never discussed it with you.

He groaned. He knew her thinking processes well enough to realize it was a possibility, a definite possibility.

But maybe, just maybe, she wanted to be away from him. After his sterling performance in the bathroom, maybe she couldn't wait to sign a contract with the network. Maybe she didn't feel anything close to what he felt about her.

When he emerged from the bedroom thirty minutes later, his agile tongue was a lead weight in his mouth. There was too much at stake, too much to lose, to go spouting off without careful consideration. He'd never felt so scared, so emptied of confidence, in his life.

What he managed to say over dinner, apart from chirpy comments on the weather, was, "Will you please come to Houston next week for the game with the Oilers? We can see Dusty, Lily and the kids while we're there, maybe stay for Thanksgiving."

Daphne looked up from her boiled potatoes after carefully shoving aside sprigs of parsley. Winterspoon loved greenery on a plate. She felt the tension radiating from him, though he spoke calmly, with no emotion in his voice. She studied the stark lines of his face, the high cheekbones, the rakish slant of his dark eyebrows. She loved him so much it hurt.

"Daphne?"

"Yes," she said finally, "I'll be there." Her voice was as calm and flat as his, but with new eyes he saw the uncertainty, the insecurity, in hers.

What to say? What to do?

He was a very physical man. Every woman he'd known intimately had teased him about being oversexed. He'd show her his love for her in bed. But later. Sex simply postponed problems; it didn't solve them.

He watched the distance stretch between them all evening. Her marvelous vivacity, her delightful laugh, had become tense wariness. They played three-handed Hearts with Winterspoon, and the supposed neophyte trounced both of them. "Well, sir," Winterspoon said, "it's only ten dollars, after all."

Much later, after careful and thorough foreplay, Brant watched her face as her body clenched with convulsive pleasure. "God, you're beautiful," he whispered. Daphne, whose body had unconsciously fought against satisfaction, felt as though she were drowning. When he entered her, gently, fully, she gasped with the wonder of it. "Brant, I—"

"I want you to be happy," he said into her mouth as he moved over her. "I want you to be happy with me."

She moaned softly against his shoulder, arching up, bringing him deeper, making him one with her.

"I want you to be happy," he said again, his words widely spaced as he gritted his teeth on the brink of his own release.

Only an absolute fool could be unhappy with him, she thought, dazed. "I want that, too," she whispered, her voice lost and helpless. She hugged him tight, feeling him explode deep within her.

Chapter Twenty

Houston was warm, too warm, Daphne thought, for the end of November, and so humid that within ten minutes of meeting the climate, she felt as though her hair had turned to damp strings about her face.

"Lily! Dusty! Good grief, the whole brood!"

Daphne smiled as she was engulfed first by Lily, then by Dusty, aware that Danny, Keith and Patricia were dancing around them. She dropped all confusing thoughts and swallowed her unhappiness, giving in to the rambunctious greetings.

"Are you still going to keep this sister of mine, Dusty?" she heard Brant asking her brother-in-law as he poked him in the ribs.

"Brant, this little gal is a dynamo. Houston wouldn't be the same without her. Yep, old boy, I'll keep her."

"Ha! Why don't you ask me, brother dear?"

Brant grinned down at his beautiful sister. "You're so easy, Lily, it never occurred to me. Besides, Dusty is so much of a man, I always knew he'd keep you in line."

While Lily was punching Brant, Dusty turned to Daphne. "And how's my gorgeous little English gal?"

Daphne felt warmed by his good nature and grinned up at him. "How about two out of four?"

"Which two?" Dusty asked.

"I never get specific about a compliment," Daphne said, giggling.

"And I'll never get another word in edgewise, not with all these hellions around. All right, kids, let's get out of here. Brant, you're staying with the team until after the game?"

"Yep, then Daph and I will invade you for a couple of days. Okay?"

"You got it. Lily and I've planned a real Texas barbecue for you right after the game. But I swear it'll be turkey and all the fixings for Thanksgiving."

After another round of hugs, Brant and Daphne took the team bus to the hotel. In the lobby, fans and reporters alike surrounded the men. Daphne shrank against Brant when a reporter she'd seen at the Dallas game spotted her and yelled out, "Mrs. Asher! Welcome to Houston! You wanna give me your prediction for the game?"

Brant felt her tension and cursed himself yet again, silently. Very gently he said, "Go ahead, love. You're loaded with predictions; give them what they want."

Brant watched her from the corner of his eye as he spoke to another reporter. She seemed at first very shy and tongue-tied; then she came alive, and he smiled to see her gesticulate as she made a point, heard her sweet laughter, her starchy English accent. He felt himself swell with pride. You utter ass, he told himself. She's a natural, and you wanted to mold her into whatever it was you wanted. Hoard was more like it. He'd wanted her only for himself. He felt sick with self-disgust.

It wasn't long before other reporters converged on her, as did teammates. It was probably the most fun pre-game interviewing he'd ever been witness to. Even Sam Carverelli was grinning like a besotted hen over his little chick.

There was only one fly in the ointment, and his name was Richard Monroe, a big sports writer from Los Angeles. He was a bastion of male chauvinism in sports and became livid when a "girl" tried to swish her tail around athletes. Brant found himself inching away from his teammates, ready to pounce if the man gave Daphne a bad time.

Which he was prepared to do. Rich Monroe had eyed Daphne's performance and felt his lips thin. He was willing to agree that she was charming, lovely, but hell, let her model if she wanted to show off. He shoved his way into the group of fools surrounding her and asked, "Do you miss all your athletes in England, Mrs. Asher? The rugby season in full swing?"

"I don't know any, and I have no idea, sir," Daphne said, turning her sunny smile and wary eyes to the tall, gaunt-faced man.

"What?" he asked, his voice dripping sarcasm. "You mean you've left all your rugby heroes for our American athletes?"

Oh no, Daphne thought, studying the man with the gleaming blue eyes and ready-to-pounce voice. He thinks I'm some sort of groupie. "Yes, sir, I did, but I don't think they'll miss me." Take that, you ill-bred jerk.

"Are rugby players so much less... inviting than our American football players? Surely you must have *known* some of them in England."

"Not more than half a dozen," Daphne said, praying he wouldn't notice that her hands had clenched at her sides. "They're not nearly as...inviting as, for example, Lloyd here, or Tiny, or Guy."

"You're a team player, then," Rich Monroe said, his pencil poised over his pad. "The more the merrier. Perhaps a team playerette."

"Perhaps, sir, you should look more closely at my husband, Brant Asher. Then, I promise you, you won't ask any more ignorant questions like that." She heard Lloyd groan in mock sorrow and tossed him a grin. Brant was at her elbow then, and she said, "My husband, sir."

Brant towered over Rich Monroe, and for a brief moment the sportswriter felt a frisson of fear at the barely veiled murderous look in Asher's eyes. Hell, he should have gotten her away from her brute of a husband.

Daphne willingly withdrew, watching Brant cut up the obnoxious man in his pleasant, utterly terrifying calm way.

"Good show, Daph," Brant said to her later. "Want me to break his neck?"

"Just his mean mouth, which you did quite nicely, thank you, Brant."

She hugged him, giving him her sweet smile, and Brant realized that she would never allow any problems between them to interfere with his game and concentration.

They beat Houston 21 to 14 in a wild and woolly fourth quarter that left Daphne hoarse from yelling, and Brant sore as hell.

"Daphne, we've got to talk."

She turned from the mirror, her pearls fastened. She gave him her special, intimate smile and said, "You are the most insatiable man! Here I am still recovering from terminal pleasure, and you—''

He slashed his hand through the air. ''Cut it out, Daph. That's not what I meant, and you know it.''

Oh yes, she knew it. She lowered her eyes a moment to her elegant Italian leather heels. ''I don't want to be late for the barbecue. Lily was in a tizzy when I spoke to her. Really, Brant, Dusty is sending the limo, and it's probably here by now.''

Brant frowned, then sighed. He saw the pleading look in her eyes and held his tongue. Later, he thought. They had to clear the air, get things straightened out between them. She had been all that was charming and supportive, wild in bed—and closed up like a clam. The wall she'd put up between them was as firm and immovable as the best offensive line.

''All right,'' he said. He started to pick up their suitcases, then changed his mind. No, he thought, he wanted to bring her back to the hotel. They had to talk, to be alone, with no interruptions from his well-meaning sister, equally well-meaning brother-in-law, and three oblivious nieces and nephews.

Lily and Dusty lived in a three-story white colonial house in the exclusive River Oaks section of Houston. The grounds were extensive, the swimming pool opulent, and the circular driveway bumper-to-bumper with cars. Almost immediately Daphne was gone from him, willingly or unwillingly he didn't know. He was, he supposed, afraid to find out.

The mood was festive, the guests in all stages of pleasant inebriation, many of them cavorting in the kidney-shaped pool.

Daphne smiled until she felt her face would crack from the effort. And she kept her distance from Brant. She'd just dipped a tortilla chip into a green substance that a guest told her was guacamole—whatever that was—when Lily said from behind her, "Daphne, why don't you come upstairs with me for a minute? I've got to make repairs to my poor face."

Daphne studied her sister-in-law's exquisite face and blinked. "What kind of repairs?"

"You'll see," Lily said briefly and, taking her arm, firmly steered her away from the crowd.

"You have a beautiful home," Daphne said as she followed in Lily's wake up the vast circular stairway.

"Yes," Lily said absently.

"The dinner was delicious."

"Yes," Lily said again. "In here, Daphne."

It was the spacious master suite, and Daphne's jaw dropped in awe. She was so used to Brant's condo. The entire five rooms could fit into this one huge L-shaped suite.

"I want to know what's going on," Lily said without preamble, waving away what she knew would be more complimentary words from her sister-in-law.

"I don't know what you mean, Lily," Daphne said, resentment clear in her voice.

"Now, don't be like that," Lily pleaded, touching her arm. "I love my brother dearly, and I thought you and he were perfect together. I know he loves you."

Daphne's eyes met hers. "I don't think so," she said quietly.

That was a shocker. "Goodness, how can you be so blind, Daph? I've been watching his eyes following you all afternoon. And you've purposely avoided being with him." Daphne said nothing, and Lily said a bit hesitantly after a few moments, "Mom told me about the miscarriage. It's a shame, but if you want children, you can have them. Is that the problem?"

Daphne raised her chin. "Brant is a very honorable, kind man. And I, well, I fully intend now to keep up my end of the bargain. I'd already decided that, regardless of what he felt or didn't feel about me. I wanted to. He's been upset that I might not...keep to my end, that is. In fact, I just realized that I'm—" She broke off. That news was for Brant first.

"What are you talking about?" Lily's voice was clearly bewildered.

"You'll see soon enough," was all Daphne would say. Lily, frustrated, allowed her to leave. Suddenly Daphne turned to face her sister-in-law again. "Do you really think so, Lily?"

"Think what?"

"That Brant loves me?"

"Don't be an ass, Daphne. I heard him tell Dusty that he was the luckiest man in the world. If I recall correctly, he said, 'And to think I almost didn't go to England. Jesus, I must have been born under a lucky star.' Does that convince you?"

Daphne thought her heart would gallop off into the sunset without her. She laughed, and at the same time a tear trickled down her cheek. She hugged Lily tightly, then skipped down the hall. She'd never been one for the grand gesture, but why not? She found Dusty, and he took her into his study, then left her alone. She picked up the phone without a moment's hesitation. It was Sunday, but why not give it a try?

Brant downed another beer. Why the hell couldn't things at least become a little blurry? All around him people were laughing, drinking, swapping jokes and unbelievable stories. It had cooled down considerably, and the Texas sky, true to legend, was clear and gleaming with stars. He watched a beautiful woman pull herself out of the swimming pool nearly as naked as the sunlit day she was born. He objectively noted her lovely breasts and long legs. They didn't do a bloody thing for him. Where was Daphne?

He saw her talking earnestly to a man Dusty had invited from one of the networks. Hell, *the* network. He watched the man shake his head and lean closer. Brant realized his hand was clutching his empty beer can, bending it out of shape, and that his knuckles were white. They'd work it out, he thought. He'd do anything not to lose her, anything.

It was Dusty who called out some ten minutes later, "Hey, folks, we've got an announcement for all of you. Come on, heads up!"

Brant felt the excitement radiating from his teammates as they shoved forward, bringing him with them. The word had leaked out sometime before. How, Brant didn't know. He hadn't said anything. "Hell," Guy had told him, "I don't mind at all if Daph sees me draped in a towel! Tiffy's accusing me of growing a fat gut, and Daph will tell the world the truth."

"I'd like to thank Mr. Donaldson," he heard Daphne say in her clear, precise voice, "and all the people who wanted to take a chance on me."

Wanted?

"I've given it a lot of thought and have decided that, as a new American, I still have so much to learn about my new home and about football. Perhaps if anyone is still interested in the next couple of years, I'll be there in the locker room to pour champagne on all your heads." She paused a moment, her eyes locked on her husband's face. "But for now, I realize that I want only to tell people just how great you guys are. Mr. Donaldson has agreed that a few short, special interviews with the Astros players is the way we'll go this year. After the Superbowl I won't be in any shape to see anyone, so we've got only the next two months.''

There was a babble of comment. "That's great—just us!"

"Lordie, an interview in English English!"

Shape? Brant stared at her, his mind refusing to function.

"Thank you all so much. You're all such good friends, and I'll do my best to see that everyone knows just how great each of you is."

There was applause, the sound of glasses clinking in toast, people crowding around Daphne. Brant forced a smile to his lips, accepted handshakes, and couldn't keep his eyes off his wife.

How the hell could he get her alone? Brant smiled grimly. He eased his way through the crowd to Sam Carverelli, clapped his arms about his coach's waist, hefted him up and, amid curses from Sam and boisterous, surprised laughter from everyone else, lifted him high and tossed him into the pool.

He was at his wife's side in the next minute. "Let's go," he said. "Now."

"But, Brant, what about Lily? And poor Sam—"

"Shut up."

Her eyes sparkled, and she said in a mocking voice, "Will you toss me into the pool if I refuse?"

"No, I'll toss you flat on your back." He dragged her out without another word.

Her laughter rang out, sweet and pure and happy.

Brant didn't say a word until they'd reached their hotel room. He closed the door, locked it, then turned to face his wife.

"Your shape is beautiful. What the hell did you mean?"

"Didn't you see how much I ate? And that guacamole stuff...I really pigged in."

"Out," he said automatically.

"But we just got here! Where do you want to go now?"

"No, damn it, pig *out*. That's how you say it."

"Oh."

Brant studied her for a long moment, his fingers stroking his jaw thoughtfully. "Take off your clothes. Now."

Daphne's fingers went to her strand of pearls.

"You can leave those on."

"But why?"

"They won't interfere with anything. I want to see your shape."

"But you saw my shape last night, this morning—"

He was beside her in an instant, his fingers on the single button at the neck of her gray wool dress. She stood quietly as he pulled the dress over her head. Bra, slip and panty hose quickly followed.

Daphne said very softly, "Are you angry with me about my decision?"

"What decision?" he managed to ask, his eyes on her breasts.

"Just to do a few interviews this season. As for the rest, well, that could be, or then again, wouldn't have to be..."

"You sound breathless, Daph." He raised his eyes to her face. "When?" he asked softly.

"Well, first you, of course—"

"That's it!" He picked her up, but unlike his rough treatment with his coach, he laid her very gently on the bed. "Now, wife, enough B.S."

"But Brant, I don't have a degree and if I did, it would have to be a B.A. I don't—"

"I guess we're going to have to retire Gwen. A station wagon, perhaps? A move to Connecticut? A shaggy dog?"

"Winterspoon isn't allergic to dogs, thank goodness."

"Do you think our baby will call him Uncle Oscar? Uncle Spoon?"

"I love you, Brant."

His eyes gleamed, and he gave her a slow, intimate smile. There was a good deal of satisfied triumph in that smile, and she poked him in the stomach.

He didn't give her the satisfaction of a perfunctory grunt. "It's about time, lady. You've had me hanging over a damned cliff so long, well, my fingers are numb."

"Just so long as that's the only part of you that hasn't any feeling left."

"Lord, would you stop treating me like your straight man?"

"I'm scared."

Brant lay down beside her, drawing her close against him. His fingers tangled in her hair and the pearls. "I feel great," he said, burying his face in a mass of hair.

Daphne felt his hand slip between them and gently rove over her stomach. She no longer questioned her intense response to him, just arched more closely against him, her fingers searching out the buttons of his shirt.

He clasped her hand. "No, love, not until you hear what I've got to say."

Daphne arched back so she could see his face. He saw her tongue nervously glide over her lower lip. "No, it's nothing dreadful, I swear. I want you, sweetheart. Now, tomorrow, in the year two thousand and twenty-five. I think I've loved you forever. It took me a long time because I just didn't know what the hell was wrong with me. I want you to be happy. I want you to keep loving me."

"I don't think I could ever stop that. Brant, I'd made the decision a while ago, but I didn't know what to do, so I didn't say anything to anybody, even the network people. I thought maybe I'd end up being a single parent and would have to earn my own living. Then Lily hauled me upstairs and told me that you said you'd been born under a lucky star."

"I said that?"

"Yes, you did, you jerk! And I was under that star, too, waiting for you."

"Forget the damned star; just make it me you're under." He lightly kissed the tip of her nose, then continued in a very serious voice, "If you want to take over Joe Namath's job as announcer, I'll be your loudest supporter. What do you say? Will you keep me around as your straight man?"

Her lashes swept down, and he couldn't see her eyes. "How straight?" came her demure question.

He groaned and kissed her.

"I love you," he said into her mouth. "Even though you've become a smart-mouthed broad."

"Bird," she said. "That's how we say it in England."

* * * * *

If you're ready for more

Catherine Coulter

Don't miss these passion-filled stories by this *New York Times* bestselling author:

#48259	AFTERSHOCKS	$4.50	☐
#48260	AFTERGLOW	$4.50	☐

TOTAL AMOUNT	$
POSTAGE & HANDLING	$
($1.00 for one book, 50¢ for each additional)	
APPLICABLE TAXES*	$ _____
TOTAL PAYABLE	$ _____
(Send check or money order—please do not send cash)	

To order, complete this form and send it, along with a check or money order for the total above, payable to Silhouette Books, to: *In the U.S.:* 3010 Walden Avenue, P.O. Box 1396, Buffalo, NY 14269-1396; *In Canada:* P.O. Box 609, Fort Erie, Ontario, L2A 5X3.

Name: _____

Address: _____ City: _____

State/Prov.: _____ Zip/Postal Code: _____

*New York residents remit applicable sales taxes.
 Canadian residents remit applicable GST and provincial taxes.

BCC3

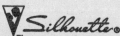

He staked his claim…

HONOR BOUND

by
New York Times
Bestselling Author

Sandra Brown

previously published under the pseudonym Erin St. Claire

As Aislinn Andrews opened her mouth to scream, a hard
hand clamped over her face and she found herself face-
to-face with Lucas Greywolf, a lean, lethal-looking
Navajo and escaped convict who swore he wouldn't hurt
her— *if* she helped him.

Look for HONOR BOUND at your favorite
retail outlet this January.

Only from…

where passion lives. SBHB